BOOK 6
CLANS
OF
MULL

THE

Wrath OF A
Scottish Blade

KEIRA
MONTCLAIR

Author's Note:

Get ready for a ride, friends! I promise it will be a great one. The novella turned into a novel, and it's a good one. This is the last book of the Clans of Mull series.

Welcome back to the world of the Grants.

CHAPTER ONE

The Isle of Mull, December 1316

BRYNJA NYBERG SPRINTED toward the cliff edge, boots sliding on rain-slicked grass as she tracked the boat rounding the point. For one heart-stopping moment, the vessel's bow swung toward shore—toward her.

Her pulse hammered.

Then the wind shifted, catching the sail wrong, and the ship heeled away behind the rocky promontory.

Gone.

She reached the cliff edge panting, wild strands of hair whipping across her face. The bastard was still hunting her. She was certain of it now.

"May your boat become grounded on hidden rocks," she screamed in Norse, the curse rolling off her tongue as naturally as breathing. "May crabs feast on your drowned eyes and your soul wander the cold depths forever!"

"Still cursing boats?"

Brynja didn't turn. She'd heard Hildi's approach because her cousin moved with the unconscious grace of someone who'd left the past behind. How Brynja envied her that.

But she could not do the same.

"It's him," Brynja said, still staring at the empty water where the boat had vanished. "The man who came for Sheona. I know it."

Hildi hung back, waiting for Brynja's temper to cool, but it wouldn't. Not today. Her Norse blood demanded she throw every curse in her mother's tongue at the fools, hoping to change their luck.

"May a tern bleed and shite all over your hair until each strand fell from your head," she yelled toward the empty sea. "May your boat run into a sea of swordfish that will punch holes in your hull, you ugly trolls!"

She glanced back at her friend, unable to suppress a smile despite her anger. Hildi's presence always pulled her back from the edge. "I'm coming. I know you're hungry."

"I am hungry," Hildi said, her mouth quirking. "But I'll never stop enjoying your Norse insults. Your mama would be proud."

The words hit harder than Hildi intended. Their mothers, Norsewomen abandoned by Scottish fathers who never returned, had raised them together on Tiree. That isle had been paradise until men came and murdered them for the cottages they wanted.

Four months. It had been only four months since Brynja held her mother's hand as life drained from her body, yet it felt like an eternity.

Brynja had never recovered from the shock of holding her mother while she took her last breath. She could still feel the weight of that cooling hand in hers. Could still hear the man who'd grabbed her braid afterward, saying, *"Aye, we'll get a pretty price for you with those golden braids and blue eyes."*

She and Hildi had escaped from the small cottage down the isle where the bairns were held. Had rowed a tiny boat until fishermen found them and delivered them to the nunnery on Iona.

Their new home. Their sanctuary.

At least, it had been until the bastards came for Sheona a fortnight ago.

They'd come in the middle of the night, but one of Brynja's dreams had woken her, drawn her to the coastline before the fools could land. She'd been waiting when their boat appeared, black against the pewter sky. Her first dagger buried itself in one man's shoulder. Her second found another's leg.

Sheona, now happily married and living on Mull, had told her later that Clyde was dead, the one who took the blade in his shoulder.

The other still lived.

And ever since, a particular boat had been patrolling near the isle. Sometimes twice a day.

Brynja came to the coast every time she spotted it. She vowed to be there when the fool dared step foot on Iona's sand again. She'd be waiting with spear in one hand and dagger in the other. This time, she'd aim for his heart.

She turned toward the nunnery, Hildi falling into step beside her. "Mayhap on the morrow I'll visit Simone, see if she's noticed anything."

"Aye, and I'd like to visit Magni again." Hildi glanced up at the fast-moving gray clouds. "We don't have much food to share, though."

"Ionaland always has food to share. The monks bring us so much bread we can spare some." Ionaland was the area of the isle where four women lived and cared for the orphans of the world—children rescued from twisted criminals who stole and sold bairns for coin.

"Rain will be here soon," Hildi said, flipping her dark braids over her shoulder.

"As long as it's not like that storm Sheona left in, we can manage."

They walked in silence for a moment before Hildi asked quietly, "Do you truly think it's the same man?"

"I'm certain of it."

"But why would he come back here? Everyone knows Sheona married Taskill and lives on MacVey land now. Eva moved to Rankin land. Why would they still search?"

Brynja shot her a look. "They aren't looking for Sheona."

"Then who?"

"Me, Hildi. They're after me." She kept her voice even, matter-of-fact. "Nearly every morning and every evening for the last week. They're searching for something. For someone. I put a dagger in the fool's leg, and he wants revenge."

Hildi pressed close, their shoulders touching.

Warmth and solidarity. "The sisters say we shouldn't seek revenge for anything."

"I'm not a nun, Hildi." Brynja's hand tightened on her spear. "You know what I must do."

Hildi sighed. "I do. But I'll worry about you. If you go alone, you may never return, and what would I do without you?"

Brynja thought about her words carefully. She had no intention of abandoning her dearest friend and cousin, but promising she wouldn't would be hollow. "Hildi, if we ever split up, I wish you all the happiness in the world. Don't worry about me. After all, I'm eight and ten now. I could leave whenever I wish."

Hildi was only six and ten—still soft in ways Brynja no longer was. She still slept through the night, no nightmares forcing screams from the deepest part of her belly.

"I know." Hildi fiddled with three braids on one side of her head, deftly weaving them into one thick plait. "You must do what's in your heart."

"Aye."

"But not today."

"Soon." Brynja lowered her spear. "I'm telling you the bastard will land eventually, and when he does—"

"You'll kill him."

The certainty in Hildi's voice should have been comforting. Instead it settled like a stone in Brynja's chest.

"I'll do what I must," Brynja said. "But come. We'll eat."

The two continued toward the stone walls of the nunnery in silence, the memories between them so powerful they rarely discussed them anymore. The gate stood open, welcoming them home. Brynja cast one final glance over her shoulder toward the empty sea.

"Do you ever wonder," Hildi said as they walked, "what we'd be doing if it had never happened? If we were still on Tiree, and our mamas were still—"

"Nay." Brynja kept her eyes forward.

But she lied. She wondered all the time. Wondered what her mother would say about the woman Brynja had become, hard and watchful and hungry for blood. Would her mother even recognize this person?

"It's not just about the man who came for Sheona," Brynja said quietly. "I have to go after the men who killed our mothers. I must, Hildi. I'll never be able to live with myself if their killers walk this land freely, able to do the same to others."

"I know."

What Brynja didn't tell her friend was that the dreams had returned. Dreams that whispered of vengeance, of blood, of a reckoning drawing near.

The dreams were growing darker. More urgent.

Something was coming. Something larger than one man's revenge for a dagger in his thigh.

And Brynja had learned to trust her dreams.

CHAPTER TWO

HAGEN

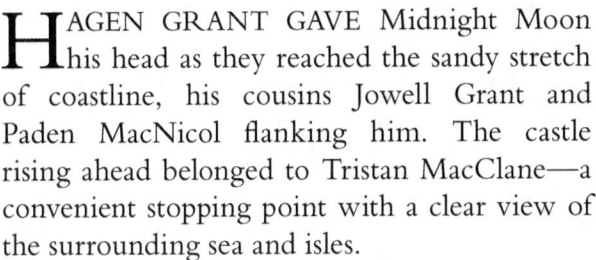

HAGEN GRANT GAVE Midnight Moon
his head as they reached the sandy stretch
of coastline, his cousins Jowell Grant and
Paden MacNicol flanking him. The castle
rising ahead belonged to Tristan MacClane—a
convenient stopping point with a clear view of
the surrounding sea and isles.

And Tristan always had boats available for
friends.

"Sorry, lads, but my sister said I'm to exercise
her horse well, and this is his favorite stretch of
beach." Hagen let the stallion choose their pace,
and Midnight surged into a gallop across the soft
sand—the kind they never had at Clan Grant.
This was one of the few times Hagen wore his
hair loose, letting the wind and salt air whip
through it.

"You'd better take good care of him," Paden
yelled, "or Dyna will have you mucking stalls by
morning!"

Hagen laughed over his shoulder. Dyna loved

her horse, but so did he. Any stallion with their grandfather's stallion'a bloodline was magnificent to ride. And Moon was glorious on the beach, his black mane flowing like a king's mantle.

"Grandda was a wise man," Jowell said, catching up as they approached the end of the beach, the horses easily climbing the crest back to the main path.

"I wish he were still here." Paden glanced at Hagen. "You're going to be nearly as tall as Grandda."

"And why are you still growing?" Jowell asked. "Neither Paden nor I have grown any taller in the last two years."

"I'm younger than you two." Hagen grinned. Nothing he liked better than hearing he resembled his sire and grandsire—Connor and the great Alexander Grant. Though he'd rather be compared for his swordplay than his height. He worked at it daily, but he still had a ways to go before he'd match his father. The man fought like his weapon was an extension of his arm.

One day, though. One day he'd look his father in the eye as an equal.

Tristan MacClane greeted them from the curtain wall as they approached his castle. "Granthams, how do you fare? Come in for a brief respite?"

Hagen glanced at Jowell, who gave a subtle shake of his head.

Paden caught their exchange. "Mayhap on the return trip, MacClane? We're headed to Iona, if we may borrow one of your midsize boats."

"Of course." Tristan leaned over the wall. "Any specific meaning to this trip? No one missing?"

Hagen shook his head, thinking back on the recent adventure—four missing MacVeys and Rankins. "Nay, all are well. We're messengers, spreading good tidings for Yuletide. We're inviting everyone to a festival at Duart Castle—the first two nights of Yule. It's customary at Clan Grant and will be soon enough at Clan Grantham. We'd love to have you join us. You know Shealee will be looking for you."

Tristan's sister Merryn had married Paden's brother Broc, and they cared for their orphaned niece, Shealee.

"I happily accept." Tristan started down the stairs. "I do miss seeing my sister. If you follow me, we'll get your horses in the stable and I'll show you the best boat to take."

"Our thanks to you."

Within a short time, they set off for Iona. Tora and Sylvi were insisting that young Magni come share the holiday with them, and they needed to extend the invitation properly.

The three climbed into a boat with three sets of oars, allowing them to travel faster. "Many thanks, Tristan," Jowell called. "We'll return shortly."

Six hands gripped the oars, slicing through the calm sea.

Hagen sat in the front seat, with his back facing Iona so his cousins couldn't see his face. About halfway across, he called out, "I may be the youngest, but why am I the strongest rower? I'm paddling about the equivalent of you two weak-arsed rowers."

"Kiss my sweet arse, you yellow-bellied whiner." That came from Paden in the back, who had the personality of his sire, Hagen's Uncle Finlay, one of the biggest teasers in all of Clan Grant.

"Are you carrying the weak-kneed knave in the middle, Paden?" Hagen glanced over his shoulder at Jowell, who always took the middle because he was the strongest rower of the three of them.

But Hagen loved to taunt his two favorite cousins.

Jowell drawled, "You should remember that I'm close enough to let my oar slip and slap any foul-mouthed buffoon in front of me or behind me, whenever I choose." Jowell was the most serious of the trio of cousins, Paden the wittiest.

Hagen didn't know what that made him, but he loved his cousins.

Paden guffawed, then twittered in the highest voice he could manage, "Oh, I'm so scared, Jowell. How did you get to be so strong? Is it from lifting that girlfriend of yours who's as big as a Highland coo carrying twins?"

Hagen snorted at that comment, his face away from his cousins. "And I could grab the oar before it hit me, shoving you out the other side of the boat. It'd be easier to row then, wouldn't it, Paden?"

Jowell snorted. "One thing I know about you, Hagen, is that you've never been a fool. I could swim there faster than you and Paden could row, and without me, you'd have to row harder, not less."

Paden and Hagen hooted and whistled over that brag.

Hagen was about to throw another taunt his way, but they were close enough to be overheard by anyone on shore, and there was one truth he'd learned after coming to Mull. Voices carried a long way over water.

As they neared the isle, Magni was the first to greet them. He flew down the path from the village, arms waving. Wee Tenney ran behind him, but Magni stopped near the edge and picked him up, the two waving as the vessel slid through the water. Magni, ten summers old, had moved here after being saved from a kidnapping. His parents had since adopted Tenney, an orphan of two.

"Greetings, Hagen and Paden and Jowell! Why are you here? We have so many visitors this day."

"Aye, aye, aye," Tenney echoed.

Once they settled the boat, Paden reached for the lad and swung him up onto his shoulders, changing his pace into a bouncing gallop. The boy giggled, grabbing onto Paden's auburn hair to steady himself.

"And who else is visiting, Magni?" Hagen asked, tying up the boat. "We'll be here for a short visit, if that's not an inconvenience."

"Brynja and Hildi are here. They brought bread, and I love bread. They're chatting with Simone and Artan." He pointed toward the archery area.

Hagen glanced at Jowell, arching a brow. He'd gladly visit with Brynja again. She was one of the prettiest lasses he'd ever met. "We'll chat with Simone too. Could you lead us to them, Magni?"

Jowell snorted. "Sure, that's who you wish to see, Hagen."

He kept his gaze forward. "I was given instructions to make sure Simone and Artan were invited. Uncle Logan insisted, if you recall."

"Invited to what?" Magni asked.

"A Yuletide celebration. We're inviting everyone to a big festival on the first two days of Yule. You'll come, will you not, Magni? Bring Tenney and your parents."

Magni stopped, looked up at the clouds overhead, then shook his head. "Nay, sorry."

"Why not?" Jowell asked. "Are you mad at us, lad?"

"Nay, I just don't wish to leave Iona."

Hagen stopped and gripped Magni's shoulders. "Now, Magni. You know we'll protect you, do you not? Who could have a chance of getting to you with the three of us surrounding you?"

"But I was stolen from Duart Castle once." The lad's messy brown locks blew in the wind, but the fear in his eyes was unmistakable.

"Good point. Because of that, we locked that hidden door in the cellars, and I promise there will be more guards. And Kelvan is gone." They'd ended the evil bastard's reign of terror not long ago, but apparently his memory survived in the lad's mind.

Magni heard a voice and pushed away from Hagen to run toward a smaller group chatting nearby.

"Can't blame him," Jowell said. "I'd think the same."

"I know, but the bastard is dead."

"What else can we say to convince him?"

"Later," Hagen muttered, wanting to approach the group quickly.

Brynja was practicing with her weapons, and he'd discovered that his new favorite pastime was watching her practice.

Especially in those tight leggings Simone had given her.

Hagen nearly stopped in his tracks, so affected by the vision before him. Brynja stood next to Simone, firing at a target. First she threw her spear, hitting dead center, then she picked up her bow and nocked an arrow, striking the target again—though not quite center.

Artan let out a low whistle. "Two right on target, Brynja. Nice. You've learned archery quickly, lass."

Hildi stood off to the side with Simone, watching her friend's skills.

Heat rushed through Hagen. The way Brynja stood, her weight balanced, shoulders square, utterly confident. The power in her draw. The deadly accuracy of her aim.

And aye, the way those leggings fit.

"That lass can shoot," he whispered to Jowell.

"Sure, her shooting is what made you hard," Jowell drawled.

Hagen picked up a clump of dirt and flung it at his cousin, who cackled with laughter. "If you've not noticed, Hildi is also a fine beauty. Which one of you are going after her? I'm staking my claim on Brynja, so stay away. Far away."

Jowell said, "I have noticed Hildi, since you mention it. She is a fine beauty and not as headstrong as her friend."

Paden let Tenney down so he could run over to Magni's side, then joined his cousins. He whispered, "I like them both."

"Jowell, good to see you," Artan called out a short distance away. "Hagen, Paden."

Hagen's gaze jumped back to Brynja, forcing him to stay behind his cousins until he got himself under control. She was just another lass, he repeated in his mind. Just like any other.

Except she wasn't.

The group greeted each other, made introductions where necessary, and Brynja placed her weapons into a sack.

"Don't stop because of us," Hagen said.

"I'm done." Brynja's expression was unsmiling. "We'll return to the nunnery."

"Nay, wait, please," Hagen called out, stopping her. "We've come to invite you all to the Yuletide festival at Duart Castle. Lots of family and friends, plenty of food. Big hunts the day before. You're all invited."

Brynja and Hildi turned to leave.

"You too," Hagen called out. "You're both invited."

Brynja stopped and spun around. "Our thanks, but we stay at the nunnery. They don't allow us to leave the isle. Too dangerous."

"I'll protect you, lass." Hagen's gaze locked on

hers. The pain he saw there took him by surprise.
Who had hurt her? He took two steps closer. "It
would be my honor to protect you."

She never smiled, never changed her composure.
He swore she had ice in her veins, but what he
wanted to know was who had put it there. Her
reply was brief. "My thanks, but we'll stay here."

Hagen bristled at her quick response, as foolish
as it was. Either way, he was going to let it pass.
"I'm telling you that you need to come. I'm
certain you'll enjoy it." He would not allow
her to stay back, hiding in a nunnery. She didn't
belong in such a place.

Brynja took two steps toward him. "Are you
trying to tell me what to do?"

Hagen noticed Simone's smile and Artan's
hand now covering his face. "I'm telling you
that anyone would be a fool not to accept such
an invitation. If you have a good reason not to,
please say so."

Paden said, "Mayhap because you're an arse,
Hagen?"

Hildi whispered, "She's had a bad day."

Jowell approached Hildi and asked, "Is there
anything we can do to help?"

Hildi shook her head, her gaze locked on
Brynja, who still hadn't spoken.

The look in her eyes told him she wasn't done
with him yet, and Hagen couldn't wait to hear
the lame excuse she was busy creating. His hands
went to his hips. "Well? Your reason?"

"My reason is that I would prefer not to spend
my time with arrogant fools who think they can

order me about. Is that what you think? That your position means you have the right to order lasses around? Do you think men are better than women too? Because you'll never tell me what to do."

Hagen glanced at Simone and Artan, realizing he'd been a bit too harsh. "My apologies, lass. I do not have the right to control you. That was not my intent. I spoke too quickly. Do as you wish." Hellfire, but that couldn't have gone worse. Now he had to find a way to make up for his crudeness. Somehow, he knew she wouldn't make it easy.

The fury in Brynja's gaze simmered until it was as cold as any he'd ever seen.

Jowell said, "Ignore him. How can we help?"

Brynja turned her back to Hagen and spoke directly to Jowell. "Since you and your friends are here, may I ask a question?"

Hildi came up to stand beside her, crossing her arms. Hildi was half a head shorter than Brynja with darker hair, but he had had to agree with Jowell. She was also a fine beauty.

"Of course," Paden said. "We'll help however we can."

"Do you patrol Mull?"

"All the time." Jowell stepped forward, eyes sparkling with interest. Jowell had always been a bit more intense.

"Have you seen any unwelcome strangers?" Brynja asked, crossing her arms. "New ones?"

Hagen looked to Artan, confused. "We haven't. Artan? Simone? Are you looking for someone in particular? Clyde is dead. He was the one who came for Sheona, correct?"

"Clyde is dead," Simone confirmed. "And Roger won't bother anyone again. He's in chains, as far as I understand. We haven't seen anyone on Mull, but we've all noticed a boat circling Iona of late. And we don't know who they are. Can't get close enough to identify either of the men in the boat. They're quite careful. No one comes near Iona that often."

"Any idea where they're from?" Jowell asked, swinging his chestnut-colored locks away from his face. "Where do they go when they leave?"

"We don't know," Artan explained. "They could be from Coll or Tiree. Ulva. The mainland. We have Thane and his men keeping watch as well."

Thane MacQuarie was chieftain of Clan MacQuarie, situated on the northwestern side of Mull.

"Any idea who it would be?" Hagen asked, his hands settling on his hips. A fury was building inside him—he had a sudden inkling of what they were going to say.

Brynja waited until the others all denied knowing the identity of the fools in the boat. Then she said with a conviction that didn't go unnoticed, "It's the other one."

"Which one?" Paden asked.

Hagen's hand ran down his face. He knew exactly what she meant, but he had to curtail his urge to bellow like a banshee.

Simone nodded, crossing her arms. "The other

one who was after Sheona. No one knows who he was. You're probably correct, Brynja."

Hildi hung her head. "I'm afraid of him."

Jowell took two steps closer to Hildi, something telling to Hagen.

"He doesn't frighten me." Brynja glanced at Hildi. "I've seen him before. I put my dagger in his upper leg. So you can all guess what he wants. Or should I say who?"

"Vengeance," Hagen whispered. "He's after you, Brynja."

"I can't discount that belief, Grant," Artan said.

Hagen knew who he was going to be after. An ugly bastard with a wound in his leg.

The buffoon was about to gain a few more wounds.

CHAPTER THREE

DUGAN

SHOLTO LANDRUM STRODE toward the cottage on Tiree, hoping to find his cousin inside. The man had been off to the mainland making deals that he didn't like. Oh, he knew all about Kelvan and Glenna of Buchan, how they'd made deals selling bairns, and they'd both died for it.

So why his foolish cousin wished to make the same kind of agreements he didn't know, but he'd come along and heard Kelvan's operation was available for anyone with enough guts to take it on. Dugan had jumped at the opportunity, but then again, his cousin had always been a blind fool about some things.

So Dugan took over the operation on Tiree, always in search of more bairns.

But then there was his friend Clyde. Was is a key part of that. Sholto had known Clyde for many years. In fact, he made it a point to come from Morvern to visit Clyde on Mull occasionally, so when he promised Sholto the taste of a fine lass, he'd gone with him willingly, even though it meant rowing to Iona.

He had no idea there'd be some bitch waiting for them, daggers in hand. She'd had strange hair and a look in her eyes that nearly made him turn around, but Clyde had insisted on going forward. The fool had thought they could beat the bitch, and they'd have two to tie up and play with.

Only the odd bitch had hit them both with a dagger, nearly amputating the most valued part of his body. Fortunately, she'd missed, but he'd been out with the fever for days. The truth was it still hurt him, though it had healed.

It took ten days for him to get his shaft hard again. That had frightened him more than anything. That odd bitch would pay. He'd see to that.

Sholto had planned to land on the back side of the isle and walk to the nunnery where the bitch lived. He had patience, and he'd studied that part of the isle because no one was ever there. She'd almost taken out his beloved lance, and if she'd been successful, what would become of him? She'd have to pay for what she did.

He strode inside the cottage, not surprised to see his cousin Dugan there, a fury on his face unlike he'd ever seen. "What's wrong?" he asked Dugan.

"Why the hell didn't you tell me?"

"Tell you what?"

Dugan got up, slamming his stool onto the dirt floor, then paced the cottage, cursing at one thing, punching what he could. "Why. Didn't. You. Tell. Me?"

"I'm not sure what you mean?" Dugan was younger, bigger, and more muscular than him, always had been, but worse yet, he had a temper that turned rampant with little warning. He often reminded him of a toddler searching for his mother's teat on a hot day.

Dugan stopped directly in front of him, leaning over to stare directly into his eyes. "Why didn't you tell me there were four or five of Alexander Grant's grandsons on Mull? And one of his sons! Here! Right here! Away from the thousand guards they must have at this point. Away from the Ramsays, the Camerons, and all the other buggered allies they have."

Sholto, totally confused, took a seat at the table and chose his words carefully. "I didn't know? Why do you care about the Grants?"

Dugan made his hand into a fist and slammed it down on the table, causing him to jump. "Why do I care? Because Alexander Grant is the one who killed my grandfather! That's why!"

"He did? I didn't know that. I just knew he died in a swordfight."

"Alex Grant is the reason my sire didn't have any siblings. He killed my sire before he could marry and have bairns." Dugan took a seat, his fist flexing over and over again.

"But…" Sholto tipped his head, wanting to say that he was here so…

"My grandsire got the serving maid with child,

my mother. He never married. He was supposed to marry some English lass."

"I still don't understand." Sholto pushed his stool away from the table, out of range of the fist in front of him.

Dugan bolted up and began to pace, muttering to himself. Sholto tried to understand his words but was afraid to move. Perhaps it would be a good time to sneak out of the cottage.

"I could have been the laird of a castle. Mayhap I'll find his daughter or take his granddaughter. Or nay, that wouldn't help me at all. I need to go after his sons. Nay. His grandsons. Or both. Son and grandson. I'll draw them out and cut them all down."

Sholto kept his mouth closed.

"How many guards have they at Duart Castle?" He scratched the few thin hairs left on his head.

"I don't know."

"Then find out! I need to know by the morrow. I'm moving on this. I have to know before they leave. Or before they bring more guards across the water. Before I lose this opportunity. Before someone else does it for me."

Sholto said nothing, just watched the man in his continuous tantrum. "What was your father's name again?"

"My grandfather was supposed to marry a MacDonald bitch, Alex's wife. Instead he slayed my grandsire in front of a crowd at Grant Castle. He embarrassed my clan, because my grandsire died at the end of Alex Grant's sword."

"Hell, I never knew that. Sorry, Dugan."

"So, you know what that means?"

Sholto shook his head, afraid to say the wrong thing.

Dugan grabbed him by the collar, pulling him forward. "It means that Alex Grant's son and grandsons must die at the end of my sword. I must avenge his death."

"What do you want me to do?"

Dugan tossed him back onto the stool. "Naught. Just find out how many guards they have. First, we'll go find that lass who stuck your leg, steal her away, then the Grants will come for her and I'll kill them all."

"How do you know they'll come?"

"Because that's the way they are. They have to help everyone. So if we steal that lass and the other one with her, then word will get around from that couple who lives on Iona, and they'll come for her."

"How will they know where we hide them?"

"We'll let the word get out."

"And then?"

"Then when the Grants come to Tiree, I'll kill every one of them."

"You'll need help."

"I'll get help. I have enough coin to hire more mercenaries with naught but evil and death on their minds. I've already bought five score. I just need another three score. I'll bring honor to my grandsire's name. I've already taken over Kelvan's job, found some of his coin, and this makes me happier." Dugan clapped his hands and smiled.

"I'm finally going to get the chance I've always wanted."

"What's that?"

"I'm about to finally avenge the death of my grandsire, Niles."

CHAPTER FOUR

BRYNJA

B RYNJA NODDED TO Hildi, letting her
know it was time to return to the nunnery.
She didn't wish to stay wherever the arrogant
fair-haired Grant was, whatever his name was.
Jowell? Paden? Hagen? She didn't know which
one, and that alone annoyed her.

Because she prided herself on having a strong
memory—every name, every face, every weapon.

But every time she saw him, something
happened to her insides. It was something she
didn't understand, couldn't explain, couldn't ask
anyone about because it was unclear.

But the Grant warrior unsettled her and pissed
her off at the same time. He tried to command
them to attend a festival, as if there were anything
to celebrate in her life or Hildi's, but at least he
apologized for his boorishness.

He had to be the one named Hagen because
he'd told her when they first met near the
nunnery that his mother was a Norsewoman.
Hagen was a Norse name, not Paden or Jowell, so
he had to be the Norseman.

"Brynja!"

She cursed inwardly, then stopped and turned around to look at him. "What do you want?"

"Tell me more about this man. What makes you think he's following you? And how close does he get to you?"

Hagen's golden hair fell well past his shoulders, not straight or curly but something in between. His blue eyes had a way of reaching inside her belly and twisting. But oddly, not in a painful way. "I know who he is because I can feel him. His anger, his hatred of me for wounding him."

"And who is he with?" Hagen's legs went to a stance that she used to see in the arseholes who killed her mother—wide, yet strong. Powerful legs if she were to bet. Then his hands settled on his hips, the image of the man something she wouldn't forget quickly.

"That I don't know."

He took two steps forward. "Let me help you."

"I don't need your help, Grant. I can take care of myself." She gripped her spear tightly, her gaze locked on his to prove that she was indeed powerful. She would never allow a man like this to intimidate her.

She'd show them all one day.

"Can you? Is that why you're at the nunnery?"

Jowell whistled from behind him, moving closer to Hildi, who'd stepped away from her friend.

Paden laughed and ran in the opposite direction. "You better get yourself far away from that spear, cousin. I'm going back to speak with Simone and Artan."

She tossed her spear into the air, then caught it again, just to keep herself from slapping him, her jaw clenching. He had no idea why she was at the nunnery or what her past was like. He'd grown up in a castle, moved to another castle, rode the best of horses probably. What did he know of the way women were treated? To him, lasses were dressed in pretty gowns and carried a fan to keep themselves calm, if she were to guess. The women in his clan probably sat by the hearth and did needlework all day, never stepping outside the keep.

She preferred to be outside. "I'm not your concern. Leave me be."

"I just made you my concern."

"You're so overbearing. Have you no one to teach you manners?"

He hid a small smirk. "I know how to treat a lass."

"Do you? I don't see it." She had the sudden realization that he was too close, so close that she could feel his heat. He was warm, too warm.

"I wish to help you. That's all. Naught more, naught less."

"And I'm telling you to let it go. Go back to Duart Castle and play your games there." Her eyes narrowed, something she'd learned to do to keep her tears at bay. "Go row your big boat back, ride your fancy stallion to your giant castle, and leave me to do what I must do. I'm sure you have more important matters to attend to."

He took another two steps forward. If he reached out, he would be able to cup her cheek.

He wouldn't dare.

"I'm not playing games, Bryn."

"The name is Brynja."

"Brynja, I am offering my assistance. We'll take this boat and see if we can find the two men who were circling the isle."

"They're gone. You're too late. They circle early in the morn and just after dusk."

"Then I'll return."

"Don't bother. I'll take care of him. Next time, I'll put my dagger in his heart." She didn't tell him that she knew her small dagger wouldn't stop the evil fool, only slow him. She'd have to be closer to get her spear where she wanted, and she wasn't practiced at shooting at moving targets. She couldn't lift a sword well enough to do any damage, which was why she was training with Simone to learn to be an archer. That was going to take time.

Hildi nodded and took two steps forward. "She can do it."

"I'm sure she can. But what about his friend? Or what if he brings two friends? Is Hildi trained to help you?" He leaned forward.

Closer, but she refused to back up.

"I'll kill them both." The lass stood like a rock, not reacting to anything he said. "Hildi doesn't need to train. I can handle them."

"You have no help at the nunnery. Sure, Simone and Artan would help you if you were here, but you're at the nunnery. I'm here to tell you that bastard is going to wait and attack you at the nunnery, and if he came from this side of the isle before, he'll attack from the back next. Why don't you come to Duart Castle until we find out who this fool is? My mother would love to meet two Norsewomen. You would always be welcome at Clan Grantham."

Hildi giggled, "I'm not a woman. I'm only six and ten. She's eight and ten. And we're not allowed to leave. Ever."

Hagen smiled. "I'll speak with the abbess, let her know that you might be in danger. I think she'd approve of a trip. Spend a sennight with us. You'll find out that life can be better."

"Better?"

"Better than a nunnery. You don't belong in a nunnery."

"And where do I belong?"

Her gaze locked on his, the pain and anger so clear that he had to know more about what her past was. "You belong with me."

"That's exactly what I expected a spoiled, arrogant fool to say. I don't belong to anyone but myself." She spun around and hurried back to her chamber at the nunnery. She didn't need to spend any more time with this overconfident man.

"Wait, please." Hagen followed her and touched her shoulder, making sure not to grab her.

"Ow!" A spark shot out from his hand when he touched her skin. "What the hell was that?" she asked, whirling back to face him. "What did you do?"

"Naught." He rubbed his fingers together, trying to make sense of what he'd experienced. "I just touched you. I don't know what you mean."

"Liar." She stalked away but waited until she was far enough away before she wiped the sweat from between her breasts. There had been something when he'd touched her, a spark, a glint of fire, of something strong.

Something that had never happened before, and she didn't like it.

CHAPTER FIVE

MAGNI

M AGNI'S MOTHER APPROACHED him
out on the beach where he played with
his brother. Tenney stood up and pointed at the
water. "Bo... Big bo..."

"Aye, that's a boat, Tenney," Magni said. "See
how smart he is, Mama?"

"Aye, he's a bright laddie, Magni, and so are
you."

"Am I?"

"Of course you are. Otherwise, how is Tenney
learning so many words? It's you who is teaching
him." His mother smiled, folding her hands on
her lap where she sat on a nearby log.

"What's wrong, Mama?" His mother never came
out to the beach. She spent her time cleaning up
their hut or cooking the night's stew. Sometimes
she helped Beatris with the other wee bairns. His
father usually went with Artan to chop wood so
they could keep warm in the winter. Sometimes
he took Magni fishing too. He liked fishing. "Do
you need me to go fishing with Papa?"

"Nay, I need you to talk with me, lad."

"About what?" He turned to her, afraid she was about to ask him those hard questions again. Where was his sister? Lia always disappeared when he needed her.

"About you. You've been through a terrible ordeal, and I'd hoped you'd get over it. I knew it would take a while, but you still seem troubled, lad."

"Nay, I'm fine."

"I don't think you are, son." She sat calmly on the log, her hands still primly folded.

"Aye, I am!" He didn't mean to yell, but he didn't wish to talk about stupid things like feelings. He was fine now that he was on an isle with the abbey and the monks and the nuns to protect him. Surely God would not allow anyone to steal him away from this isle. Someone had told him once that even the villains would never hurt a nun or a priest.

"Then why don't you wish to go to the Yule celebration? I thought the bairns were all your friends. Sylvi and Tora and Sandor and Alana. Don't you miss Alana? She surely misses you."

He scowled because he didn't wish to admit how much he missed his friends. And he wouldn't cry about it. Only wee bairns cried. Why, Tenney hardly cried at all anymore, only when he fell and hurt himself. "I like it here."

A boat approached, catching their attention. He looked out over the sea to make sure it wasn't anyone evil. "Who is it, Mama?"

"Your eyes are better than mine, Magni. Who does it look like?"

"I think it's Thane. I'm so excited! I wish he came more often." Whew! He got away from that talk with his mother. He didn't wish to discuss it. He was staying here on the island where he was safest and that was it. "Thane! Over here! Mama," he turned around and motioned to his mother. "Watch Tenney and I'll help Thane." He raced out to see his dear friend, then clapped when he saw Mora was with him. "Greetings, Mora. I'm glad you came."

"Greetings to you, Magni. I see your brother is over there. And your Mama too. Are you still happy here? I miss you so much. Don't you miss us too? And you should see Tamsin's belly. Do you think she'll have a boy or a girl? I'm hoping for a girl. We need more girls at our castle."

Thane put his arm on his sister's and said, "Greetings to you, Magni. Would you hand me that rope, please?"

Magni grabbed it and handed it to Thane, who secured the vessel.

"Why are you here, Thane?"

"Because we miss you, Magni," Thane said, stepping out of the boat and holding his arms open. Magni leapt into them with a shriek of joy.

"I miss you too. Papa is busy. Come see Mama, and I think Simone is here." He shot back across the landscape, not wanting to look at Thane. He missed him too much. And Mora too. And Brian. And their parents and Alana and Tamsin. If only...

"Come, Mama," he snagged her hand and pulled her toward the beach, though she wasn't moving quickly.

"Magni, my back has been bothering me a wee bit. They're coming this way." His mother's hands did that thing she did, leaning them both against her back and bending backwards.

Simone came along next. "Greetings to you, MacQuaries. So nice to see you. Are you ready for winter?"

"Aye. We brought some extra vegetables for the wee ones. And Mora has some fruit tarts for someone special."

"Me! Me! Please! They don't make them here." Even though he'd begged Beatris to have their cook make fruit tarts, she hadn't made any yet, just baked apples.

Once they found their way to a table in the small hut, they found seats and Mora took a fruit tart out of her sack and set it down in front of Magni. He let out a big sigh, taking a whiff of the wonderful delicacy. "Apple. I love it," he whispered. "May I?"

His mother said, "Should you not share it, Magni?"

He frowned, not having thought of that, but he said, "They have fruit tarts, and we don't." Tenney came in behind him, his hand in the air for something to eat. "Tenney. I'll share with Tenney." His brother didn't eat much yet. He could give him a small bite, but just a small one.

They sat while Simone and Magni's mother got everyone something to drink, broth and mead both available. "Why are you here, Thane?"

Mora looked at her brother, who gave her a

small nod, then she said, "We wish to invite you and Tenney and your parents, Magni. We'd like you to come to live with us."

Magni nearly spit his fruit tart out, but he couldn't lose it, so he swallowed, nearly gagging, then shouted, "Nay, we cannot!"

"Why not?" Mora asked.

Magni set the fruit tart down and said, "Because Mama wants to stay here." That should convince them.

His mother gave him that look she did, the one that told him she was on to him. "I'd be pleased to go to MacQuarie Castle. At least for the winter, Magni. The floor is cold in winter."

Thane said, "Magni, there are ten of you living in this small hut, and they cannot build a new one before winter. Next spring, we can all help build another one, but until then, you will be cramped all winter in this tiny home. Why don't you live with us for a while? We have several big hearths and a fine cook. You and Tenney can have your own chamber, and you won't have to sleep on the floor."

"I don't mind sleeping on the floor. Nay. I'm not going." He stormed out, slamming the door on the way out, tears now running down his face. He didn't want the big chieftain seeing him cry. He wasn't a baby, just afraid sometimes. He swiped the tears away when he heard the door close.

Thane shouted, "Magni, wait for me, please."

He did, but he wouldn't look at the big laird. It hurt his neck sometimes to look up at someone as big as Thane. And Connor Grant was even worse.

Thane came up behind him and led him over to a boulder. "Sit with me a moment, please?"

"All right." He sat down, scowling. He knew he would try to convince him to move to Thane's castle, but he didn't wish to go. He'd get stolen away again.

Once they were both seated, Thane said, "Tamsin misses you verra much, and so does Alana."

"They why didn't she come?"

"Because her belly is getting too big. She was afraid she'd tip the boat over."

Magni laughed with a hoot, slapping his knee at that thought. "Would she?" He'd laugh if she did, but then he would feel badly.

"Nay. Do you think I would let Tamsin tip over?"

"Nay, because you are an honorable Highlander. I know it. I can't come back to your castle. Mama won't let me." Mama wasn't here to hear that lie so he thought it was worth a try.

"I think your parents might consider it. Your mother looks like her back is bothering her, and I can guess why. Can you?"

He knew why. The small pallet she had to sleep on. And Papa slept with her. Magni and Tenney slept on the floor, and Tenney complained all the time that it was too cold, so Magni always cuddled him to sleep. But he wouldn't leave. And sometimes they both climbed in next to Mama. It was verra crowded.

"I'm not sure," he lied again, feeling a sudden wave of guilt for telling so many lies.

"I think she would be more comfortable in that big bed in the chamber that has no one in it now. And you could sleep in the same chamber as Alana or with your parents. I'd give you your own bed, Magni."

"You would?" He'd never had his own bed. He always slept with someone else—Rowan or Sandor or…"

"I would. If you decide you can't come, I hope you will at least come for a Yule visit, Magni. We might have special treats for the holiday season."

His eyes grew big. "What kind of special treats?"

"I'm not sure yet. You'll have to come and see."

He got up from the log and stared at Thane. Then he said, "Nay, we can't come."

And he ran off toward the nunnery.

CHAPTER SIX

HAGEN

———⚬⚬———

HAGEN PACED IN the great hall of Duart Castle after the morning meal was finished three days later. "Why, Mama? Why would the lass be so foolish as to not want my help? You're Norse. Are they different?"

"Hagen, I'm not sure if you know this or not," his mother, Sela Grant, said with the odd sense of patience she often had. "But you're also Norse."

"I know, but you know what I meant." He'd tried to figure out how to convince the lass to come to Duart Castle, but after the way she'd stormed off, calling him spoiled, he'd had to tamp down his own temptation to argue with her.

But deep in his belly, he knew she was right. He'd had a much easier life than she'd had, and he wished to fix that, if he could.

His father, Connor Grant, youngest son of Alexander and Maddie Grant, came down the stairs and asked, "Who's Norse?"

His mother said, "Hagen is…intrigued by a lass at the nunnery who is Norse. She's refusing his help."

His father arched a brow before taking a seat by the hearth after speaking with a serving lass about some porridge. "You're interested in a nun, Hagen? Truly?"

"Nay, she's not a nun." He gave his father a look of derision.

"Not yet. It could be she plans to become one if she's at the nunnery," his mother said.

"Fill me in, please," his father said, his gaze locking on Hagen's.

Hagen took a seat and explained, "She's not a nun but living at the nunnery. I'm not sure why, but I'm guessing she and her friend are orphans. Like Beatris and Geva's place with all the orphans, but she's older. Do you recall when Clyde and another tried to attack Sheona Rankin?"

"Aye."

"This lass knew they were coming for her, so she hit both men with a dagger, one in the leg and Clyde in the shoulder. Scared them off. There's a boat that's been circling Iona every day, and Brynja thinks it's the other man coming after her for revenge."

"Brynja. That is a fine Norse name. Especially for one who can hit two men with near deadly aim." His father leaned back in his chair and grinned.

"Da, be serious. Tell me what to do. The man is coming for her. Simone noticed the boat also, though he has a new partner with him. They come around twice a day, are not fishing, and Brynja thinks it could be that man coming for revenge."

"So what do you need? More men to go after him?"

Sela smirked and said quietly, "Brynja is refusing his help, Connor."

His father broke into a wide grin. "A Norsewoman refusing help from a Scot with good intentions? Where have I heard that before?" He tipped his chair back and balanced on two legs with a large guffaw. Then he set back down and stared at his wife before leaning over and kissing her cheek.

"You know he's part Norse, not just a Scot."

"Aye," his sire replied. "Sela, you have to answer him. I can't explain why women can be so stubborn. Why would she refuse him?"

Sela twirled a lock of hair that escaped her plait. "A few reasons pop into my mind. First, she might not like being around you, but since you just met, I doubt that would be it. Second, she doesn't wish to bother you. Women have a hard time asking for help, especially from strangers. Third, she's stubborn and thinks she doesn't need your help. That's my guess. If she's that good with a dagger, she's fairly accomplished for a young lass. How old is she, Hagen?"

"She's eight and ten. Her friend Hildi is two years younger."

"Is Hildi her sister?"

"I don't think so. Brynja is fair-haired and Hildi is dark-haired."

His mother tipped her head at him. "Think about that, fair-haired brother to two dark-haired people."

Hagen rolled his eyes. "True, but they don't look alike."

His mother sent his father a lopsided smirk. Hellfire, but the two had a language he didn't understand.

Hagen got up to pace again, grabbing an apple from a basket to chew on. "She is the one who used a dagger, hit both men, and she can use a spear too. She's equally talented at both and now she's trying archery."

His father asked, "A spear? That is impressive."

His mother said, "A common weapon for a lass in the land of the Norse."

"And she's good at it?" his father asked before taking his first sip of the broth that Murreal brought him, nodding his thanks to her.

Hagen said, "She is. She hit a target at twenty paces with a spear and an arrow."

His father stared at his mother again. "You left out a possible reason, wife."

"And what is that, husband?"

Hagen watched the two as they did that odd thing of communicating by staring at each other and not speaking.

His father's gaze still locked on his mother's, he said to Hagen, "You unsettle her."

Hagen frowned, glancing from one parent to the other, his mother wearing a soft smile now. Fortunately, his sister Dyna came down the stairs, interrupting the three. "It's the last one, Hagen. She likes you."

"She does?" Was that what his father meant about unsettling her? Why didn't he just say that?

Dyna paused on her trip to the kitchens. "Aye. She's too stubborn to admit it, so she just denies you. That's what happens when the heart becomes involved. It makes you do stupid things. Things that you have no explanation for. Why else would I have tripped Derric and put my boot on his chest when he was the only man to ever set my heart fluttering?"

"Is that what it was, Sela?" his father asked.

His mother, still locked on his father's eyes, whispered, "You know exactly what it was, Connor Grant."

Dyna headed toward the kitchens. "Get out now, Hagen. Run for your life. When they get like that, you don't want to be witness to the worst of it."

Hagen, confused, got up and followed his sister into the kitchens. Once they were on the other side of the door, he whispered, "Then what do I do?"

Dyna made three bowls of porridge, taking the kettle from the serving lass who had a bowl for his father and left. "Don't listen to her. Be persistent. And use your head. She can't hit two men with a spear at the same time, and she can't stop them both with daggers. She needs help from someone. It may as well be you. You like her?" Dyna asked, waggling her brow at him.

"I'm not sure. I'd like to know her better, but she doesn't live here, so how do I get to know her when she refuses everything I offer?"

"Ignore her and go anyway. Watch the boat. Go to MacQuarie land and see what Thane says about her. Has he noticed any strange boats? Ask Artan if he thinks you'd have a chance when she's not around. Don't give up if you are truly interested."

Hagen turned around and headed out the door. "My thanks, Dyna."

"Where are you going?"

He stopped at the door and smirked. "MacQuarie land. I'm after a Norsewoman."

"Good. I'd like to learn how to throw a spear."

Then he stepped out into the hall, surprised to see his parents had disappeared.

CHAPTER SEVEN

BRYNJA

SISTER ADA STROLLED along the coastline behind Brynja, who paced the shore, hands on her hips, spear not far away. "Are you certain the boat will be here?"

Brynja answered without turning around, focusing on the sea around them. "Of course. He always comes in the morn. Sometimes he comes at night and other days he doesn't."

Hildi came running toward them. "Sister Ada, why are you here this morn?"

The nun sighed. "The truth is that I worry about you two."

Brynja stopped her pacing and turned to face the woman. "There is no need to worry about us. I'll protect both of us."

"But I worry for your soul, lass, not that you will be attacked. I know that's your primary concern, but I trust our Lord to keep us safe, along with the assistance of you and Simone. I think you spend too much time out here, chasing a boat that may come or may not. But what's inside of you?" She patted her hand to the middle of her chest. "This is what worries me about you."

Brynja turned away so she could roll her eyes, something her mother hated, but it was a perfect way to express how her insides felt without speaking. "I'm fine, Sister. I missed the fools this morn. I overslept. We'll come help cut vegetables for the pottage." It was something they did nearly every day, and she didn't mind at all. It helped her deal with some of her feelings that she couldn't put words to.

"I would appreciate that. You neglected your chores yesterday and it's not the first time this has happened. I don't want you to be so immersed in revenge that you forget everything else around you, Brynja." The sister folded her hands in front of her. "God is always watching, lass."

She knew she'd missed once, but twice? What would happen if they rejected her? Sent her away? The thought was too frightening. "My apologies, Sister. I'll see that it does not happen again."

"We will forgive you this time as you've had much to deal with." Sister Ada turned away, her robes billowing in the wind as she headed back to the hallowed grounds. "Follow me then. We can talk inside."

How she dreaded this. Why did everyone insist on worrying about her? All she had to do was put her spear in the heart of the two men who killed her mother and her aunt, then put her dagger in the other man's belly. Then he would leave her alone.

She had to do it. Every night of the past four

moons, she had nightmares of the men who attacked her mother and aunt, stealing their cottage, and then taking the two lasses to another cottage on Tiree.

It was there they learned why. The bastards were going to sell the two young girls to men across the water. She didn't understand exactly why, but she heard different words from the fools who guarded their cottage.

Mistress, love slave, plaything.

She hated men, every spitting part of their bodies. They lied and connived and beat people. How many others had they stolen away? How many more would be their victims?

And most of the ruffians smelled horribly. Did they never wash their clothing in the sea?

"Come along," Sister Ada said.

"I'll be right there. I'll put my weapons away, then I'll be along." She waved Hildi off with the nun.

Brynja trudged into their hall with the multiple beds, thinking about Sheona and how much she missed her. Iona was now the home where she and Hildi lived, their days filled with praying and working and worrying.

A far cry from the days when she and Hildi would help their mothers with chores, then spend the rest of the time swimming or hiking the isle of Tiree. They loved to watch the birds, climb the hills to overlook the sea, or fish for their dinner.

They laughed and giggled and spent their days doing whatever they wished. Then at night, they'd listen to their mothers tell tales of the

Norse and the goddesses. Freya was her favorite, mostly because she was her mother's favorite.

How she missed her mother, her gentle touches, her soft-spoken ways, her warm hugs.

They never laughed on Iona unless they played with the bairns at the nearby Ionaland.

She tidied up her bed, put her weapons away, and left, strolling across the courtyard to the kitchens of the nunnery. It was beautiful here, the stone arches and walkways something she'd never seen before. The abbey wasn't far from them, the structure the largest on the isle, but they didn't go there often.

She opened the door and heard Hildi's voice immediately. "Over here. Carrots to cut."

Bryjna joined the two at the workbench, grabbing a knife and chopping with her usual vigor.

"Brynja, perhaps it might be better if you forgot about the boat. It may be simply a fishing vessel," Sister Ada said. "Have you considered that possibility?"

"Why? I think it's wise to make sure they aren't coming to attack us." She gripped the knife harder and sliced a carrot with a precision others didn't care about. *Chop, chop, chop, chop.*

"I've known others who carry a hate and a vengeance deep inside them for too long. What I fear is that it could draw your focus too much. I think your time would be better spent praying or meditating."

Chop, chop, chop, chop, chop, chop.

"Or you could join the group where you can

learn to read. Those nuns study the Bible and use their studies to teach others. Does that sound like something that might interest you?"

"Nay, sorry."

Chop, chop, chop.

"Tell me about your time living here at the nunnery. Have you or Hildi decided if either of you are interested in taking your vows? Perhaps one of you would like to dedicate your lives to serving our Lord."

Chop, chop, chop, chop, chop.

Hildi said, "I think I would prefer working at Ionaland when I'm old enough."

"And that is an admirable vocation, my dear. Perhaps next winter we can make that arrangement for you. I am pleased you can see that in your future, Hildi." Then the attention turned straight to her. "Brynja? What about you?"

Chop, chop, chop, chop, chop, chop, chop, chop, chop.

She tossed the knife down on the table. "I've told you many times, Sister. And I'm sorry that you do not approve of me and my ways. But I am focused on two things and two only."

"Aye?" The nun looked at her as if she had no idea what she was about to say. As if she'd never heard her the other ten times she'd told her.

If she had to say it again, she would.

"I need to put a blade in the heart of the men who killed my mother and my aunt. And then I'm going after the man who came here for Sheona, who would have used Hildi and me after he finished with her."

"Please consider letting this go, child."

"Nay!"

"Why not?"

"Because he's coming for me next!"

Brynja whirled around and ran out the door, allowing it to slam behind her.

At least Hagen hadn't told her she needed to change her ways.

The nuns told her all the time. They just didn't understand that she couldn't.

Anger for their situation possessed her and wouldn't let go until she got what she wanted.

What her soul needed.

Vengeance.

Vengeance was her soul now.

CHAPTER EIGHT

SHOLTO

———～～———

THE WOUND IN Sholto's thigh throbbed with every step, a constant reminder of the Norse bitch who'd put her dagger there. It has festered for nearly a fortnight, not the flesh, which had healed after a fashion, but the humiliation. The rage.

He limped to the window of the cottage they'd claimed on Tiree's western shore, watching storm clouds gather over the sound. Behind him, Dugan sat at the table, counting coins with the focused attention of a man who worshipped nothing but silver.

"You're brooding again," Dugan said without looking up. "It's tiresome."

"She stabbed me." Sholto's hand went to his thigh, pressing against the scar through the fabric. "That golden-haired witch put a blade in my leg and laughed about it. Then she threatened to put another one there."

"Aye, you've mentioned it. Several times a day for nearly a moon." Dugan stacked his coins with irritating precision. "What you haven't done is anything useful about it."

Sholto spun from the window, nearly losing his balance as his bad leg protested. "I've been watching. Following. Learning where she is."

"Watching the nunnery from a boat like some lovesick fool." Dugan finally looked up, his pale eyes cold and assessing. "All you've accomplished is letting her see you. Letting her know you're coming. That's not hunting, Sholto. That's announcing yourself."

"I want her to be afraid. I want her to lie awake at night knowing I'm out here. Knowing I'm coming for her." Sholto's voice dropped to something darker. "I want her to remember what I'll do to her when I finally get my hands on that pretty throat."

Dugan's expression didn't change. "And after you've strangled her and satisfied your wounded pride, what then? You'll still be a landless mercenary with a limp and a reputation for losing to women half your size."

The words hit like stones. Sholto's fists clenched. "Careful, Dugan."

"Or what? You'll kick me with the leg she already wounded?" Dugan returned his attention to his coins. "Face the truth, Sholto. You're obsessed with one woman who humiliated you. I'm interested in building an empire."

"Empire." Sholto spat the word. "You're a hired sword. Same as me."

"For now." Dugan leaned back in his chair, lacing his fingers behind his head. "But I won't be for long. See, while you've been nursing your wounded leg and your wounded pride, I've been gathering information. Making contacts. Learning who matters and who I can trust. I'm not interested in finding bairns for long."

Dugan had found these cottages nearly four months ago, getting rid of the owners and sending their bairns off to a cottage where he could get coin for them. But the truth was he was tired of handling bairns. And now that he'd found coin he hadn't expected, his aspirations had grown. Now he had a plan.

Despite himself, Sholto's interest piqued. "And?"

"And your little Norse bitch won't be on Iona for long." Dugan's smile was thin and cold. "She'll be at Duart Castle soon, they're telling me. With the Grants."

Sholto's pulse quickened. "How do you know?"

"Because I pay people to know things. Fishermen. Merchants. A serving girl at the MacQuarie holding who's verra fond of coin and verra talkative after a few cups of ale." He gestured dismissively. "Your golden-haired prize is hoping to keep company with one of the younger Grants. I'm guessing he is one of Connor Grant's sons. Grandson of the legendary Alexander Grant."

The name meant nothing to Sholto beyond another obstacle between him and Brynja. But Dugan's expression had sharpened with something like hunger.

"The Grants," Dugan continued, his voice taking on a strange intensity. "Do you know what killing a Grant would do for a man's reputation? What it would mean in the Lowlands, where the mercenary companies compete for the best contracts?"

"I don't care about your reputation—"

"Then you're a fool." Dugan stood, pacing to the window where Sholto had been brooding moments before. "Think, fool. The Grant name carries weight from here to Edinburgh and beyond. They're legends. Alexander Grant fought at the Battle of Largs against the Norse. Connor Grant has held the Highlands together through wars and rebellions, their clan now one of the largest in all the land. And there's a new generation—grandsons, all carrying that blessed name."

He turned back to face Sholto, his pale eyes gleaming. "If I—if we—were to kill one of those precious heirs? If we were to strike at the heart of the Grant legacy?" He spread his hands. "Every mercenary company in Scotland would know my name. Dugan, the man who brought down a Grant. I could command any price. Lead any force. Build something that lasts."

Sholto stared at him. "You're daft. The Grants would hunt you to the ends of the earth."

"Let them try." Dugan's smile widened. "By the time they realize what happened, I'll be in the Lowlands with a company of two hundred men at my back. Men who respect strength. Men who follow the leader who proves himself most deadly."

He moved closer to Sholto, his voice dropping

to something almost confidential. "Don't you see? Your obsession with that girl—it's small. Petty. But if we make it part of something larger? If we use her to draw out a grandson or Connor Grant, and we kill him along with her?" He laughed softly. "That's not revenge. That's legacy."

Sholto's mind churned. He didn't care about legacies or reputations. He cared about the look in that bitch's eyes when she'd driven that dagger into his thigh—fierce, unafraid, victorious. He cared about wiping that look away forever. About making her afraid. About hearing her beg.

But if Dugan's ambitions could help him get to her…

"What are you proposing?" he asked slowly.

Dugan's smile turned predatory. "I'm proposing we go after the lass. Once they know we have her, they'll come to us. The youngest Grant will come and so will his sire. They can't help themselves. They travel in groups. Then I'll kill both of them and you can have the girl."

"You'll allow it?"

"She's yours." Dugan's expression was indifferent. "Do what you want with her. Keep her, kill her, sell her—I don't care. My interest is in the Grant name. Once Connor Grant is dead, I'll have what I need." He moved to the window again and stared out over the sea, his mind churning with ideas. Sholto had seen him like this before. "They'll be ripe for an attack and they'll be too busy grieving." The man smiled and rubbed his hands together, a smile nearly gleeful dancing across his face.

Sholto's hand went to his thigh again, rubbing the scar that ached in cold weather. His permanent reminder of the bitch who'd bested him. "How many men can you gather?"

Dugan turned away from the window. "Mayhap three score with the coin I found. Men who won't ask questions. Men who'll follow orders when the blood starts flowing." Dugan crossed his arms. "But I need your agreement. And I need you to stop this ridiculous brooding and start thinking like a warrior instead of a jilted lover."

The insult stung, but Sholto forced it down. Dugan was right about one thing—watching from boats had accomplished nothing. If he wanted Brynja, he'd have to take her. And if taking her meant helping Dugan kill some legendary Grant heir…

He could live with that.

"When?" Sholto asked.

"Soon. The weather's turning worse, which works in our favor. First we get the lass here." Dugan's smile turned cunning, "Then her lover will follow, and if we're verra lucky, we might get two Grants for the price of one."

Something cold moved through Sholto's chest. Killing some young warrior in his prime was one thing. But Connor Grant was a legend, an old man who'd fought in wars before Sholto was born. "That's—"

"Brilliant." Dugan's eyes gleamed with ambition. "Can you imagine? Dugan, the man who killed Connor Grant. Or at the verra least, who was there when the old legend finally fell. My name would echo in every tavern, every mercenary camp, every lord's hall from here to the Borders."

He began pacing again, energy crackling off him like lightning. "Every petty lord with a grudge will want to hire me. Every ambitious merchant will pay for my protection. I'll build a company that rivals any in Scotland—nay, in all of Britain."

His voice dropped, taking on an almost reverent quality. "Do you understand what I'm offering you, Sholto? Not just your petty revenge on one girl. But a chance to be part of something that will be remembered. A chance to matter."

Sholto didn't care about mattering. He cared about the smell of fear, the satisfaction of breaking something that had dared to wound him. But he understood ambition well enough to recognize it in others. And ambitious men were useful—they planned, they organized, they got things done.

"You really think you can kill a Grant?" Sholto asked.

"I think I can kill anyone if the price is right and the planning is sound." Dugan turned to face him fully. "Grants bleed like anyone else. They die like anyone else. They just have more coin."

He moved back to the table, pulling out a rough map he'd been working on. "And once they are grieving, we move on to taking over their castle on Mull. Duart Castle sits on a promontory. Good defensive position, which is why the MacDougalls chose it. But it also means limited escape routes. If we come at them from the land side with enough men, we can bottle them up. Force them to either fight or surrender."

"They'll fight," Sholto said with certainty. "Men like that don't surrender."

Sholto studied the map, but his mind was elsewhere. On golden braids and blue eyes. On the sound a blade made sliding between ribs. On the way Brynja would look when she realized she'd lost.

"I want her alive," he said. "At least at first."

Dugan glanced up, his expression calculating. "How long do you need?"

"Long enough to make sure she understands what it cost her to cross me." Sholto's voice was flat, emotionless. "Long enough to hear her beg. To break that spirit that made her think she could put a dagger in my leg and walk away."

"Fine. Just don't let your…plaything interfere with the larger plan." Dugan rolled up the map. "I'll start gathering men. Good fighters who won't balk at attacking Grants."

Sholto's jaw clenched. "When this is over— when I have her—I'll be the man who broke the girl who thought she could wound me. I'll be the man who taught her what happens when you cross the wrong person."

"Small ambitions for a small man." But Dugan's tone was almost cheerful now as he counted coins. "Still, small ambitions are easier to achieve than large ones. You might actually succeed."

They worked in silence for a while, Dugan calculating, Sholto brooding. Outside, the storm was building, dark clouds rolling in from the west.

Finally, Dugan straightened, closing the chest. "One or two more days before we grab the girl. Then we'll bring her here. By then I'll have the men and supplies. Then we wait for the Grants to arrive. Have you found out their number yet?"

"Nay, I haven't been able to get over to Craignure yet. On the morrow I'll go."

"Good. I need to know how many men to hire. Find out."

"And if the Grants have more men than we thought? If we can't separate the grandson or Connor?"

"Then we adapt. I didn't survive ten years as a mercenary by being inflexible." Dugan's smile was cold. "But one way or another, I will have my reputation. And you will have your revenge. The only question is how many Grants have to die to make it happen."

He moved to the door, pausing with his hand on the latch. "Oh, and Sholto? Stop patrolling the coast in that damned boat. You're warning her we're coming. Let her think she's safe. Let her relax into that false security. It'll make the surprise so much sweeter."

Then he was gone, leaving Sholto alone with his thoughts and his aching leg.

Sholto returned to the window, staring out at the gathering storm. Two days. In two days, he'd have his hands on that golden-haired bitch. He'd show her what happened to women who thought they could fight back. Who thought they were stronger than the men who owned them.

His hand went to his thigh one more time,

pressing against the scar. She'd marked him. Left her signature on his flesh like some kind of brand.

Soon, he'd return the favor. And his mark would be permanent.

He smiled at the thought of having complete control over the lass. Let Dugan have his ambitions and his empire. Let him chase his precious reputation.

Sholto would have something better.

He'd have her fear. And that was worth more than all the fame in Scotland.

CHAPTER NINE

BRYNJA

THE NEXT DAY, Brynja made her way around Ulva, the place they traveled to because not many lived on the isle, yet it held the most beautiful apple trees she'd ever seen. She and Hildi had rowed over with two monks from the abbey. They needed a good supply of fruit for the winter and there were still a few apples that hadn't dropped yet, even in this cold weather, because the trees were so well-protected from the cold wind of the sea.

They searched for nuts and any other food that could feed them through the long winter season. Ulva was much larger than Iona, so they often followed the coastline of Mull with their boat to make their way over to forage for food. They'd put their boat on the south end, the monks heading in one direction with their sacks while she and Hildi headed in the opposite direction.

"What think you of Hagen?" Hildi asked, hiding her smirk by turning her head immediately after asking.

"I see that, Hildi. I know you're amused, but

there's naught to get excited about. Hagen is no different than Jowell, Paden, Alaric, or Broc to me. They're from Clan Grantham and all the same." She noticed a tree with apples on the ground and pointed, the two heading in that direction.

Hildi said, "I think Hagen thinks you're special."

"And what if Jowell thought you special? Would it please you?"

Hildi scrunched her face up, then broke into a wide grin. "Aye. I think he's cute."

She squelched the impulse to roll her eyes, then scanned the area, always protective of the two of them. "It matters not to me," she said, finding a few edible apples and placing them in her basket that she would put in the sack once it was full. The sound of voices caught her, and she held her hand up to her friend. "Hush."

Brynja froze, unable to make out the voices, but she knew they were not the monks. "I'm going through there to see."

Hildi nodded, the two setting their baskets on the ground as Brynja led the way through the thick trees. They both stopped at the same exact time, the boat traveling in front of them close enough that they could actually see the inhabitants.

One was the bastard who'd tried to hurt Sheona, but the other one had his head turned away from them. Brynja was certain of the one. She nodded to Hildi to let her know they were the ones she feared but held her hand up to keep her from speaking. There was a line of trees along the coastline that they were able to hide behind.

The two were involved in an avid discussion, something she hoped would keep them from noticing her presence.

Brynja followed the boat that held the two men rowing down the coastline. She stayed hidden in the tree line, listening to the conversation between the two. Apparently, neither one knew how well voices carried across water.

"What's your plan, Dugan?"

"On the morrow. We'll come back just before dark. Catch her unaware. Throw her in the boat and take her to Tiree. And what did you find out about the Grants, Sholto?"

"I haven't yet, Dugan. I've tried, but you cannot just walk up to the gates of the castle and ask."

"Then I suggest you get your arse over there as soon as we return. I need that number. I can't attack until I know how many guards they have. Even if I choose to wait on Tiree, I need enough men to fight them off."

"Why the Grants? I thought Duart was Clan Grantham?"

"I told you. Alexander Grant killed my grandfather, and I want vengeance. It is Grantham, but Clan Grant is part of Grantham, idjit. Just find out. Go to Craignure and ask in town. They'll know. I'll leave you there and return after I check out Mingary. And ask if Connor, Kyla, or Jamie Grant are there. I want as many of Alexander's heirs as I can."

"Connor, Kyle, and James?"

"Nay, fool. Just ask how many of his sons are there." The man spit off the side of the boat.

"What was your grandsire's name again?"

"Niles…Wait. What the hell was that?"

They pulled the oars in and slowed so Brynja motioned for Hildi to move back, but she tripped and landed with a groan.

"What the hell? Someone's over there."

"Through the trees. I see them."

"Run, Hildi!" Brynja and Hildi took off toward their boat, running through the trees as fast as they could. Hildi dropped her basket and bumped into a tree just before the man roared toward her, laughing as he charged down the open path next to her, catching up.

"Faster!" Brynja shouted, her hand on the dagger in the fold in her trews.

But the smaller man appeared next to Hildi, and he grabbed her arm, yanking her in front of him and setting his knife at her throat. "Come on out, bitch. I have your friend, and I'll keep my knife at her throat until you appear. Or I could just kill her first."

Brynja paled, hiding in a clump of bushes about fifteen paces away. She didn't have her spear, but she had two daggers. If she fired one off, she might hit him, but she might hit her dear friend too.

"Brynja, help me." Hildi's cries carried to her, the shaking in her legs visible from the bushes.

What the hell could she do? She couldn't use her weapons with Hildi as his shield.

Brynja came out of the bushes, standing tall, refusing to let the ogre intimidate her. "Let her go and I'll come to you." If he did, and Hildi ran, she could hit him with one dagger before he managed to get close to her.

He let Hildi go, so Brynja moved forward, but then he reached for her cousin again, laughing.

Hildi screamed, shoving at him, and Brynja raced over, her blade ready to launch but she had no clear target.

Before she could get close enough, he grabbed Hildi by the arm and threw her against a tree. Hildi hit hard, her head snapping back as she fell to the ground. The man kicked her, and she rolled down the ridge to the beach.

"Hildi!" Brynja launched herself at the man, pulling her knife out as she cut his arm.

Surprised, he cursed, grabbing her by the braids. "I've got one of them, Dugan."

The cruel bastard snatched her by the arm and dragged her toward the beach where their boat sat.

He was too strong for her.

Brynja was about to be taken captive, and Hildi wasn't moving, blood leaking all over her hair.

CHAPTER TEN

HAGEN

HAGEN AND HIS two cousins headed out
for MacQuarie Castle before dark, the
three chatting when they could ride abreast on
certain sections of the path.

Jowell was the first one to speak. "So exactly
what is our purpose for this visit, Hagen?"

Direct as usual, Hagen paused to gather his
thoughts.

Paden didn't hesitate. "This is when Hagen asks
Thane to speak to him privately, then tells him to
make Brynja fall in love with him. That he can't
live without her..."

Hagen slowed his horse and dropped back so
he could follow Paden, who chuckled over his
shoulder, his teasing continuing in the usual
MacNicol way.

"I love her, Thane. Make her love me. And
could you please allow me to use one of your bed
chambers after you convince her I'm the most
skilled swordsman in all the land?"

"You are such an arse, Paden."

His voice reached up to its highest point again.

"But I love you so, Hagen. Marry me, please. Make me the happiest lass ever. I'll follow you around and do your bidding for all eternity."

"I'm going to knock your arse right off your mount and feed a fist into that sweet voice of yours."

Paden snorted and stopped. "Seriously, just go after her, Hagen. She's drawn to you."

"I don't know that. I think the opposite. The look in her eyes speaks more of hate than attraction."

Jowell waited for the other two to finish, speaking last as he often did. "Hagen, I'm not sure that Paden was still there when it happened, but I was. If that spark that lit up the sky when you touched her shoulder isn't a sign, then what is? I wish I'd received a similar sign about Hildi. I know she's a bit young yet, but I'm drawn to the lass."

Hagen sat up straight, slowing his mount. "You saw it? It was truly a spark? Because I thought mayhap my eyes were playing trickery on me."

"I saw it. Heed the sign. Ask Thane whatever you need to, but you need to pursue the lass."

Paden said, "All jesting aside, I saw it from afar. You need to listen to Jowell. I've never seen a clearer sign."

Hagen wrestled with his cousins' opinions and his memory of what happened. There had been a visible light, some gleam or glitter or spark. But it wasn't just something to see.

He'd *felt* it. A power shot through his hand and landed deep in his belly. He had no idea what to make of it, but he was glad to receive their confirmation.

He wasn't daft after all.

They arrived at their destination and Bearnard let them through the gates without question. "The evening meal just finished. We've got some pottage left."

Hagen said, "I'd like to speak with Thane first, if you don't mind. I have a few questions for him." MacQuarie Castle offered one of the best views on Mull. From the parapets, Coll and Tiree lay to the right, Ulva, Iona, and Staffa to the left. The castle sat nearly opposite Duart on the island.

Bearnard said, "Climb on up to the parapets. He's up there."

Jowell said, "I'll gratefully accept the pottage."

Paden followed Jowell. "Sorry, Hagen. I have to eat first. Let me know if you see anything."

Hagen shook his head, not surprised at all that his cousins didn't view this issue as anything truly important. But they didn't have the interest he did.

The image of Brynja striding away from him ate at him. He had to do what he could to help her, then convince her that he was sincere. That he might be spoiled a bit, but that didn't make him a fool.

A short time later, he found Thane leaning over the edge, staring at the waves in the distance. "Hagen, you're alone?"

"Aye, my cousins are hungry. But they understand you have an excellent cook. Her reputation is known all over the isle."

"My mother has passed all of her recipes along to Agnes, who has done so well that we hired another to do the housekeeping. Now, I see the worry on your face, so please tell me what concerns you so."

"We were on Iona when Brynja shared that there are two men circling the island often. She thinks they originate at one of the other isles and are searching for her."

Thane rubbed his chin. "Specifically, for her? Why?"

"Brynja believes one of the men is the same man she wounded when they were searching for Sheona."

"Ah. That makes perfect sense to me." He grinned at Hagen, shaking his head. "That lass thinks like a seasoned warrior."

Hagen couldn't hide his smile.

Thane added, "But she's more than a warrior to you, I see."

Hagen couldn't deny his interest. "I'd like to get to know her better, but she pushes me away. I'd like to see if I could find a way to assist her. She refuses to leave the island, but I'm wondering if we could arrange a patrol from your land. End their torture of the lass."

"She's no weak lassie looking for a man to save her, but you know that."

"I do. But that doesn't mean she doesn't need protecting. Some assistance."

"Spoken like a Grant. Your sire taught you well. I'm happy to lend you any boats you need to patrol. When did she say they circle Iona?"

"Dawn most days. Dusk on some. She waits every day."

Thane shook his head. "She reminds me of my wife, poor lass. Always looking over her shoulder. You and your cousins are welcome to stay here for a few days and do your own patrolling with my boats."

"I think we will accept your offer with my gratitude. Tamsin had a difficult time, I heard." He sighed, arranging his thoughts before asking the question his cousins would mock him for if they overheard. "How did you convince her you were interested? I mean…" He scratched his head. "I know how to court a lass on Grant land, but here? How the hell do you court someone focused on vengeance?"

Thane smiled and turned around, leaning his back against the parapets. "You ask a great question. It takes a great deal of patience, and all I can say is that when her defenses finally come down, she'll see you, but only if you've been there for her all along. I never aggressively pursued Tamsin, and our circumstances are different, but when she was ready, she nearly fell into my arms. I'll be honest with you. I didn't have much experience with lasses, not like MacVey or Rankin, but I knew what I wanted, so I devoted myself to supporting her whenever she needed someone. It worked, fortunately."

A sound caught Thane, and he stopped, his gaze going to the water as a small boat entered their visual field, headed toward Ulva. "Let me get my spying implement."

He stepped to the end of the wall and took something from a crate, holding it up.

"What is that?"

"Something the Norse left in the boat they deserted that I took. It enhances your vision." He squinted as he looked through the device. "Two men. Headed directly to Ulva. Here," he said, handing him the odd shaped object. "Look for yourself."

He lifted it to his eyes and pointed it out to sea. "Och, this is impressive. Two men and I don't like the looks of them. Do you know them?"

"I do not. What's the fastest way to Ulva? Boat from here?"

"Nay. Take your horse down the second path until you see the small port. It's the closest to Ulva. You'll see fisherman there, and you can take a boat across for a coin or two. The sea is a bit rough to go from here. It's a short distance from the port. Have you any coin?"

"Aye. I'm leaving. Tell Jowell and Paden to follow."

Thane clasped his shoulder. "Godspeed. For both of your endeavors."

Hagen found his mount and headed down the path, reaching the spot Thane indicated with no problem. Two men stood guarding the boats, but as soon as he chose the one he wanted and paid coin for it, Jowell and Paden came behind him.

Paden said, "You and Jowell go. I'll watch the stallions."

Hagen and Jowell climbed in, heading toward

Ulva just as he heard a scream. And it was definitely a young lass's scream.

"Not Brynja," Jowell said. "That was Hildi."

Hagen feared what they would find. "I have to agree." He glanced over his shoulder and said, "The boat I saw that held two men is sitting on the edge. Do you recognize the man in it?"

Jowell peered at it and replied, "Nay. But he's waiting for the one running down the path. He must be after the girls."

When they reached the isle, it was nearly deserted, so Hagen jumped out, grabbing the sheathed weapon he'd set in the bottom of the boat so he could row faster. "I'm going that way."

"No need," Jowell said, pointing. "He's dragging Brynja behind him. Ready yourself and I'll take care of the man in the boat. I hope Hildi's not here too. I'll go look around once I've taken care of the man."

As soon as the man in the boat heard Hagen jump out and unsheath his sword, he set off in the water, yelling at his friend. "I hope you can jump because I'm not coming closer to those two blades."

Jowell and Hagen made it to shore, Hagen saying to his cousin, "Stay with the boat. I'll get her." Then Hagen took off toward the man dragging Brynja.

"Let her go or die!" Hagen bellowed, heading straight for the fool who let go of Brynja, shoving her down a steep embankment toward the sea.

And a short distance away, another body lay near the water, not moving.

Hagen dropped his sword and ran.

CHAPTER ELEVEN

DYNA

DYNA SAT ON the rushes in front of the hearth, her head in her hands. Sandor ran in circles, sobbing, "Unca Shakee, come an' chase me." Then he ran in a circle, falling down and bursting into tears when nothing happened. "Mama, I wan Unca Shakee."

"Uncle Jake, please!" The lad had been doing the same thing for half the hour with no success. Sandor had grown quite fond of his games with the ghost of his great uncle, Jake Grant.

Her father said, "He's not here, Sandor. Shakee is sleeping."

"Good try, Da."

Sylvi said, "He's not sleeping, Mama. He's helping someone else."

Dyna nodded, frustrated with all that had happened of late.

Maitland came in from the tower, Grant strapped to his chest while Maeve followed. "Maitland, mayhap he'd like some apple."

But the lad knocked it out of his mother's hand.

Maitland stilled the lad's hand and said, "We do not hit your Mama, Grant. Nay. We love Mama."

Grant cried harder. Then he kicked his legs and mumbled, "Wia, Wia, Wia."

Dyna stared at Maitland, wide-eyed. "What the hell does this mean? I don't like this at all."

Tora came over to her mother and whispered, "He wants Lia."

"I know, sweeting. But Lia isn't here."

"But she's coming soon. And so is her friend."

Then Tora ran over to the blocks, sitting with her sister.

Her father whipped his head from Tora to Dyna. "Who is Lia's friend? Is there someone out there that I missed? Is there another angel?"

"I don't know, Da. These bairns have never been the same ever since the chaos of Kelvan and friends. It's as if every so often, they all remember what it was like to be stolen away, sent off on a boat, locked in a dark chamber, fed nothing…" Dyna closed her eyes and said a quick prayer for things to go back to the way they were before the chaos.

Sandor let out a loud squeal and took off running toward the far end of the hall. "Unca Shakie can't catch me! Nay you can't." He giggled and swatted at the air. "Top it, Unca Shakie."

Connor said, "Jake? Where have you been? The lad missed you."

Tora ran over and jumped on her grandsire's lap, cupping his face with one small hand. "He said he was busy hepping someone else." Then she hopped off his lap.

"Who, Jake?" Dyna shouted, giving her father a side-eye of fear.

Tora raced back over, climbed up, then said to her grandfather. "He hepping Hagen."

Off she went again.

"Wait, Tora. Helping Hagen with who?" Dyna asked.

Tora looked at her mother, then scowled before moving back over to her grandfather, who shrugged his shoulders, but then the lass climbed up again to her trusted grandfather. "Unca Shakie hepping Hagen and Bria."

Grant wiggled and squealed, "Bwia, Bwia, Bwia!" He clapped his hands and giggled.

Derric looked at her and asked, "Diamond?"

Her father asked "Dyna?"

Maitland finally announced, "What is happening?"

Dyna had no idea.

CHAPTER TWELVE

BRYNJA

———— ⌇ ————

BRYNJA ROLLED DOWN the hill, heading straight toward the water, the stones ripping her skin in places, but she couldn't stop herself. She closed her eyes in fear of losing her sight to a stick or a stone.

Two strong arms grabbed her, lifting her instantly, keeping her from landing in the sea. She opened her eyes and stared up at blue eyes.

"I've got you." Hagen Grant.

She let out a breath, so glad to see him, but then said, "Hildi, she's hurt."

Hagen set her on her feet, then ran over to the shape on the shore, still not moving. He knelt down next to the body and rolled her over.

"Is it Hildi? Is she dead?"

The sound of the two men laughing as they left in their boat irked her more than anything. "I'll kill you both someday," she shouted. "You'll see." She recognized the one man, then caught a quick glance of the other one.

Could he be one of the men who'd killed her mother? She tried to get a better look, but she was more worried about Hildi. She couldn't follow, but she could still curse the bastards. "May the biggest eels from the deepest depths of the sea slither over the side of your vessel and strangle you both until your eyeballs pop out of your head!"

"Hildi, wake up," Hagen said, gently prodding her.

Brynja tried to walk but found her ankle weak, nearly falling. "Hedgehog's warts."

"Do you need help?"

"Nay, I'm fine. Fix Hildi."

"She's not waking up. I'll get her in the boat and get her back to Iona. I think Aunt Brenna is visiting. If not, Beatris can help her." Hagen lifted Hildi without a struggle and carried her, handing her over to Jowell, who settled in the boat the best he could.

"I've no furs or extra plaids." Jowell shrugged his shoulders.

"We can't get to Iona from here," Brynja said, her gaze moving to every area around her as if someone were to jump out at her. "Not in this small boat."

Hagen said, "We'll get her to MacQuarie Castle, then get a larger boat. It's the only way. This is not our boat."

Brynja sat next to Hagen and stared at her friend, tears coming to her eyes. "My dearest Hildi."

Hagen said, "Brynja, I cannot row with you next to me. Can you sit in front of me, mayhap hold Hildi's head on your lap?"

"I can do that." Brynja nodded, unable to think much of anything. "Just save her. Please."

They set off, Brynja cradling Hildi's head. Though she continued to speak with her, the lass didn't awaken.

"What happened?" Hagen asked once they were headed back to Mull.

"We saw the two men approaching by boat, so I crept over to the edge to identify them and to listen in on their conversation, but Hildi tripped and they heard us. The next thing I knew one of them was chasing us through the woods. When he got close, he grabbed Hildi and threw her hard against a tree, snapping her head back. Then he pushed her down the hill. I feared she would land in the water and drown. The monks are still there somewhere."

She looked back, noticing one on the shore watching them depart. She waved to let them know she was hale.

Hildi was not.

Once they arrived on Mull and returned the boat, Hagen lifted Hildi and handed her to Paden who settled her in front of him as they headed back to the castle. Jowell explained to Paden what had happened, while Brynja rode with Hagen. She leaned back against him and whispered, "Do you think she'll die?"

Hagen said, "Nay. She's young, she's strong. Head injuries need time to heal. That's what I've been told before."

"How will we get back to Iona?"

"Thane MacQuarie will let us borrow a boat. I'll leave Paden here with the horses. Jowell can travel with us."

"Many thanks to you, Hagen. Why were you on Ulva?"

"Because I was talking with Thane when we saw the suspicious boat go by. You were right, then. Those men are looking for you."

They rode slowly in the dark, and to her surprise, Hildi's voice carried to her when they neared MacQuarie Castle. "Brynja, are you hale?"

She spun around to the horse behind them. "Hildi? Is that you?"

"What happened? Where are we, Brynja?"

"The bastard threw you against a tree. Hagen came along and scared the two away. Are you hale?"

"Nay, I don't feel well."

They approached the castle and Thane called out to them. "What happened?"

"Let me down," Hildi said. Paden set her down and she fell to her knees and heaved all over the bushes. Jowell followed her and helped her back up when she finished, talking quietly to her.

Brynja hopped off Hagen's horse and moved over to Hildi, who hugged her friend and then passed out, Jowell catching her from behind.

Thane joined them, letting out a sharp whistle. "Artan, we need you."

Artan arrived a few moments later and said, "We need to get them both back to Ionaland. Get one of the larger boats. Beatris will take care of her."

Thane said, "I'll send a few men with you to row. You'll have to hold her, Brynja."

"I can do that. Is she going to die?"

Artan arranged for the men to ready the boat, then the group headed to the shore to climb on the boat. Artan barked orders while Brynja went from Hagen to Jowell to Paden. "Is she going to die? Will she wake up? Please tell me she'll live."

Hagen said, "I think she'll be fine, but she may not awaken until the morrow. The moon is bright so we can head across the water, but don't wake her up. She needs her sleep." He peered out over the water. "At least it is calm. We should get there quickly."

The large boat headed toward Iona, four men rowing. Jowell held Hildi on his lap while Brynja leaned against Hagen. She could hardly keep her eyes open. Upset that her dear friend was hurt, she held onto Hagen's arm as if she were about to be tossed out of the boat.

Once they arrived on Iona, Hagen got out first and helped Brynja, standing her next to him. Brynja watched as Jowell and Paden got Hildi out of the boat as carefully as possible, though she did not awaken.

"Which hut, lass?" Jowell asked, lifting Hildi into his arms.

"The small one on the end belongs to Beatris and she is the healer." They headed that way, knocking on the door quietly. Beatris answered, cracking the door just a touch. "Beatris, I think Hildi is dying."

Beatris opened the door, clutching her night rail

around her, tightening the belt. "What happened, Brynja?"

"An evil man threw her against a tree. She hit it on her front and snapped her head back before she crumpled to the ground. She woke up once, heaved all over, then she went back to sleep. Can you fix her?"

Beatris said, "Please put her down here. I see she has a bump on her forehead. That's probably why she's still sleeping. I need to undress her and look at all her injuries. I'll ask you all to step out while I do that."

Brynja nodded, squeezing Hildi's hand before she left.

The group stepped outside and Hagen asked, "Shall we escort you back to the nunnery or do you wish to stay here?"

"Neither one."

He frowned, but then said, "What next then?"

"I have something I must do before Hildi dies." She gripped the front of her tunic as if it were about to fly off into a raging storm.

"What? Can we be of assistance?" Hagen asked. "We will if we are able."

"Not long ago, we lived on Tiree until evil men came to kill both of our mothers, who were sisters. Our mothers were Norse, and they told us that if we ever found ourselves in dire need, there was something hidden for us. The instructions were simple: dig behind our cottage in a specific spot, and we would discover something meant to help us, no matter the challenge we faced. I think we need it now, whatever it may be."

Jowell, wide-eyed, asked, "And you wish to go now, in the middle of the night, in the dark?"

"Aye, we have the rowers. The moon is bright. I have to go now. If Hildi dies, I'll never forgive myself. Besides, the cruel ones left and went in the opposite direction. They are not there now. It's the safest time. Please. We've never been able to go before. No boat and no one to help us. We need a bigger boat to get to Tiree than what the monks have."

Paden said, "Can't argue with that reasoning."

"On one condition," Hagen said, crossing his arms.

"What?" she asked.

"You have to promise that if we take you to Tiree that you will visit Duart Castle after we return. If you can go off the isle for Tiree, you can go off the isle for Duart Castle."

She glared at him, giving his words careful consideration. "I'll agree, but you must help me dig."

"We will," Hagen said. "And you will go to Duart within a sennight."

She thought for a moment, then whispered, "Agreed. Take me to Tiree."

CHAPTER THIRTEEN

LIA

L IA KNOCKED ON the door, pleased to see
it was Dyna who answered the door. "Dyna,
may I come in for a chat?"

"Of course. The girls can't wait to see you. I
hope all is well. You don't have bad news, do you,
Lia? We haven't seen Hagen, Jowell, or Paden
since last eve."

"Nay, all is well. They are assisting in another
matter."

"My brother? Is he close?"

"Aye, he is with Brynja. Do not worry about
them, but they have a task to do before he returns.
He should be here on the morrow." The lass of
six summers, who claimed to be a guardian angel
and thought of by some as a green faery, strode
past Dyna and into the great hall. The bairns were
playing near the hearth and wee Grant took one
look at her and squealed.

"Thank the Lord above," Maitland said. "Grant
has been calling for you, Lia."

She moved right over to the lad who was tied
to his father's chest, facing outward so he could

see everyone. His chubby legs kicked as if he were chasing down two deer so Maitland took a seat in a nearby stool to get the lad to her level. Lia took both of Grant's hands in hers, something that stilled the boy instantly. "Grant, have you been upset about something?"

"Wia, Wia." He stuck his fist into his mouth.

"Come, sit down next to me. You weigh too much for me to hold you. I fear you would toss yourself from my lap in three breaths."

Maitland said, "He would. You are not strong enough for him, Lia."

"He is a most special bairn, my lord."

Tora, Sylvi, and Sandor raced over to her side, all anxious to give her a hug. Sylvi asked, "Are you staying with us for a time, Lia? Please?"

Lia took a chair near the hearth, folded her hands in her lap, and said, "You know I cannot do such a thing. But I wish to know how you are doing. Have you been well or sickly?"

"Well. We are all well," Sylvi answered.

Dyna said, "I'll tell you my thoughts. Sylvi and Tora have had terrible nightmares. Grant spends all his time whining for Lia and Bria. And Sandor constantly asks for Uncle Jake as if he is only happy when he is around. And if any one of them is disappointed, they cry and carry on for hours."

"Oh, dear. I'll see if I can do something about that."

"I wish you would. I'm lost and don't know how to help any of them."

"You love them and must be nearby in case they need you. That's not so difficult, is it? she asked with a wide smile. "Your love is truly all they need."

"But I don't want them to be so troubled," Dyna said.

Lia sat down on the floor on a special rug for the bairns. "Come sit with me, all of you." She motioned to Sylvi and Tora, then Sandor followed while Maitland set Grant in her lap.

"He won't fall far since you're on the floor." He looked at Maeve to see if she approved, and she nodded.

Just the opposite happened. Grant stuck his thumb in his mouth and leaned back against Lia, as calm as he'd ever been.

"Good, I was hoping to talk with all of you. You're having nightmares, lassies?"

Tora nodded, Sylvi scowled.

"Magni tells me how much he misses you."

"We miss him too," Sylvi said. "Would you please bring him along next visit?"

"I would love to, but he refuses to leave the Isle of Iona. I don't know why. What do you think about that?"

Tora nodded. "He's afwaid."

"What is he afraid of, Tora?"

"Bad men. They took us all before, and I don't want to go again."

"You think they'll find you again?"

Sylvi nodded. "I don't want to leave here again. They stole us away when we were on horses. What if they come back for us?"

"You think Magni is afraid to leave too?"

"Aye."

"Shall we go visit him to make him feel better?"

Both girls shook their heads furiously.

"You won't go?"

"Nay, I don't want to," Tora said, moving over to sit on her mother's lap.

Lia said, "That saddens me."

Maitland asked, "Are you here for someone in particular, Lia? Is someone in danger? Please not the bairns." He leaned down and picked Grant up again.

"I am here for someone, but I cannot say who. I can ease your mind and say that it is not a bairn."

"Why can you not just tell us?"

Lia got up and moved over to the door. "I must go. I hear you are having a Yuletide festival? Is it true?"

"Aye, and we would love to have you join us, Lia. As a friend." Maitland chuckled and looked to Dyna and Maeve for help. "About that person you are helping…"

"I must go, but I will probably see you all soon."

And she was gone.

Maitland cursed. "Who this time?"

No one answered.

CHAPTER FOURTEEN

HAGEN

THE BOAT RIDE to Tiree was rough, the winter sea churning beneath them. The moon was full, the clouds disappeared, and there was no boat near the area where Brynja wished to land.

"Here," she whispered. "This is Gott Bay. Our cottages are on this path, but a distance from shore."

Hagen motioned to Jowell. "You stay here. Paden and I will go with Brynja to dig for her."

"Got it. You'll hear my bird whistle if I see anyone."

"Paden will be in front of the cottages. Brynja and I will be in back. That's where we're digging, correct, lass?"

"Aye. Under a tree in the back. Mama made me tell her so at least ten times every sennight."

They set off, Brynja between them as they headed down the dark path. "Tell us the story again, lass."

Brynja cleared her throat. "All right. Mama said she had some valuables that she'd saved from long ago, but she wished to make sure they were never stolen from her, especially one piece in particular."

"Did she say how big the piece was? A necklace? A ring? A brooch?"

"She never said, just that she wished for us to dig it up if we ever left. But of course, the idiots who killed her didn't know what was here and I had forgotten too. I will be grateful if anything is still there."

"Have you any idea what it might be? A spear, mayhap? Did she teach you how to use a spear?"

Brynja smiled, the warmth of the memory of her mother the first time she threw a spear washing over her. "Aye. She was so good with a spear, but I doubt she hid one. She wanted the men to know she had many of them. In fact, she used them on a few fools who thought to sneak up on her at night. She left one under her bed so she could grab it before her attacker even knew she was in the bed."

"Truly? She sounds like a powerful woman."

"She was. And she killed two men who tried to sneak up on her."

"Who taught her?" Hagen asked.

"Her sire. She brought three with her when she traveled with the Norse. She was to hunt with them, her father also, and they joined a group traveling to the land of the Scots. They were told there were riches everywhere, so twenty of them came to the Highlands, surprised that they found no riches other than wood. Her father died when they landed on Arran. They lost another five to the same fever, then the Scots found them and stole my mother and her sister away. Hildi is my cousin. They kept them for a while, then dropped them on Tiree and left. Mama said they tired of them, and she'd never been happier than that day."

"A forced relationship," Hagen said, his gaze narrowing as he stared off over the sea. "I'm sorry you had to deal with such a life, lass. Every bairn should know their father and their mother."

"I need nothing from my sire. He was just a man who planted a seed, no more."

"That's a bit harsh, is it not?"

She shrugged. "I've not seen evidence of any great sires. Sheona's father treated her horribly. The poor lass sobbed after he left."

"Dermot Rankin can be difficult. I wish for you to come to Clan Grantham or Clan Grant, so you see how others live their lives. I look forward to the visit you agreed to take if we are successful on this journey." Hagen patted her arm, but she quickly pulled it away from his touch, glaring at him.

She pointed up ahead. "Those are our two cottages. Ours is the first one, Hildi's the second one, so it should be planted under the apple tree behind the closest hut."

"Have you a shovel for digging?"

"There should be two behind the cottages."

Hagen and Paden checked the cottage, pleased to see both were empty, though they both showed signs of recent visitors. The men were probably still on the boat, as Brynja had said.

They located the shovels, and Hagen said, "I'll start, Paden. You keep watch out front. If we have to dig up too many spots, I'll switch with you for a bit."

"Any time you need a break, just ask. I'll switch."

The area was deserted, but Hagen glanced in three directions before making his way over to the tree. Brynja already had a shovel in her hands, pointing to an area directly under the apple tree. "There." She pointed, and he nodded.

"I see it. In fact, I think the dirt looks like it's soft. Why else would anyone dig back here?"

Brynja stuck her shovel into the soft dirt and hit something hard with a clunk. She glanced at Hagen who reached down, easily pushed the dirt aside and pulled out a small box. He set it on the ground and said, "Go ahead, open it and I'll see if there's anything else."

Brynja tipped it sideways to knock all the soil from the top of the box, then opened the latch gingerly, lifting it up. She gasped, grabbing Hagen's arm. "Oh, my word, look." A wide smile crossed her face at the number of coins inside. "They're gold and silver, both. How much are they worth?"

Hagen stopped and lifted a few of the coins, allowing them to drop through his fingers. "These are old coins. Probably worth a fortune. But I'm confused by the soft dirt."

"What do you think it means?" she asked, looking over her shoulder at nothing.

"I think it means someone in that cottage found it but is keeping it hidden. Probably taking some to get supplies, then hiding it again. Mayhap there were others inside he didn't wish to see."

"Who are they? The ones you saw on the isle. You think they are living here? The same men that were in the boat?" Hagen asked.

"One was named Sholto. He's the one I hit with my dagger. He and his boss went in the opposite direction. And I thought that other man might have been the one who killed my mother and my aunt. I need to get a better look at him. I would wager they are both living here, but I also think they'll be back. I think we take it and leave.

"Wait." Brynja said. "I think there was more. Mama said there was something special. Please dig a wee bit more?"

"All right." Hagen began to dig, the soil much harder to dig through. "What makes you think there is more?"

"Because my mother always said there were two things for us. And this crate is only one. She always referred to it in multiples. When you find them, not it. When you see them, not it."

"I'll keep digging."

Hagen dug for a while, so Brynja joined him. "Brynja, if we don't find something in the next quarter hour, I say we take what we found and leave. They could be back shortly and I'm not in the mood for another battle."

"I agree."

They continued to dig, and to their surprise, they both struck a piece of metal at the same time, staring at each other. "What do you think it is?" Brynja asked.

"I don't know but it's much larger than that

crate." He moved the soil aside, moving in her direction. "Brynja, this is for you, I think."

"Why?" She stood back out of his way because the object was so large. He tugged on one side of it and lifted it slowly. When he got half of it out, she helped him, tugging the bottom out of the deep spot it was in.

He held it up and she nearly screamed with excitement.

It was a beautifully crafted set of gold armor.

Made for a woman.

CHAPTER FIFTEEN

BRYNJA

B RYNJA COULDN'T WAIT to show Hildi her find. The plate of armor made to fit a woman's body was so beautiful that she was in shock still. And with Hagen's help, she'd held it up to her own body and it fit perfectly. There were straps to hold it on, but it was a little too uncomfortable to wear on the boat, so she decided to carry it back.

Hagen picked it up to carry it for her, then said, "Look, it's in two pieces, meant to split at your waist." So she carried the top piece, and Hagen carried the other piece.

Jowell and Paden were surprised to see her find. "Aunt Gwyneth will love it," Jowell said.

"And so will my sister," Hagen said.

"Dyna will love it, I agree. And Eli, if she wasn't carrying a bairn," Paden added.

"Eli will still try to put it on. I'll warn Alaric," Jowell added with a laugh.

Brynja cleared her throat and said, "It's staying with me. It's a gift from my mother. It probably came from the land of the Norse, my ancestors."

Hagen said, "But you agreed to come to Duart Castle if we helped you find the treasure. And we did, and you found a hell of a treasure, so now you must go to Duart Castle with us."

"Are you ordering me again?"

Hagen growled but said nothing.

She cleared her throat again and said, "Only if Hildi is better."

They climbed into the boat, setting her discoveries carefully at the bottom of the boat. Hagen said, "That was not part of the agreement."

Jowell said, "But I think we can allow her a couple of days for Hildi to wake up."

Hagen made another odd growling sound and said, "We'll see."

"Did you just growl?" Brynja asked.

"Nay," he said, turning his head away from her.

"You did. You surely did growl."

Hagen ignored her and so did the others. Whatever. She didn't care. So pleased to have found what she did, she knew that Hildi would be excited at the coins. Their mothers had always promised that if they wished to go north to the land of the Norse, they could find a way.

Here it was, right on her lap. "Is this enough to take us on a big ship north?"

Paden said, "Probably. I'm not sure what coins those are. They are different."

"Mayhap," Hagen said. "But probably not enough for what you need, because if you choose to go, you should take guards with you as escorts. Two women alone on a ship full of men would not be good."

"You always think the worst will happen."

"It will, in this case. Would you feel safe on a ship with two score men on it?"

She frowned, having not given it much thought before, but he was right. "I don't know."

They arrived a short time later, Magni running to help them out of the boat. "What is that thing? It looks like a monster of some kind." He pointed to the armor in the bottom of the boat.

"Nay, it's armor built to protect my body." Brynja lifted it carefully out of the vessel.

Magni stared at the protruding breast plates. "Aye, it would not fit Hagen, would it?"

"Nay, it's for Hildi or me. Mama buried it for us, and we found it with Hagen's help. How is Hildi?"

Magni didn't answer, instead running back to the cottages. "Tenney, stay over here!" The boy liked to play chase, and he giggled until Magni caught him.

"Why are you two awake? Isn't it Tenney's bedtime?" Hagen asked.

"We stayed up in case you returned."

Brynja stopped, remembering her manners. "Hagen, Jowell, Paden, I cannot thank you enough for taking me to Tiree. Hildi and I have always wished to go but never had an escort. I will pay you each a coin for taking me."

"No need," said Jowell. "We were happy to help. Just remember the arrangement you made."

She blushed because she knew this part would be difficult.

Hagen said, "We'll wait for you to gather your belongings, and to check on Hildi."

She nodded, knowing full well she had no plans to go with them. She'd only agreed in order to convince them to take her to Tiree. It was the only thing in her life that she had to see to fruition. It was done and she'd apologize, but she was not going to Duart Castle. There were too many people there and she'd never leave Iona. Well, unless she was going to the land of the Norse.

She made her way into Beatris' cottage, trying to be quiet, though Beatris sat at the table. Hildi was sound asleep.

"Is she better, Beatris? Did she awaken yet?"

Beatris started at her entrance, but replied, "Nay, lass. She sleeps on and the bump on her head hasn't gone down much. I don't know what to do for her."

"May I sleep here with her?"

"Aye."

"We found a bit of treasure. Where would be a safe place for me to hide it?"

"I have the perfect place. My father insisted we build a hiding spot into the hut when the men built it for us." She pulled a chest out then removed two boulders. "Put it in here. No one will ever touch it."

Brynja set the box full of coins inside the hiding spot, then closed it up, pushing the chest in front of it. "I must tell the Grants to go home, then I'll return."

Beatris asked, "Didn't you promise to go with them if they took you to Tiree?"

"Aye, but only if Hildi was better."

"Oh, of course. I didn't hear that part."

"I'll be right back." Beatris never heard it because she never said it before. But she would now. She made her way straight to Hagen and said, "Hildi is no better. She has not awakened yet, so I cannot leave her."

Hagen said, "If she hasn't awakened then this is a perfect time to go. She'll never miss you. Many people with bumps on their head sleep for a few days. We'll have you back in two days. Magni will tell her where you went."

"I'm sorry, Hagen, but I'm not going."

Hagen settled his hands on his hips. "You never intended to go, did you?"

"I might have, but surely not with Hildi still sickly."

Jowell said, "We'll wait for you in the boat, Hagen." He and Paden disappeared toward shore.

"You lied to me."

She didn't like that comment, even if it were true, but she should be used to his overbearing nature at this point. It wasn't intentional but a slight lie. "Nay, I just forgot to mention that I needed Hildi to be better before I could leave."

"And if she were better right now, would you leave?"

Now he was just pissing her off, so she might as well tell the truth. If she did, perhaps he'd go home and never return. Her life would be much easier at the abbey if he disappeared. She tipped her head to the side and pursed her lips. "Nay, probably not."

"Why? Do you have something against me? Or do I just frighten you?"

Hellfire, how had he guessed the truth? But she'd be damned before she'd ever admit the truth to him. He scared the hell out of her because he made her insides do strange things. "I'm not afraid of you." Another lie.

"Then why won't you come to Duart Castle?"

"I already told you."

"Nay, you told me a lie. But the truth is you'll never come. Why? You at least owe me that much."

"I don't owe you anything."

"We risked life and limb following you to Ulva. And then to Tiree. And you don't appreciate any of it. You called me spoiled and a fool, but how are you acting now?"

She didn't know how to argue that, so she resorted to what she did know. "May a venomous viper come through your walls this eve and bite your toes off."

He snorted. "Norse cursing. I can't believe you're resorting to that instead of telling the truth."

"May a pus-headed toad climb inside your breeches and die."

He shook his head and moved two steps closer. "You are afraid of me, but not for a reason others would suspect. You're afraid of how I make you feel."

"May the shite of four score birds land on your head on your journey back."

Brynja wished to step back because he was too close. His heat caused her warmth to increase. She could feel the sweat between her breasts, an odd tingling between her legs, feel the increase of her pounding heart. It wasn't just that she was afraid of him. Going to Tiree brought too many memories back. The murder of her mother, the stealing away of her and her friend, the situation of being at the mercy of evil men was fresh in her mind now.

He stepped close enough that if she reached out, she could take his hand in hers. But he changed tactics, and that bothered her more than anything. It was as if he could read her mind.

"Who hurt you?" he whispered.

She shook her head, fighting the tears—of exhaustion, of exhilaration, of fear of losing her friend. "May a dung-spattered cur seek out your mother."

"Who? Give me a name and I'll make sure you never have to fear him again." His fingertips traced her jawline with a touch as soft as the fur of a red squirrel.

"My father, for one. I was there when he finally returned to Tiree and asked my mother if I was a lad or a lassie."

"And?"

Her words came out in a yell that she hadn't intended. "And he said he wanted no part of a lass."

"And if you'd been a lad?"

This time it was more of a scream. "He would have taken me with him. Leaving my mother with no one after she raised me alone. Selfish bastard. I was glad he left. I wouldn't have gone with him anyway."

"I'm sure that was a painful experience for you, but there's more, isn't there? Who was he?"

Brynja thought to deny him, but why not be honest? She'd never have the chance to tell anyone else. No one else would care what happened to her. Now that her mother was gone, the only one in her life who cared for her was Hildi, if she ever awakened again. "I can't tell you," she whispered. "I don't know his name."

"How did he hurt you?"

"He touched me. When we were taken from Tiree to Ulva, the man who abducted us rubbed his hand over all my body. I fought him but he punched me, then punched Hildi. I hate him."

"Ah, you're after vengeance then, are you not, lass?"

She nodded.

"Be careful. I hear vengeance can rot your insides. I don't fault you for it. I would do the same. If you ever decide you'd like some help, I'm happy to be of assistance to you. I'm truly sorry to hear of all you've had to deal with. More than you should have."

Her voice was quiet. "I hate all men."

"Nay, you don't, but I can wait for you to figure that out. I'll be waiting for you, whenever you're ready." He leaned over, lifted her chin with his fingers and brushed his lips against hers.

She nearly pulled away, but for some unknown reason, she liked it.

Probably because no matter how she wished to fight it, she liked this man. This man who reminded her of her mother and Hildi's mom. This man who had gone out of his way to help her.

Help her, not hurt her.

He didn't say she wasn't wanted, he didn't tell her to shut her mouth, he didn't tell her that because she was a lass that she had no worth, no value.

His lips were soft and warm, enough that she tugged him back for another kiss, and Hagen growled, wrapping his arms around her and pulling her close as he angled his mouth over hers. She parted her lips and his tongue met hers. But that scared her. She pushed him away.

"You growled again."

He chuckled and said, "I did, for a good reason." Then he leaned down and whispered in her ear, "I'll be waiting. Whenever you are ready to accept me in your life, I'll be there."

Brynja turned away, heading toward the cottage. She didn't tell him that she thought the man who'd touched her was the other man in the boat, but she wasn't certain, so she kept that inside. Well hidden from everyone because she would find revenge for what he did to her and to Hildi.

But most of all, she refused to let Hagen see her tears because they were a sign of weakness.

She was not weak.

CHAPTER SIXTEEN

LIA

LIA STROLLED OUT of the woods the next morning, looking for two people. This assignment was going to be very different for her. Usually, she was the protector of the bairns, but not this time.

She was the protector of an older man who was tied to many of the bairns she was assigned to watch over. But she had to get things arranged properly or the universe would be a mess. Closing her eyes, she hummed, calling to a certain person who could always hear her, summoning her to Lia's side.

A wee bit later, Simone came through the trees with Artan. "Good morn to you, Lia. I didn't expect to see you here."

"Good day to both of you. I'm pleased you are here. I could use your help with something." Lia liked the idea that she could send a message to Simone, and she accepted it without realizing it. It was something guiding angels used often. It came through to Simone as a sudden urge to go somewhere, and she was the type of person who always followed her intuition.

If only more people would do the same.

Artan said, "It is a nice day, Lia. Simone said she had to come here, though she couldn't tell me why. I think I have an idea what compelled her forward. Do you know?"

Lia smiled and said, "I might. I need your help with something, though I believe Simone will be of more assistance than you, Artan, but I'm glad you came along."

Simone closed her eyes and whispered, "Lia, please, not my sire again. I couldn't handle it."

"Nay, not your sire. Someone I visited long ago, though they have not recognized me yet."

"Who? Do tell, please." Simone's face lit up with excitement.

"I cannot tell, but I'm certain you will be able to discern who my target is. But for now, I need you to convince Brynja to go to Duart Castle."

"Is she your target?"

"Nay, not directly. She is an important part of what needs to happen though, and right now, she is being a bit stubborn."

"How do you define stubborn as an angel?" Artan asked.

"She's ignoring all the inklings I'm sending her way. Brynja must go to Duart Castle. It's in her best interest, but she's refusing to listen. I don't wish to have her kidnapped so I'm hoping you'll convince her to go with you."

Simone thought for a moment, then asked, "Does Hildi need to go with us?"

"Aye, you need to take Hildi to Brenna, the healer. She'll know how to fix her. I fear she could have long-lasting effects from her injury if she stays here."

"We'll see it done."

Lia said, "My thanks to you both."

Sometimes, people on Earth were quite dense.

CHAPTER SEVENTEEN

CONNOR

———⚬⚬⚬———

CONNOR SAT ON a stool in the parapets, a glass of mead in his hand. He couldn't help but think of his sire every time he came to the parapets. How he loved it here.

Alex Grant loved the parapets and his special place on Grant land where he chopped down trees to get rid of his anger. Connor never had the temper his father did. Jake, Kyla, and Alasdair did, but he and Jamie escaped it. That's why Alasdair now kept the area open for anyone who needed it.

How Connor missed his parents, but he was reminded of them in so many places. He saw his mother in Kyla's ministrations to everyone in the clan, in Elizabeth whenever she read stories to the bairns. His youngest son, Morgan, was the image of his father and acted like him too. So much so that at times, it would haunt Connor, as if he were watching the ghost of his father in front of him. Hagen also acted much like Alexander Grant because he had the fierce quiet that his father had. Something Morgan lacked. Hagen's power was in his words and his actions, Morgan's power was in his sword.

He missed Grant land, but he also loved Mull. Looking over the sea was something he'd never had the pleasure of doing from Grant Castle. They had a loch to overlook, but never the sea. And it was quite a view. The Sound of Mull and Ben Buie were his favorite sites to look at. The mountains and the hills, the water, the forests. Mull was a beautiful place to live. Now if he could get the rest of his bairns here, he'd feel complete.

To his surprise, Dyna came out into the courtyard with her three bairns. Sylvi ran ahead while Sandor swung his play sword, but Tora?

She stopped down underneath him as if she knew exactly where he would be. She spun around and looked right at him. "Gwandda!"

"Good morn to you, sweet Tora. What is it?"

"Come down, Gwandda! I need you."

Dyna looked up at him and shrugged.

"I'll be right there, Dyna."

He didn't like it one bit, but he wasn't going to ignore his granddaughter when he knew she could see what was to come. He set the stool back, grabbed his cup of mead, and headed down the stairs until he made it outside.

Tora ran straight at him, holding her arms up to him. "Uppy, Gwandda."

Connor sat on a nearby bench and held his arms out to the sweet lass. "Come to me, lassie."

Tora climbed up, giggled, then became serious. She cupped his face and said, "You have to help Bwia."

"Bwia?"

"Bwia. Hagen's Bwia. You have to help her. She comeen later." Then she shoved at his chest, just like she always did. "Down."

Hagen had returned from Iona last eve but hadn't said much. It was quite late when he'd heard him return and the lad looked exhausted. Connor had waved to him as he climbed the stairs, Jowell and Paden behind him.

He had to seek him out this morn.

Something was up.

Dyna came over after Tora left and whispered, "What now, Da?"

"Something about Hagen's Bria. Do you know her?"

"Nay, but I've heard of her. The one with the spears. She's Norse, I think. Brynja."

"Your daughter says I have to help her." Connor glanced around, looking for his son. "I'm going to go find him. Time to get up."

He returned to the great hall, pleased to see that Hagen was eating a bowl of porridge, the only one in the hall at the moment. "You got in late, son?"

"Aye, we were on Iona, helping Brynja and Hildi, but Hildi was hurt and Brynja refused to come here."

"From the beginning, Hagen. The last I heard, you were headed to MacQuarie land."

"When we arrived, we told Thane about all we knew, and while we were on his parapets, he noticed two men headed toward Ulva. So we went after them and sure enough, the evil bastards went after Brynja and Hildi, who happened to be on Ulva gathering apples. The bastard grabbed Hildi, used her as a shield against Brynja, then threw her against a tree and she hasn't awakened yet. We took Hildi to Beatris, then Brynja asked us to take her to Tiree, where we found the place where her mother lived and helped her find something buried behind the cottage, a cache of coins. It was her mother's, but the soil had been loosened so we think one of the men found the coins and kept them hidden. We took it with us so now they may be after her for taking what is rightfully hers. And she refused to come to Duart though she promised if we took her to Tiree she would come to Duart."

Connor nodded, then said, "Start from the beginning. Everything."

Hagen sighed, but repeated everything, filling in with the missing details. "Now do you understand?"

"Somewhat. What is this lass to you? Is she the one you asked about? The one you are interested in? At least you thought you were. Is it any clearer to you now?"

Hagen's gaze darted to five places around the hall. "Aye. I hope to make her my wife, Da."

"From one or two times you met her?"

"How many times did you see Mama before you knew?"

"That is not the same thing."

"How many times did Grandda see Grandmama before he knew?"

"That is not the same thing either."

"Uncle Brodie and Aunt Celestina?"

Connor cursed. "You made your point. You say she's refusing to come here. Tora had one of her moments a short time ago."

"And?"

"And she said I have to help Bria. Hagen's Bria were her exact words."

"Shite. I don't like that, but I'll take you there to be safe. Those men could come for her."

"Nay, no need. Tora said she's coming here later."

Hagen frowned. "She made it clear she had no interest in coming here. Something would have to change her mind."

"Or someone."

"Who are you thinking?"

Logan came down the staircase. "Simone will bring her here later. Avelina already told me so."

"She's coming here? Truly?"

"That surely brightened your day, Hagen. You are besotted, are you not?" Logan had the famous crooked grin on his face.

"I guess I am. And I'm happy about her coming here."

"Why do you wish for her to come here, Hagen? That's not something you've ever said about any lass before." His father knew there had to be much more to this story, so he decided to probe a little bit without being direct.

Hagen sighed and pushed himself away from the table. "Because... Her father is a Scot who got her mother with child and deserted her. The bastard came back when she was older and asked her if the bairn was a lad or lassie. Brynja overheard the conversation when her own sire said since she was a lass, he wanted naught to do with her. And he left again."

Logan whistled and said, "Oh Lord above, please let me find this bastard."

"And when the men came along and killed her mother, they stole her away, started rubbing her, she tried to stop one, so he punched her. Punched her! She hates men, Da. And I don't know how to convince her that there are good men in the world other than to get her here."

His father and uncle had a look pass between them. Uncle Logan paced a bit, but his sire stayed in his seat.

"I tried to talk her into coming here, but she refused. Said she couldn't leave Hildi."

Logan stared up at the rafters. "You know what's next, right, Grant?"

"I do, but I'll listen to your thoughts, Ramsay."

"If Simone doesn't bring her here, I'll go for Hildi."

His father grinned. Great minds came to the same conclusions quickly.

Hagen said, "Nay, go get Brynja. Make her come. She needs to come here."

Connor and Logan both laughed. "Nay, son. If you do that, she'll hate you."

"She'll hate me if I bring Hildi here."

Again, that look passed between the two. "What?"

His father said, "If you bring Hildi here, Brynja will follow."

Logan said, "She'll insist." He shook his head. "We still have things to teach you, lad. But that happens to besotted men. The right woman will twist your insides in five score ways."

Connor didn't say what he thought. He was glad his son was besotted.

But he wasn't glad that Brynja was on Tora's mind. That couldn't be good.

CHAPTER EIGHTEEN

BRYNJA

———— ✺ ————

BRYNJA SAT IN the boat with Hildi's head in her lap, Artan, Simone, and one of Thane's guards rowing them across to MacQuarie land. "Can Lady Brenna fix her? I can't lose my best friend, Simmy."

"If she can be fixed, Lady Brenna will find a way. She's the best in all the land."

When they arrived at MacQuarie land, Thane told Artan, "If she hasn't awakened yet, take the larger boat and four more men down through the Sound of Mull straight to Craignure. You can use a cart to get her to Duart from there."

They'd switched boats, Hildi moving from one set of hands to another and then another, but she never awakened.

Once in the new boat, Brynja did her best not to cry, because the look on Hildi's pale face saddened her more than anything else could right now. How could she still be sound asleep after sleeping the night through?

Oh, she knew Hagen would have something to say about her coming with Simone, how she'd refused him. But he'd have to deal with it. What else was she to do? Hildi was no better, and Simone had been forceful about bringing her to another healer.

Beatris had wholeheartedly agreed.

It took them longer than anticipated to arrive at Duart Castle, but the weather had been good, and it was the middle of the day, so she was pleased.

But she hadn't expected to see how spectacular Duart Castle was, sitting majestically on a promontory, turrets, parapets, and castle walls all making it appear as though it could touch the sky. It overlooked the Sound of Mull and the sea, a true rarity.

Simone must have caught her staring as they climbed up the hill, riding mares abreast. "Quite regal, is it not, Brynja?"

"I've never seen anything like it." She was unsettled riding her own mount because she hadn't ridden much, only the small ponies at the nunnery. Simone held the reins of her mount when she needed assistance, and Brynja was grateful. But the castle was unlike anything she'd ever seen.

As they drew near along the coast path, the fortress changed from a dark silhouette against the sky into a formidable mass of weathered walls, its square keep rising defiantly above the Sound of Mull, surrounded by a thick curtain wall. The waters below churned gray-green against black rocks, and gulls cried in the salt-laden wind. The castle seemed to emerge from its crag, as though it had stood watch over these waters since the beginning of time, its stones bearing the marks of years of rough storms and clan warfare.

"It's monstrous," Brynja whispered. "How many live here?"

"It changes daily because of the Grants and Ramsays. It's their way to travel back and forth to the Highlands. It was built by the MacDougalls, but King Robert took it from them and gifted it to the Ramsays, and they gathered with their allies to choose the chieftains. There are two lairds, Maitland Menzie and Dyna Grant."

"A lass is a chieftain?" Brynja couldn't have been more shocked.

"Aye, and the two in charge of the fighting forces are husband and wife, Alaric and Eli Grant, who is my niece. He trains the swordsmen, and she trains the archers."

Brynja said nothing, wishing Hildi could hear what they discussed. Would she be as shocked as Brynja was to hear that lasses were part of their fighters? "The castle looks so tall."

"The tower house is four stories, and the main keep is three stories tall. The Grants know how to manage chambers, putting three or four beds in each chamber, some meant just for bairns. They have two stables, one for the horses and the other building is where most of their guards sleep."

"I cannot wait to see inside. It must be beautiful."

Simone nodded, squeezing one of her hands. "There are two hearths just in the great hall. Tons of tables, benches, tapestries, along with various weaponry on the walls. You'll see, but I think you'll be more impressed when you see the courtyard and what's inside the curtain wall."

Brynja tipped her head, puzzled by the comment. "Why?"

"After the recent attacks, they moved the archery field inside. It's smaller than the outside one, but Alaric wouldn't have his wife practicing outside the walls. There's a small area for the guards to practice, but the primary lists are outside the wall. You'll see."

Once they were at the gates and inside the wall, handing their mounts to the stable lads, Simone said, "Artan will carry Hildi to Brenna. I would like you to come with me. Let Brenna take a good look at Hildi before we join her. Do you agree?"

"Why can't I go with Hildi?"

"You will, but healers like to see the sick person alone at first. I'd like to show you around the castle, so you know where you're going. And there are some special people I'd like to introduce you to first."

Brynja stood inside the curtain wall of the huge castle, looking up at the parapets and the windows of the stone keep. It was surely a glorious place overlooking the sea. Just inside the gates stood a tall man with dark hair peppered with strands of gray. He stood taller than anyone, and he approached them. "Simone," he said. "Is this the lass I've heard so much about?"

"This is Brynja Nyberg," Simone said. "She and her friend live at the nunnery, but they were attacked on Ulva by unknown assailants. Hagen and his cousins were there. Hildi is still not well so we brought her to see Brenna. Brynja, this is the past chieftain of Clan Grant, Connor Grant. Also Hagen's father."

"Greetings to you, my lord," she said, not knowing what else would be appropriate. She'd never seen so many men in one place except at the abbey with all the monks. But monks didn't talk so this was definitely different.

There were men everywhere.

"Welcome to Duart Castle. If I can be of any assistance to you, Brynja, please let me know."

"My thanks to you," she said, kneading her tunic a little too hard. Being this close to men who weren't monks did make her a bit uncomfortable, and she stepped back two paces. What if one of them tried to touch her inappropriately? Should she ask Simone about such a situation?

"I'll leave you to your tour." Connor headed back to the keep, almost as if he'd picked up on her state.

Simone said, "Come, I'll show you the archery practice field. The butts some call it."

Brynja approached the small archery field, Simone behind her. The closer she got, the more shocked she was. Brynja had never seen anything like it in all her days on Tiree or Iona. Nothing could have surprised her more.

It wasn't the castle or the keep that held her attention, but the people. This was the world she'd always dreamed of, a world she thought only existed in the land of the Norse. Surely there was something special going on.

Off to the side of the keep stood two lasses, one with red hair and the other with brown hair, both dressed in tight leggings, firing arrows at three different targets. They fired so fast that it made her gasp.

What shocked her even more was the older woman with only one leg who appeared to be teaching them. She had an odd contraption on one leg while a man stood behind her, catching her and setting her to rights whenever she began to lose her balance.

The older woman said, "Merryn, watch me for a moment. Watch my hand movements. I arrange my arrows like this so I can grab them faster." She fired five arrows pulled out of her quiver so quickly that Brynja covered her mouth to hide her gasp.

Then the poor woman teetered on her odd leg contraption, and the man behind her caught her, righting her at the same time she bellowed, "Logan!"

"I have you, love," the man said. Then he shouted over his shoulder. "Dyna! We need you!"

Simone whispered, "Those are my adoptive parents, Logan and Gwyneth Ramsay. I'll introduce you later, but first I'd like you to see exactly what you could have if you moved here with them. I promise they will accept you. They saved me and many others from the exact type of evil men who killed your mother, Brynja. We will help you."

The red-haired lass shot again. "Was that better? It felt better."

Simone tipped her head toward the archers. "That's Merryn, married to Broc Grant. She's just learning, as you are, and she lost her sister and her parents to some cruel bastards. Watch and see who you think the best is. And the other is my niece, Eli, married to Alaric Grant. She's a feisty lass."

Gwyneth said, "Try again, Eli. You were a wee bit slow."

Eli did as instructed and hit the center of her target four times, but missed the fifth one.

Logan whistled. "Nice job, but what happened to the last one, granddaughter?"

The door of the keep opened and a nearly-white haired woman exited, hurrying over and grabbing a bow and quiver with ten arrows, her suppressed giggle erupting. "Mama has the lassies. My turn, please." She stretched the last word out as long as she could.

Logan glanced at the blonde and drawled, "You need practice like Gwynie does, and you know it, Dyna."

Brynja held her breath. She glanced over her shoulder at Simone, who nodded and whispered, "Aye. Hagen's sister and the best in my opinion. I watch her moves verra carefully. She's as graceful as she is powerful, something you don't often see."

Brynja had to hold it together because she couldn't believe she could have the opportunity to learn from these women. These strong, powerful women who were allowed to be themselves and not forced to wear skirts and be delicate and dainty. No man stood near them barking orders except the one helping his wife supervise the training session.

Dyna set herself while the others stood back. She fired every arrow she had, pausing twice, every one hitting the center target. Gwyneth laughed and applauded. "Nice job, Dyna."

Dyna let out an unladylike snarl as she ran over to the target. "I missed with this one."

Eli shouted, "Hellfire, nay, you witchin' bitch! You nailed every single one!"

Brynja whipped her head to look at Simone. Had she really heard that cursing in front of her own grandfather? "Truly?" she whispered.

"Da doesn't care how she curses as long as she hits that target."

Dyna picked up her arrows and began to take her stance again when the door to the keep opened and a woman stood in the doorway, waiting for two young lasses to join her.

The most regal woman Brynja had ever seen stepped out, a long, dark blue mantle flowing behind her, her nearly white hair braided so uniquely that Brynja was fascinated. She held the hands of two wee lasses, both carrying miniature bows and arrows. The tall, statuesque woman headed toward the archery field with the two girls, her smile brilliant. "Watch your Mama shoot, lassies."

Brynja stepped back into the shadow of a nearby tree, not wishing to be seen. Was this her?

Was this the woman named the Ice Queen? The one who she and Hildi had heard about and idolized for years? The one who'd helped save hundreds of lasses and bairns by standing up against the cruel men of the land? Stopping a shipment of lasses tucked into crates to be carried across the waters and sold as if they were trinkets? The tale was that she teamed with a group of men known as the Band of Cousins to stop the most atrocious group ever.

Simone whispered, "Aye, that's Sela Seton Grant, Norsewoman known as the Ice Queen, who caught the man no Scot could catch, so Grandda says. She married Connor Grant, whom you met. Parents of Dyna," she tipped her head toward the archery field. "Also Hagen, Astra, and Morgan. She's the reason Dyna is not just powerful but graceful, the power of a Grant with the grace and force of a Norsewoman."

Then Simone stared at Brynja and tipped her head to her. "Dyna is exactly like you, part Scot, part Norse."

Brynja couldn't stop the tears from running down her face at seeing her inspiration, the one who motivated her to want to be more. More than a wife, more than a mother, a woman of her own strength and constitution.

A woman who mattered.

"Can I see Hildi now?" She mopped at her tears, looking away so she wouldn't be moved to tear up again.

"Sure. We'll go inside. We need to find something to eat. I'm starving."

Simone led her across the courtyard and up the steps to the keep. As soon as the two stepped inside, the entire place quieted. It was still the midday meal for some, but the squeals of a wee laddie overpowered everyone.

"Bwia, Bwia, Bwia!"

Simone led her over to a man with a bairn strapped to his chest, kicking like he was running down a hill. "Maitland, this is Brynja. Brynja, this is one of the chieftains of Duart Castle along with Dyna, Maitland Menzie. What is he saying?"

The wee lad reached for her, but Brynja wasn't sure what to do.

"Welcome, Brynja," Maitland said with a nod of his head. "This is my son, Grant, and I think he's been waiting for you for a long time. He seems to know you."

"Waiting for me?" She couldn't have been more surprised.

"Bwia, Bwia…" he reached for her so Brynja lifted her hand, setting her finger against the palm of the lad's hand, the boy gripping her tightly. He smiled and whispered, "Bwia."

"He knows you." Maitland's brow furrowed. "But how?"

"I don't know. I've never been here before." Brynja stared down at the small hand gripping her finger.

"I think he'll never let you leave."

Simone said, "Talk to him, Brynja. Tell him why you're here."

She tipped her head down and said, "Greetings to you, Grant. I have to go see the healer to make sure my friend is hale. I hope she's fixed now. I miss her already."

Grant calmed down and waved at her, his

thumb going into his mouth after he let go of her finger.

The door opened, and three men entered, one coming straight to her. Hagen approached while Jowell and Paden went for food from the sideboard.

"You've arrived, Brynja. Welcome to Duart Castle. I have to admit that I'm surprised to see you here. You came with Simone?"

"Aye," she replied, biting a fingernail. "Hildi is no better. Simone said Brenna could fix her, that she was still here for a visit. She didn't know when Brenna would be leaving so we came right away."

"I'd be pleased to show you around," he said.

Dyna flew over with a laugh. "We have guests, I see, Maitland. Are you staying the night, lass?"

"I will, if you don't mind. But I can sleep with Hildi in the healer's chamber."

"Absolutely not. I'll find you a chamber that you can share with Hildi when she improves. Hagen, would you introduce us, please? Or should I guess her name?"

"Brynja, this is my sister, Dyna Corbett, Chieftain of Clan Grantham. Dyna, this is Brynja from Iona."

Grant popped his thumb out of his mouth, suddenly kicking and reaching for her again. "Bwia, Bwia, Bwia."

Dyna reached for the laddie, taking him out of his father's fashioned sling over his chest. "You wish to see Brynja, Grant?"

"Bwia, Bwia."

"Do you like bairns, Brynja? Would you like to hold him? He seems to like you."

"I've been to Ionaland many times, and they always have bairns. I'd love to hold him." She put her hands under the lad's arms and lifted him, settling him on her hip. Grant set his head on her shoulder and closed his eyes.

Dyna whispered, "Oh my." She peeked up at Maitland.

Maitland said, "I'm shocked. He loves you, Brynja. You must be special."

Brynja took in the boy's sweet scent and smiled, but then she froze.

"Who is this lass?" Hagen's mother headed straight for them.

Brynja panicked, handed Grant back to Maitland and ran over to the only other door besides the door the serving lasses came out. She prayed it was the healing chamber.

She couldn't handle meeting the Ice Queen yet.

CHAPTER NINETEEN

HAGEN

———❧———

"MAMA, YOU SCARED her away. Don't do that. I told you she was petrified of coming here."

"Why? We're friendly."

Simone said, "Brynja lived a verra protected life until a few months ago." Simone's voice grew somber. "She and Hildi lived on an island with their mothers—next to each other in small cottages on Tiree. Then men came. Killed both women right in front of the girls."

She paused, letting that sink in. "They took Brynja and Hildi to another cottage where they held stolen bairns. The girls were to be placed on a ship and sent away, God knows where. That's all Brynja knows because she and Hildi escaped in a wee boat. Fishermen found them and took them to the abbey. They've been at the nunnery ever since."

His mother said, "Hagen, you didn't tell us all of that."

"I didn't know all of it. I learned more when we went to MacQuarie land, and I told Da.

Right now, she wants vengeance against the man chasing her… the one who was with Clyde, who wants to kill her. His name is Sholto. And she also wants to find the man who killed her mother and aunt."

"The girls are cousins then. Poor lasses," his mother said. "I pray that Hildi heals quickly."

"Mama, she's stronger than you'd think."

"Of course she is. She's part Norse." Her mother arched a brow at him.

Dyna said, "What I want to know is why does Grant seem to know her?"

Maitland shook his head. Grant pointed to the healing chamber and said, "Bwia."

"I know. Bria is busy, Grant. She'll be back."

Dyna put her face in front of Grant's and asked, "How do you know her, Grant?" Then she tickled his chubby belly until he giggled. "Bwia? How do you know her?"

Grant pointed to the door again and said, "Bwia."

Dyna stood up and crossed her arms. "I don't know what it could be, but there's something between those two. I can't wait to learn what it is."

"Mayhap she's a seer too?" his mother asked.

"Or an angel?" Dyna suggested.

"Nay, not an angel," Simone. "There's nothing other-worldly about Brynja like there is Lia."

Hagen didn't like that comment. He would defend the lass for any slight. "You cannot be certain of that."

Simone drawled, "Did Brynja live under a frond until Hildi found her?"

Hagen rolled his eyes and laughed. "Good point. Seer then."

"Mayhap. We'll have to wait and see," his mother said.

"I think," Dyna said. "I think she has another power, but she's too young to have developed it yet. It's yet to be determined." Then she wiggled Grant's foot. "Just like you, wee laddie."

The group, in unison, all turned to stare at the door.

Hagen's father approached and said, "Oh, I wish to know exactly what caused that."

His mother said, "Hagen, tell him about Grant and Bria. I'm going to see Brynja."

Simone stopped her and said, "Sela, you need to know that as a daughter of a Norse woman, she heard all about the Ice Queen…"

"She did?" The expression of surprise on his mother's face was unlike any he'd ever seen before.

"Aye. And she idolizes you. That's why she left so quickly. She saw you coming and wasn't prepared to meet you yet. Coming to the castle with all the people, seeing the archery field, it's been much for her to absorb."

"Mama!" Hagen said. "And she was up late last night with us on Tiree."

His mother arched a brow at him, but then he caught the twinkle in her eye and that small grin of hers.

Simone touched his arm. "Nay, let your mother

go. It's a great way for her to get to know Brynja, and being Norse, I think she'll be good for both girls. I'd also guess we're all going to see much more of Brynja and Hildi."

"'Struth," Dyna said with a nod of emphasis and a glance at Grant. "Especially Brynja. I mean Bwia."

Hagen stared at the door, still doubtful. "Brynja is tough to talk with. She has all these walls built up to protect herself from everyone."

Dyna reached over and clasped her brother's shoulder. "Think about our mother's background and how it compares to Brynja's."

Hellfire, his sister was correct.

CHAPTER TWENTY

BRYNJA

B RYNJA SAT DOWN on a stool next to the bed Hildi lay on and looked up at Brenna. "Is she fixed yet, my lady?"

"You must be Brynja. She is not fixed yet, but I think she'll get better. And please call me Brenna."

"How do you know, Lady Brenna?" She rubbed her hands together so tightly that she had to stop after a few moments.

"I'll show you. Then you'll know what to do if it happens again." She lifted one of Hildi's eyelids and held it open. "Do you see the middle part of her eye that is black?"

"Aye."

"If she were truly bad, that part would be huge. It's not. That is a good sign. Here's another one. Watch when I pinch her arm." Brenna pinched and Hildi jerked her arm away. "Did you see that? People whose brains are really sick don't feel pain. She does."

"That's good?"

"Aye. That's verra good. She has a sizeable bump on her forehead still, but it looks to be getting smaller. Once it shrinks, I think she'll wake up. And she will be quite hungry. In fact, I may go get her some broth. Do you know where the kitchens are?"

She shook her head. "But I can find it."

The door opened and the Ice Queen entered.

Brenna set her hand on her forearm, stopping her from going to the door. "Nay, I'll go. Sela will stay with you. Sela, have you met Brynja yet?"

Brenna introduced the two and Brynja stood up, backing away.

Sela said, "I'll stay with the two, Brenna. You go. I've wanted to meet Brynja."

Brenna left. Brynja stood, backing away until she hit the wall, her hands pressing against the stone. She didn't know what to do. Would Sela be nice like Hagen and Dyna? Or cold, like her title suggested?

Sela sat down and patted the stool. "I won't bite. Please sit down, Brynja."

She did what the woman asked, her gaze never leaving the beautiful woman's face as she crept over to take the seat next to Sela.

Sela said, "Simone said you've heard of the Ice Queen. True?"

Brynja nodded, swallowing hard. "My mama talked about you often."

"You know I'm not overly fond of that title, but I'd love to tell you a story. Do you mind?"

Brynja shook her head.

"I was verra cold when I met Connor Grant. Do you know why? Was that part of the tale you heard from your mother?"

She shook her head, interested in hearing the answer. She would listen to anything this woman had to say, especially if it was something she hadn't heard about the Queen.

"The evil men held my three-summers-old daughter away from me. They threatened to hurt her if I didn't do what they asked. Connor followed me when he first met me, and I feared my daughter would be punished because of Connor's actions. But fortunately, she wasn't. However, Connor and I were both punished."

Brynja, puzzled, hadn't heard this part of the story before. "Punished? Both of you?"

"Those evil men, who probably numbered around fifty, beat Connor, then beat me, leaving us both to die in the forest. If not for Connor's friends, who searched for him, we would both be dead. There would be no Dyna or Hagen or Morgan or Astra. But we survived. They took me to Grant Castle, and I met Connor's mother, the kindest woman I've ever met. Maddie Grant taught me to love, to trust…" she stopped to clear her throat, the tears in her eyes clear, "to believe Connor when he said he would protect me from the bastards who killed for coin and for entertainment."

Totally enraptured, Brynja couldn't speak because she had the oddest feeling that Sela's life was much like hers.

"You see," she continued, wiping her eyes, "men killed my parents in front of me, then took me to be their plaything. I had my daughter Claray, but I was forced to do their bidding for three years.

"Until I met Connor."

Sela stood and paced, her voice carrying across the chamber. "And do you know that Connor's mother, the woman known as Maddie, was the woman I most wished to model myself after? She wasn't an archer, or a queen, but a woman who loved bairns and devoted herself to protecting them. Have you heard the story of the day my daughter was saved from the man known as Hord, the spider man?'

Brynja shook her head. She hated spiders so much that her skin crawled just from the mention of them.

"It was one of the most glorious days I've ever lived in my life. I rode in front of Connor on his magnificent stallion. Behind us rode at least a hundred Grant guards, Maddie riding with her husband, Alex. She'd told Alex that she would not leave without my daughter. I couldn't believe she would do what no one else could do, get my wee lassie away from those evil men. But we approached the castle, and out came about fifty of the bastards, all carrying their swords and ready to fight. Alex demanded my daughter back, and they laughed, saying they didn't have any little girls."

Sela chuckled, tipping her head forward for a moment, then standing up with a smile, the tears now flowing down her cheeks.

"Do you know what that tiny woman said? Against all those cruel, evil creatures, she said, 'You bring me that child, or I will have my husband hold you down while I stick my needle in the middle of your eye.'"

Brynja said, "Truly? She said that? But why would they be afraid of a woman with all those men?"

"It wasn't her size but her words and the way she said them. She spoke with a conviction unlike anyone I'd ever heard. Anyone who listened to Madeline Grant speak of my daughter knew that she wouldn't hesitate to give her life for my lassie. And fools that they were, they were witnesses to the fire in her eyes. I saw that gaze myself, and it frightened me."

"And she only had needles? No sword or daggers?"

"Aye, she threatened the bastards with two needles. After hearing her speak, and I will add, looking at her husband behind her, a powerful warrior who would do whatever his wife asked of him, the villains passed looks amongst themselves and then motioned to one man who brought my daughter out." She tipped her head again and then lifted it back up, swiping at the tears on her cheeks before she continued. "That wee woman ran to grab my lassie just as the battle broke out, swords and bellows everywhere. But my sweet girl was safely in Maddie's arms, a place that became one of her favorite places to be. Now, I tell you this story for two reasons."

"Why?" Brynja asked, her hands trembling.

Sela came over and sat down in front of her, cocooning Brynja's hands with her own. "I tell you because you need to know that Clan Grant and Clan Grantham are the safest places you could ever be. Trust what they tell you. My husband, my son, my daughter, and I will protect you from those bastards."

"And the other reason?"

Sela reached up and brushed the stray hairs away from her face, then cupped her cheek. "Never doubt your value as a lass. That woman controlled over a hundred warriors and men with her words and two needles. You don't need the muscles or the size of a man to be powerful. Use your words, your mind, and the strength that you have within you. That is your power, lass." Then she placed her hand on her chest. "And here. Maddie Grant's strength was in her heart."

Sela leaned forward with a smile and whispered, "And never forget your Norse heritage."

Brynja fell into Sela's arms and sobbed her eyes out.

For her mother, for her aunt, for her dear friend Hildi.

And for herself. She'd found her people and her place.

CHAPTER TWENTY-ONE

HAGEN

———❧———

THE NEXT DAY, Hagen had spent most of his time on patrol, looking for evidence of the men who'd attacked Hildi and Brynja. They were nowhere to be found. He'd gone to MacQuarie land and talked with Thane, and he'd seen nothing.

Brynja had spent the day at Hildi's side, but Hildi hadn't awakened yet. Brenna had told him quietly that the longer it took her to awaken, the worse her chances were that she would recover.

He couldn't imagine living his life as Brynja had. She'd watched her mother and aunt die, been kidnapped, escaped to a nunnery, and lived there.

Alone except for Hildi.

Oh, she'd made friends. Sheona and Simone and Magni and Beatris, but no family but Hildi.

Only one cousin.

Hagen sat by the hearth thinking on that one thought.

Jowell came in and took a seat next to him.

"What are you thinking on? I can see the steam coming out of your ears."

"Cousins. How many cousins do you think we have?"

Jowell's eyes widened as he chuckled. "More than I can count?"

"I'm going to try. You, Alaric, Paden, Eli, Alick, Eli, Alasdair, Merelda…"

"Maryell, Broc, Chrissa, and then there are the Ramsays who we consider to be cousins, Ysenda, Errol, Thea, and then Brin… I could go on and on. What's your point?"

"Brynja only has one—Hildi. Her mother's dead, her aunt is dead, and that's it. She lives in a nunnery. What the hell would it be like to only have one in your family?"

Jowell tipped his head in thought, steeping his fingers in front of him. "Ask your mother what it's like. Didn't she only have Claray when she met your father?"

Hagen scowled. "You're right. I hadn't thought of that. Both her parents were killed. Shite. What an awful life to live."

Jowell stared at him. "You're going to be careful with her, are you not?"

"What do you mean?"

His voice dropped, taking on an edge. "She's not some prize to be won, Hagen. She's not a challenge or a diversion. She's a woman who's been broken and put herself back together with spit and rage. And she deserves someone who sees that. Who understands what it cost her to trust anyone again. Don't play with her feelings."

Hagen forced himself to breathe. To think before responding. Because Jowell wasn't wrong to be protective. If anything, Hagen respected him more for it.

"You're right," Hagen said quietly. "I'm beginning to understand why Grandda was known for protecting women."

"Absolutely true. Now that we're clear on that, I'm going to bed. Paden is already there." The three shared a chamber with three beds in it since there were so many living or visiting at Duart at present.

"I'm going to check on Brynja, then I'll be up."

Hagen headed to the healing chamber, opening the door slowly in case anything that required privacy was happening, though he'd seen Brenna take her leave earlier. "Brynja?"

She sat next to Hildi, the saddest expression he'd ever seen on anyone's face—a look of loneliness and defeat. "Brynja, may I come in?"

"Aye, please."

"How is she?" he asked, entering and closing the door behind him.

"No change. She's sleeping."

"She'll probably sleep all night, do you not think so?"

Brynja's gaze went to her friend, and she reached over to brush a few wild strands of hair back from her face. "I suppose she will."

"Would you go for a quick stroll with me? I'd like to show you something."

She sighed and stood. "I do need to stretch my legs."

He held the door for her, and they stepped into the great hall.

"Where are we going?" she asked.

"To a special place I'd like to share with you." He pointed to the staircase.

She scowled. "Not your chamber. Your cousins are there."

"Nay." He laughed. "My sire would kill me first and then my mother. The parapets. They are spectacular here because of the Sound of Mull." He led her up the first staircase, then down the passageway to a door at the end. "May I take your hand? It's a dark staircase."

She nodded, so he tucked her hand in his and led her up the stairs, pushing against the heavy door and holding it for her. There was a slight breeze that greeted him right away and he smiled.

"This place makes you happy," she said.

"The smell of the sea does. It's so different than our castle in the Highlands. It's why we stay. There's something about the water." He led her around the parapets until they overlooked the Sound of Mull.

"It's chilly. I should have brought my mantle."

He said, "If you'll allow it, I'll tuck you in front of me and you'll be protected from the wind."

To his surprise, she agreed, stepping in front of him. He wrapped his arms around her, yet making sure it wasn't too tight. He didn't wish to frighten her. "I'll tell you a story. My grandfather always loved the parapets. It's where he spent much of his free time. But he would also come up whenever he had to decide on battle plans, or whenever he had to decide who was to be in charge of certain things. He loved it so much that it was one of the last things he did before he passed. My father would carry him up to the parapets where they kept a chair for him. He loved the wind in his hair, but his favorite part was the view. He swore he could see all the way to the edge of the land of the Scots, though I doubt it."

She scanned the area from one way to the other, a sight she'd never seen before. "It's beautiful. I've never seen anything like it, Hagen. My thanks for bringing me here. Tell me more about your grandsire. How did he meet your grandmother?"

"He was out patrolling, something he loved to do. He always wished to know who his neighbors were. He was a distance away with one of my uncles when he stopped at a manor home, but the owner was not friendly. They went inside, decided to spend the night, and he claims to have been compelled to open doors in the middle of the night. Said he came upon the most beautiful woman he'd ever seen in a chamber, sound asleep, but he knew he could never leave her."

"Why not? She was sleeping."

"She'd been badly beaten. He left because her maid chased him out with a broom, but he couldn't leave her. He and his brother were sent out by the owner, but they snuck back inside later, and he caught him whipping her, so he stole her away."

"And they married right away?" she asked.

Hagen chuckled. "Nay. She didn't trust him, but she didn't trust any man. She was quiet, reserved, and afraid of men. Grandda said it took him forever to convince her that he would never hurt her."

"And your sire found Sela, also someone held against her will. And they married."

"That took him a while too. She stayed in an abbey because she didn't think she deserved to marry Connor Grant. But he convinced her."

"She's so happy now."

"Oh, naught makes my mother happier than grandbairns. She keeps hinting at me and Astra that she needs more. Morgan is too young yet."

"How many summers are you?"

"Two and twenty. And you?"

"Eight and ten. Old enough to leave the abbey, but I have nowhere to go." She stared out over the landscape and asked, "Have you been to all those places out there, Hagen Grant?"

"Nay. I've visited many, but not all. You?"

She smiled and said, "None. This is my first time on Mull. I've only been to Tiree and Iona."

He stood back and turned her around to face him. Cupping her cheeks, he said, "Brynja, I'll take you wherever you'd like to go. But may I kiss you first?"

She smiled and nodded.

His lips melded with hers, slowly and cautiously at first, not wanting to frighten her. It was clear to him that she hadn't been with a man before. Everything about her was hesitant. His tongue teased hers and she opened for him, giving him access to the sweet cavern inside. He teased and taunted her until her curiosity got the best of her, dueling with him until he was panting with a need he hadn't felt in a long time.

A need to know more about her, taste her, make her his.

She surprised him by leaning into him, her curves fitting against him so perfectly it was as if they were made as one. Her arms slipped around his neck, and he deepened the kiss, growling with a need that was so fierce he feared what he would do.

He ended the kiss and she whispered, "You growled again."

He laughed and kissed her forehead. "All your fault, lass. You inspire me."

The door opened around the corner, and he moved enough to see his cousin there. Paden held the door open and said, "Hildi's awake. Aunt Brenna woke me up."

Brynja squealed and headed down the staircase, Hagen right behind her. "My thanks, Paden. Go back to bed."

Brenna was already at the bottom of the stairs waiting for Brynja.

How he prayed her cousin was healed.

CHAPTER TWENTY-TWO

BRYNJA

B RYNJA BURST THROUGH the door into the healing chamber. "Hildi?"

Brenna made a motion with her hand to lower her voice or slow down or something. Was she not awake? What did that mean?

Hagen entered behind her, his hand at the small curve in her back, something that encouraged her to move forward. "Is she awake?" she whispered.

"Brynja?" a scratchy voice called out to her.

Brenna nodded and pointed to a stool for her, so she sat down, reaching for Hildi's hand. "Hildi, how do you feel?"

"Where are we, Brynja? And who is this nice lady?"

"She's a healer. We're at Duart Castle. Simone thought you should come to see Brenna because she's one of the best healers, and I was so afraid you'd never awaken. You are well?"

Hildi moaned and closed her eyes. "My head." Her hand reached up to cradle the side of her face. "It hurts."

Brenna said, "You took a terrible blow to your

head, Hildi. It will hurt for a while, but it will go away. I can give you something to help ease the pain."

Brynja asked, "Are you hungry? Do you want something to eat?"

"Just something to drink. My throat is too sore to eat."

"I have some warm broth for her. It will help her throat. See if you can get her to drink it, Brynja."

"I can't lift my head," she said.

"Here, I'll help you." Brynja set her hand behind her neck and helped her lift her head, then set the cup to her lips. Hildi took two sips before her head fell back.

"Please, will you stop this aching in my head?"

Brenna said, "I'll give you the potion, but it will make you verra sleepy."

"Good, because I'm tired."

Brenna left and Hildi whispered to her friend, "Where are we? And who is she?"

"I told you…" Hagen's hand settled on her shoulder, telling her not to correct her. She glanced up at him and he shook his head.

Brenna returned and said, "I'll give her the potion." She gave Hildi the concoction she'd made. "This should ease the pain in your head. Do you hurt anywhere else?"

Hildi swallowed and said, "Nay, just my head. It's terrible." Then her friend rolled over on her side and closed her eyes.

Brynja couldn't believe that her friend had turned away from her. She looked to Brenna for

help, but the healer waved her over to the door,
Hagen following. She set her arm around Brynja's
shoulders. "Do not be concerned by anything she
did. She's been asleep for several days now. She
has to catch up with everything, and her body
is still healing. The best signs I'd hoped for were
for her to wake up, recognize you, and ask for
something to drink, and she did all three. She'll
be fine, Brynja. You just have to give her time. It's
going to take her a while to heal."

"My thanks to you, Lady Brenna. I think I'll go
to bed." Brenna nodded to Hagen, who ushered
her out the door.

Once they were alone in the hall, Brynja looked
at Hagen and said, "I forgot, but I heard those
men talking about Grant men. I should probably
tell Connor, shouldn't I?"

"Aye, we'll tell him first thing in the morn."

"I'll have to push myself to recall their words.
I was so worried about Hildi that it completely
left my mind."

"Just focus on getting some sleep. You'll
remember on the morrow, and we'll speak with
my da."

She nodded, giving Hagen a small smile.
"There's only one thing I wish to do now."

"Say the word and I'll help you, lass."

"I want to kill the bastard who did that to
Hildi. I want vengeance against him and against
the men who killed our mothers. Will you help
me?"

"I will, but you have to promise me you'll not
go alone."

She wasn't sure she could promise that, but she nodded her agreement.

One way or the other, those men were dead men.

And she'd be wearing her mother's armor.

CHAPTER TWENTY-THREE

BRYNJA

THE NEXT DAY, Brynja stood at the edge of the training yard, watching Hagen work with a chestnut mare. The horse was young, still learning, and clearly testing the boundaries of her handler's patience. Hagen murmured something too low for Brynja to hear, and the mare's ears flicked toward him, her stance shifting from defiant to curious.

"She trusts you," Brynja said.

Hagen glanced over his shoulder, a smile tugging at his mouth. "Not yet. But we're getting there." He ran a hand along the mare's neck. "Want to try?"

Brynja hesitated. She could ride, the nuns had kept a few ponies for travel to the abbey, but those had been placid, elderly creatures content to plod along the coastline. This mare was different. Young. Powerful. A warrior's mount.

"I won't be verra good at it."

"Then you'll learn." Hagen led the mare over, reins loose in his hand. "Besides, if you're going to stay at Grant holdings, you need a proper mount. Can't have you stuck afoot when there's trouble."

The practicality of the argument appealed to her. She hadn't had the opportunity to excel at horseback riding at the nunnery or on Tiree. Learning to ride well meant one more skill, one more way to control her own fate.

"All right."

Hagen's smile widened. "Good. First, you need to understand her." He handed Brynja the reins. "What do you notice?"

Brynja studied the mare. "Her ears keep moving. Listening."

"Aye. She's paying attention to everything— you, me, that lad by the stable, the wind in the trees. Horses are prey animals. They're always watching for danger."

Something in Brynja's chest tightened. She understood that. Being always alert, never quite at ease.

"So how do you make her trust you?"

Hagen moved closer, close enough that she could feel the warmth of him at her back. "You show her you're not a threat. That you're calm. That you notice what she needs." His hand covered hers on the reins, adjusting her grip. "Too tight and she'll think you're afraid. Too loose and she'll think you're not paying attention. Like this."

His fingers were warm against hers, callused from sword work. Brynja's breath caught. She forced herself to focus on the mare, not on the way Hagen's voice had dropped lower, more intimate.

"Now stroke her neck. Let her learn your scent, your touch."

Brynja reached out with her free hand. The mare's coat was warm and smooth, her muscles shifting beneath the skin. "She's beautiful."

"Aye." Hagen's voice held an odd note. When Brynja glanced back, he wasn't looking at the horse.

Her cheeks heated. She turned her attention firmly back to the mare.

"What's her name?"

"Doesn't have one yet. She's too new. Da just had a few more brought over from Oban. They don't like the ship so I'm trying to calm her, get her used to her new world." Hagen stepped back, giving Brynja space. "You could name her, if you'd like."

"Me?"

"Why not? You're going to be the one riding her."

The casual certainty in his voice, that she would stay, that she would need a horse of her own, should have rankled her. Instead, it felt like a gift. Like he was offering her an opportunity she hadn't dared imagine.

"Freya," Brynja said softly. "Freya is a goddess in my mother's tongue. She looks regal the way her coat catches the light."

"Freya." Hagen tested the word, his accent making it sound different but no less lovely. "It suits her."

The mare's ears flicked toward Brynja at the sound of her new name, as if she approved.

"Now," Hagen said, all serious again, "let's get you in the saddle. Come here."

He led Freya to the mounting block. Brynja climbed up, suddenly aware of how high the horse's back looked from this angle.

"Put your foot in the stirrup. Aye, that's it. Now swing your other leg over. I've got you."

His hands steadied her as she mounted, one at her waist, one at her elbow. The contact was brief but sure, and then she was seated, looking down at him from an unfamiliar height.

"How does it feel?" he asked.

"Strange because I'm so high off the ground. Powerful." Freya shifted beneath her, and Brynja gripped the reins tighter.

"Easy." Hagen's hand covered hers again, loosening her grip. "Remember, she feels everything you do. If you're tense, she'll be tense. Breathe."

Brynja drew in a slow breath, then released it. Freya's ears swiveled back toward her, listening.

"Better," Hagen said. "Now we'll walk. Just around the yard at first. Press with your legs, gently, and she'll move forward."

Brynja did as he instructed. Freya moved into an easy walk, Hagen keeping pace beside them, one hand resting lightly on the mare's shoulder.

"Good. Keep your back straight, shoulders relaxed. You're doing well."

They circled the yard, and with each circuit, Brynja felt more confident, more attuned to the mare's movements. It was like learning a new language, subtle cues and responses, a conversation without words.

"Want to try a trot?" Hagen asked after a few rounds.

Brynja nodded, her earlier nervousness replaced by something close to excitement.

"Press a bit more firmly with your legs. She'll speed up. And you'll need to post, rise and fall with her rhythm. It takes practice, so don't worry if it feels awkward at first."

Brynja pressed with her legs. Freya's walk shifted to a bumpy trot, and Brynja found herself bouncing uncomfortably in the saddle.

"Try to find her rhythm," Hagen called, jogging alongside them. "Up, down. Up, down. There. You've almost got it."

It took another full circuit before Brynja found the timing, and then suddenly it clicked. She rose and fell with Freya's gait, the bouncing smoothing into something almost graceful.

"That's it!" Hagen's grin was infectious. "Now you're controlling her on your own."

A laugh bubbled up from Brynja's chest, surprising her with its lightness. When was the last time she'd laughed like that? Not the bitter, angry sound she'd grown used to, but genuine joy. This was different than riding a pony or riding with Hagen. This was a relationship between her and Freya.

After another few circuits, Hagen signaled for her to slow. Freya slowed to a walk, then halted. Brynja's heart was racing, her cheeks flushed with exertion and pleasure.

"Well done," Hagen said, reaching up to help her dismount. His hands spanned her waist as she swung her leg over and slid down. For a moment, she was pressed against him, close enough to see the silver flecks in his blue eyes, close enough to feel his breath against her forehead.

Neither of them moved.

Then Freya nudged Hagen's shoulder with her nose, breaking the moment. He stepped back, his hands falling away, a faint color rising in his cheeks.

"Now for the important part," he said, his voice slightly rough. "Horse care. Come with me."

He led Freya toward the stable, Brynja following. The interior was dim and cool, smelling of hay and leather and the warm, dusty scent of horses. Hagen led Freya into one of the stalls at the far end and began removing her saddle.

"Always tend to your horse before yourself," he said. "She's given you her strength, her trust. You owe her care in return."

They worked together, Hagen showing her how to brush Freya down, check her legs for heat or swelling, give her fresh water and grain. The repetitive motion was soothing, almost meditative. Freya stood patiently, her eyes half-closed in contentment.

"My grandsire used to say," Hagen said after a while, "that you can tell a man's character by how he treats his horse."

"What does that make you?"

He looked up, meeting her eyes across Freya's

back. "I hope it makes me someone worth trusting."

The weight of the words settled between them. He wasn't just talking about horses, and they both knew it.

"You are," Brynja said quietly. "Worth trusting."

Something shifted in his expression, relief, perhaps, or hope. He reached across Freya's back, his hand finding hers on the mare's withers, his thumb brushing across her knuckles in a touch that could have been accidental but wasn't.

The strangest thing happened. A heat suffused her that was different. She'd had similar reactions to Hagen's closeness, his touch, but this was something almost otherworldly. "Hagen?" she whispered, staring at his face to see if he caught it too.

He swallowed hard, his gaze following his hand as he reached for hers again. As soon as they touched, the same thing happened.

Warmth, heat, something shot from his hand to hers in an instant, a burst of light illuminating the small area.

"Did you feel that?" he asked.

She nodded, afraid to speak. "I saw it too. Just like the first time."

He did it again, this time gripping her hand and holding her, and an intensity shot through them that made them both take a step back, breaking their bond. "Hagen, what was that?"

"I don't know." His gaze locked on hers while he reached for her again, but this time, nothing happened. "I've never felt anything like it before."

This time, it was a simple touch. Hagen shrugged. "Must be something odd in the air. Mayhap a storm is coming."

She accepted his explanation because she had no other explanation for the oddity.

They finished caring for Freya in companionable silence, then walked out into the afternoon sunlight. Brynja's muscles ached pleasantly from the ride, and her hands smelled of horse and leather. She felt… grounded. Present in her body in a way she hadn't since before that terrible day on Tiree.

"Many thanks to you," she said as they walked back toward the keep. "For the lesson. For…" She gestured vaguely, unable to articulate all that the afternoon had meant.

"For what?" he asked.

"For treating me like I'm capable. Like I'm more than just…" She trailed off.

"More than just what?"

"Broken," she said quietly.

Hagen stopped walking. He took a step closer, his expression serious. "Brynja. You're not broken. You're a survivor. There's a difference."

"It doesn't always feel that way."

"I know." His hand lifted, hovering near her face, then dropped back to his side as if he'd thought better of the touch. "But I see you for what you are, Brynja. Not your past. Not your scars. Not your losses. You. And what I see is someone strong. Someone brave. Someone who rides a strange horse for the first time and laughs."

Her throat tightened with unexpected emotion. "I haven't laughed like that in a long time."

"Then we'll have to make sure it doesn't take a long time before the next one." His smile was gentle. "On the morrow, we'll work on cantering. And then, if you're willing, we'll take Freya out on the trails. There's a path along the coast that's bonny this time of year."

"I'd like that," Brynja said. And she meant it.

They walked back to the keep together as the sun began its descent toward the western sea. Brynja's body ached in unfamiliar places, but her heart felt lighter than it had in longer than she could remember.

Perhaps trust wasn't something you gave all at once. Perhaps it was something you learned, like riding—one careful step at a time, until suddenly you found yourself moving forward with confidence.

And perhaps Hagen Grant was exactly the teacher she needed.

CHAPTER TWENTY-FOUR

MAGNI

———◆◆◆———

MAGNI STOOD IN front of his cottage, watching his younger brother again, but this time he was frustrated. "Tenney, stop going over to the pile of horse poop. I told you to leave it alone."

The boy was fascinated by this hunk of what appeared to be dirt, but Magni knew by the odor that it had been left behind by Simone's horse when she arrived a short time ago. She was inside chatting with his mother and Lia at the moment, but he surely could use some help with the lad.

"Tenney, it smells. You cannot play with it."

Tenney laughed and giggled but ran away from Magni as if it were just a game to him. Finally, Magni thought of something. "I'll fix you." So he chased after him, grabbing him like a sack of vegetables, then carried him over to the horse. Magni climbed onto the mounting stone, then set him up on Simone's stallion, who was busy munching on some grass.

Tenney landed on the saddle, and her horse lifted its head to look at Magni who patted him.

"He just wants a wee ride. Simone will be back soon."

The animal ignored him and went back to eating his snack.

Tenney, in the meantime, was having the time of his life. He sat on the saddle, grabbing the front of it to keep himself balanced, then bounced up and down as if he were really riding the beast across the beach. He laughed and giggled and carried on so much that it made Magni smile.

"I wish I could forget everything and have fun again, Tenney." He sighed thinking of all the fears he still held onto, the ones his mother kept telling him he had to let go.

Fear of kidnapping, of smelly rooms and cellars, of mean men who hit you for no reason. Of old boats that could carry you to an unknown land and leave you all by yourself.

Of boats that could leave you on the shore of Mull, where you ran away with the hope you could find someone. And he had. His sister, who wasn't truly his sister, but she loved him and protected him. Lia.

But then the cruel men could leave him somewhere else, where he didn't know anyone. He wished Thane lived here with him because he would protect Magni when Lia was gone. And Connor Grant could live here too because he was the biggest man he had ever seen. And when he used his sword it scared Magni.

But so could Broc and Alaric. Their swords were bigger than Thane's sword. And Lennox's wife, Meg, could live with him too. She protected him once with an axe. And she hit the man right in the forehead, and he fell to the ground and never moved after that.

Mayhap he could get his grandfather to move here. Logan wasn't really his grandfather, but he adopted him. Could he convince him to live here for one moon? And then Thane for the next moon. And then Lennox and Meg. And then Connor. And then Alasdair and John. They had that big blue sword.

And then there were the archers. Simone lived here already so he needed another one. Would Eli come and stay for a moon with Alaric? Or would Gwyneth come with Logan and protect him? Or Dyna. Aye. Dyna could come with Tora and Sylvi and Sandor, and they would tell him if any bad people were coming for him. They were all seers. Or Dyna was and Tora too. And mayhap Sylvi. But Sandor could talk with dead people. Or was it only some dead people?

"Magni," his mother called out. "Would you please carry my bag for me?"

Magni took Tenney down from the horse and carried him over to his mother. "Where would you like your bag, Mama?"

"In the boat, please."

All set to do as she asked, something stopped him. He stared at the bag and then back at his mother. "Where are you going, Mama?"

"I've decided to go stay with Thane for a while. And your da will help me get there. Would you like to come with me?"

He took two steps backwards. His head shook

before he could even shout his answer out. "Nay! I'm not leaving here, ever. And you can't leave me ever again."

Simone came out behind his mother and said, "Now, Magni. I heard that. You know Thane will protect you. Your mother is having a terrible time with her back, and I think if she spent some time on a good bed at night that she would heal. And she wouldn't have so many chores at MacQuarie Castle. Here she helps with all the bairns, and it is wearing on her. Why don't you come along with us?"

"To MacQuarie land? Nay. Never. I'm staying here. Mama, you cannot go. Please."

His mother came over and set a hand on his shoulder. "Magni, I'd like you to come with us. I'm not abandoning you. You belong with me, so please come along. Your sire will take me, but he'll return."

"But you can't leave me."

"Child, if I don't heal my back, I won't be able to walk much longer. Brenna gave me something to put on every day, but I have to figure out exactly what my problem is. Come with me."

"Nay." He stopped to think for a moment. He didn't want his mother unable to walk. She needed to be fixed. Mayhap in a day or two she could return, and as long as his father was returning, it might be all right. "Will you come back when it's better?"

"If you'd like me to, I will. But Da is coming with me. He'll return for you if you insist on staying here."

He wanted to cry but he was getting too big to cry. "I want you to come back as soon as you're better."

"All right. If it will please you, then I'll do that."

"And Papa."

"Fine. I'll have him return to you once I'm settled."

"Lia will stay with me." He looked around because he hadn't seen her in a while. Where was she? "Lia?"

Lia came out of the house and strode right up to him. "Magni, I'm going with your mama. She needs our help."

"Nay, you cannot go too, Lia. You're my sister."

"I know that, but I have something I must do on the isle. I promise to return."

Magni felt his world fall apart. He glanced over his shoulder to see if someone was waiting for him. Or mayhap there was someone hiding in the trees waiting for everyone to leave. Or was there a boat approaching? One with ten men who would grab him and Tenney and steal them away?

Lia approached him and took his hands in hers. "Magni, I will not let anyone hurt you. I told you I'd protect you. But if you're that uncomfortable here, then come with us. Thane and Tamsin would love to see you and so would Mora and Brian."

The tears flooded his cheeks, and he couldn't stop them, so he hugged Lia, hoping no one would see his tears. He wasn't a baby, so he didn't know why he was crying. "Please don't go, Lia."

Simone came out and took Magni by the hand. "Say good-bye to your mama. Your father is going to take her there, and he will return. We all have to get her to Thane's safely. Then Artan and I will return. Your da will probably return in a day or two, once your mother is settled. Lia has other places she has to go."

"But you promised, Lia."

"I promised I would always protect you, Magni, and I will hold to that promise."

"But you didn't before. I was stolen away."

"And you were saved each time."

"But I don't want that to happen ever again. I don't like being stolen away."

Simone waved his mother and father over to the boat. "Magni, come sit with me for a moment."

"All right. Are you going to stay with me, Simone?"

"Nay, but I'll be back soon. I will still live in our hut, but I'll visit every day while Lia is gone. I promise."

"But why is everyone leaving me? Don't you still love me?"

Four voices cried in unison. "Of course we do!"

His tears turned to sobs, something he couldn't stop. His nightmares were getting worse, and he hated it when he woke up in the middle of the night scared, but he would go lie in bed next to his mother and all would be fine.

Now he wouldn't be able to do that.

"Magni, your mother's back is hurting her verra badly. Brenna came to check on her and said if she didn't find a better place to sleep that she might not be able to walk in a few moons. You wouldn't want that to happen, would you? Your mother wouldn't be able to hug you from her bed if she had to stay flat all the time."

"Nay, I don't want Mama," he said with a hitch, "to be hurt so bad. But why can't she get fixed here?"

"Because she needs a solid bed like Thane has. She's going there for a while. And you don't have to be alone. You may go with them right now. You and Tenney can climb in the boat."

"But Tenney doesn't want to go either."

Simone arched a brow at him. "He doesn't? Are you sure about that?"

Magni let out a huge sigh. "Nay, but I don't want to leave, and I don't wish for Tenney to go. I'm too afraid. God is here on Iona."

Lia leaned over and kissed his cheek. "God is everywhere, child. I've told you that before, but I promise to return. You take care of Tenney. We have to go now."

Simone gave him a big hug. "Artan and I will return before darkness descends. I promise."

"Will you stay here with me?"

His father yelled, "I'll be back on the morrow, son. Beatris, Geva, and Emma are all here too, Magni. Henry will be back soon."

"Would you and Tenney like to sleep in our hut this eve?" Simone asked.

"All right."

Simone waved and headed toward the boat.

Magni's biggest fear had come true. He was all alone.

CHAPTER TWENTY-FIVE

DREW

REW MENZIE MADE his way down to the tavern. It was late at night and poor Lina had suffered from another bad headache.

The kind of headache that told him something bad was about to happen. The only thing he could think to do was go outside the walls of Duart Castle and find out what else was happening on the Isle of Mull.

Because something was definitely brewing. They could all feel it.

Connor would go to MacVeys and Rankins. Dyna would go to MacQuaries and MacLeans, but he knew where the best place was to gain information from the undercurrent of the world—the local tavern.

He stepped inside the tavern at Craignure, not surprised to see it nearly full. He took an empty seat at the bar, ordered a drink, tossing the man a coin while he crafted his story in his mind.

"Where you from?" the man behind the bar asked.

"I just came across the ferry this eve. I heard

there was someone paying good coin for warriors. Know you of who I could see about it?"

"Aye, I might," he said, nodding to a man leaning against the wall.

Drew stayed where he was, waiting to see if the man would approach. He had unkempt brown hair with a beard that appeared to be new. He wasn't tall, but he had broad shoulders and carried a sheathed small sword.

And he had a strut that tried to impress everyone.

It didn't impress Drew.

When he finally approached, Drew gave the man the same story. "Are you the man hiring?"

"Aye, but we don't need you yet. In about a sennight. We're gathering forces now."

"Against whom?"

"You don't need to know. You just have to show up and fight. Bring a good sword."

"Where?"

"Not certain yet. You can get word back here in two days. I'll let the man behind the bar know where you will meet us."

Drew said, "Suits me fine. I love a good battle." He noticed the man had a scar on his right cheek, not recent. He also had recent scratches as though he fell into a pile of nettles. "What's your name? So I know who to ask about."

"You don't need to know. Just ask the man about the force. He'll know."

Drew took a swig of his ale, waiting with the hope that he would say more. The man didn't move, taking a swig of his own drink. Finally, the scarred man asked, "Know you much about the Grants?"

"Not much. A little."

"How many guards at Duart? And how many fighting Grants are there?"

Drew shrugged and said, "I heard someone on the ferry say he was a Grant. He was bragging to everyone about the force they had. And that there were a few Grants here."

"Alex's sons here?"

"Just one. Mayhap some grandsons."

"How many total?"

"He said they had four score, and that two score more were coming in a sennight. Don't know if he was being honest or bragging. Didn't know the man."

The man turned to take his leave, but the man behind the bar said, "You need to pay, Sholto."

Drew hid his smile. Now he knew the man's name, and when he walked away, he noticed something else.

Sholto walked with a limp, and his hand went to his thigh when he stopped.

Probably rubbing the same spot where Brynja hit him with her dagger.

CHAPTER TWENTY-SIX

CONNOR

———⚬⚬⚬———

T HE NEXT DAY, Connor sat in the solar with Drew, Alaric, and Maitland. Drew had shared what he learned at the tavern last night. It seemed they were about to be attacked again. But why?

"I need to know what they're after. Did he give you any idea about that, Drew?"

"Nay. Naught. Just that it would be happening within a sennight."

A knock interrupted them. Connor said, "Enter."

Hagen stepped in, someone behind him that he couldn't see.

"What is it, Hagen? We're busy."

"Brynja has some information for you. She heard the two men talking when they were in the boat."

Connor nodded. "Please, escort her in."

Hagen ushered her inside, and the four men all stood. By the shock on Brynja's face, he knew that she'd never been treated like this before.

The expression on his father's face told him he thought the same.

Brynja blushed and said, "Good morn to you all."

Hagen said, "You've met my sire and Maitland. This is Grant's grandsire, Drew Menzie, Avelina's husband and Maitland's sire, and this is Alaric, another cousin, husband to Eli."

"How is Hildi, lass?" Connor asked, waiting for her to sit before taking his seat again.

"She awakened last night and this morn. She's improving slowly." Hagen ushered her to a chair in front of his father's desk. Even though it was technically Maitland's or Dyna's chair, Maitland and Dyna both allowed Connor to sit behind the desk when he joined the conversation out of respect for his previous lairdship.

Dyna stuck her head in and said, "Sorry, Sandor is being a wee devil this morn. Have I missed anything?"

"Nay, Brynja has something to tell us. Go ahead, lass." He waved Dyna inside.

Dyna took a seat and nodded to Brynja, so the lass began. "When we were on Ulva, I heard the two men talking before they saw us. One wanted to know how many guards the Grants have."

"Did you hear their names?" Maitland asked.

She thought for a moment, tipping her head. "I did. Sholto and… Dugald? Nay, Dugan. That's it. Dugan."

Connor looked at Drew. "Is that the name you were given last eve?"

"Aye, his name was Sholto. Brown hair, long,

short brown beard. A head shorter than me but broad shoulders. Scar on one cheek."

"Aye, the same. That's the man I hit with my dagger."

Drew smiled and winked at her. "And you're still causing the man pain from it, lass. He was limping last night and rubbing his inner thigh. Well done."

"There aren't many with aim like that," Connor said. "I hope you are proud of yourself for that."

She blushed but said naught, moving her chair a wee bit closer to Hagen's. Connor wondered if his son knew what a telling movement that was. Probably not, but he surely did.

Connor said, "Continuing. Do you know why he wished to know how many guards we have?" Suddenly he felt so tuned into the lass that he had to calm himself. He had the oddest inkling that nothing could prepare him for what she was about to reveal.

"He told Sholto that if he didn't attack, that if he stayed on Tiree, he still had to know how many you would bring."

"Did he say anything else that you recall? Anything at all."

She nodded, swallowing hard. "He asked if any of Alexander Grant's heirs were here. He said your name and asked about Kyle and James, I think?" She looked at Hagen, who turned wide-eyed to his father.

Connor held his hand up to Dyna, who jumped out of her chair. "Might he have said Kyla and Jamie?"

"Aye. One said Kyle and James, the other said Kyla and Jamie. He wanted to know if any of you were here and if any grandsons were here."

"That bastard," Dyna said, pacing the floor now. "Why? Did he say why he wanted Connor? And what about granddaughters? I'm right here waiting for him." Her fist came up from her side as if she were about to punch someone.

Brynja paled, so Connor motioned for Dyna to sit again. They needed this information as accurately as possible. Brynja was exhausted and in strange surroundings. Connor said, "Let's give Brynja the time she needs to recall everything."

Dyna sat and muttered, "My apologies, Brynja. Take your time."

Then Connor gave his attention back to the lass in front of him, the trembling in her hands evident. "Did he say anything else that could be important? Why he was interested in the Grants? Or in me?"

Brynja cleared her throat. "Dugan said Alexander Grant killed his father."

"Oh hellfire," Maitland said. "That could be a hundred different men, Connor."

Drew said, "Could be another Buchan."

"Or a MacNiven," Dyna said.

"Brynja," Connor asked. "Did he say who his father was? An earl, a baron, a jarl, anything like that?"

She shook her head, glancing at Hagen seated next to her. Connor heard him whisper to her, "You did a great job. No worries."

Then his son squeezed her hand. Connor

glanced at the two faces, noticing something there that hadn't been there before. The two were definitely in a relationship, and it was more than a simple friendship.

His son was falling in love with Brynja. And she was returning his feelings.

Connor wasn't surprised. She was beautiful in a different way. There wasn't a dainty bone in her body. The lass's constitution was tougher than the hide on an old buck, and she was feisty as hell. She reminded him of Eli Ramsay, Alaric's wife. She wasn't going to let anyone bowl her over with lies. He'd wager she's tossed a few punches before, though her prowess with a dagger was already known. She just had to get used to a wild, but loving, bunch of Grants.

He was confident she would.

The chatter continued amongst the group as they tried to guess who Dugan could be, laughter here and there at the memories that surfaced of Connor's father and his many battles. But out of the corner of his eye, he caught the change in Brynja's countenance, the expression on her face changing with the rest of her body.

"I remember." She bolted up from her chair, looking at each one in the group.

"What is it?" Connor asked, his voice quieter than it had ever been, the group silent and waiting to hear what she had to say. Dyna stood up and gripped the back of the chair next to her.

"Sholto asked him who his grandfather was. He didn't say the whole name, just his first name. He said his grandfather's name was Niles."

Everyone in the chamber stilled, Dyna fighting to keep herself from charging out the door. Connor could feel the tension shoot up at just the thought that this could be who they initially thought of.

Who they were all thinking about.

Poor Brynja looked at all the shocked faces. "Did I say something wrong?"

"Nay, lass. You are doing beautifully." Hagen squeezed her hand again.

Then Connor asked, "Did you hear the name Niles Comming?"

"Nay, just Niles. Alexander Grant killed his grandfather, Niles. He wants vengeance."

"Oh my God in Heaven," Dyna whispered.

Drew said, "Connor, don't let this change how you handle anything. It should have no bearing on anything."

Maitland said, "That's not possible, Da." He looked at his father and arched a brow.

Brynja looked at Hagen. "Who is Niles?"

Connor said, "Niles is the man who raped my mother. And aye, my sire killed him for it. He deserved worse."

CHAPTER TWENTY-SEVEN

BRYNJA

~~~

BRYNJA FOUND HAGEN in the lists, working through sword forms with a focused intensity that spoke of anger rather than practice. His movements were sharp, aggressive, each strike against the practice post harder than necessary.

"You'll break your wrist if you keep hitting that hard," she called out.

Hagen paused mid-swing, chest heaving. Sweat dampened his hair despite the December chill. "Mayhap I wish to break something."

She crossed the yard to him, noting the white-knuckled grip on his sword hilt. "What happened?"

"It's about this whole possibility of the grandson of Niles Comming wanting to attack my clan. I see what it does to my father, then my mother's reaction too. And it upsets Dyna. I'm glad Astra and Morgan are still at Clan Grant. They'd be upset too and Astra was already subjected to too much.

Brynja understood that rage. It lived in her

chest too, burning hot and constant. "Then you go after him. Why wait?"

"It's not that simple."

"It is that simple." Her voice hardened. "He did evil. He should pay for it."

Hagen looked at her, something shifting in his expression. "You sound verra certain about that."

"I am certain." She met his gaze squarely. "Justice doesn't wait for convenience or politics. Either you believe in it or you don't."

"Is that what you call it? Justice?" His tone had shifted, grown cooler. "Or is it vengeance?"

Brynja stiffened. "There's a difference?"

"Aye. There is." Hagen pulled his sword from the ground, wiping the dirt from the blade with deliberate care. "Justice is about making things right. Vengeance is about making yourself feel better."

Heat flared in her chest. "So when I hunt down the men who murdered my mother, I'm just trying to make myself feel better?"

"I didn't say that—"

"You did." She took a step closer, anger thrumming through her veins. "You just said vengeance is selfish. Well, I want those men dead, Hagen. I want the bastards' blood on my hands. Is that selfish? Aye, mayhap it is. But it's also right."

"Right for who?" He faced her fully now, jaw tight. "For you? Or for your mother? Because she's dead, Brynja. Killing her murderers won't bring her back."

The words hit like a physical blow. "How dare you?"

"How dare I what? Tell you the truth?" His voice rose to match hers. "You think I don't understand? You think I don't lie awake at night imagining what I'd do to the men who hurt my family? The Buchans, the Commings, so many have attacked my clan over the years. But wanting something and it being right aren't the same thing."

"So you'd let them go free? Let them live while good people died?"

"I didn't say that either."

"Then what are you saying?" Brynja demanded. "Because it sounds like you're saying my quest for justice—"

"Vengeance."

"—is somehow wrong. That I should just forgive and forget and move on like a good little lass."

"That's not what I'm saying!" Hagen's shout echoed across the empty yard. "I'm saying I'm terrified you're going to get yourself killed chasing ghosts. You don't know who the guilty men are yet. How many will you have to kill to find out who killed your mother and aunt?"

Silence fell between them, sharp and sudden.

Brynja's breath came hard. "My mother's murderer is a ghost, but Sholto isn't a ghost. He hurt Hildi."

"True, but he might as well be. You've been watching the horizon for weeks. Every boat that passes, every stranger who comes to port, you think it's him. You're living your life waiting for another confrontation that might never come."

He took a step toward her, his expression raw. "And if it does come? What then? You fight him? You kill him? And then what, Brynja? Does the hole in your chest fill up? Do the nightmares stop?"

"I don't know," she said, her voice shaking. "But I have to try. I have to." She broke off, fists clenched. "You don't understand."

"Don't I?" His laugh was bitter. "I now know of a man who wishes to kill me and my father? How can I not go after Dugan? You think I don't imagine it every single day?"

"Then why don't you?" The question came out sharper than she'd intended.

Hagen went very still. When he spoke again, his voice was quiet, dangerous. "Because I know the difference between justice and revenge. Because I know that killing him won't bring anyone back. And because—" He stopped, jaw working.

"Because what?"

"Because I'm afraid of what I'll become if I do it." The admission seemed wrenched from somewhere deep. "I'm afraid I'll like it. I'm afraid the rage will feel good. And then what? Where does it stop?"

Brynja stared at him. "So you do nothing."

"I do something. I protect the people I love. I make sure it doesn't happen again. I fight when fighting is necessary." He met her eyes. "But I don't chase vengeance dressed up as justice."

The words stung more than they should have. "You think that's what I'm doing."

"Aren't you?" He took another step closer.

"Brynja, I understand the need for it. I do. But I'm watching you consume yourself with this need for revenge, and I'm terrified of what happens if you get it. More terrified of what happens if you don't."

"You stand here and tell me not to chase revenge while you're beating a practice post to splinters because you can't get to the man you want to kill. You say you're afraid of what you'll become, but you want it just as much as I do. You're just too afraid to admit it."

Color rose in Hagen's cheeks. "That's not true."

"It is. You want your revenge. The rage inside of you is barely contained. You just dress it up in noble words about protection and justice. But at the core? You want him dead as much as I want Sholto dead. The only difference is you won't let yourself have it."

Hagen's hands fisted at his sides. "Mayhap because I fear nothing could be enough. Will you be satisfied if he's dead? If you find the man who murdered your mother and you put a spear in his chest, will it be enough?"

"I don't know, but I surely don't like the alternative." Brynja's voice cracked. "I should just let them live? Let Sholto and the others walk free? They murdered my mother, Hagen. They would have sold me like cattle. And you're telling me I should just... what? Forgive them?"

"Nay." He closed the distance between them, his expression fierce. "I'm not telling you to forgive them. I'm telling you that revenge won't heal you. It won't give you peace. And I'm terrified that when you finally get it, you'll realize that too late."

"You don't get to decide what will heal me."

"And you don't get to throw your life away on a mayhap!" His voice rose again. "Because that's what you're doing, Brynja. You're so focused on killing Sholto that you're not living your own life. You're existing in this tiny space, waiting for him to come so you can—what? Die trying to kill him? Because that's what might happen. He's not going to come alone. He'll bring men. And even if you win, even if you kill every last one of them, what will it cost you?"

"Whatever it costs, it'll be worth it."

"Even your life?"

"Even my life."

"Well, it's not worth it to me!" The words exploded from him. "Your life is worth more than revenge, Brynja. It's worth more than Sholto's death." He broke off, running a hand through his hair in frustration. "You're worth more than that."

Tears burned behind Brynja's eyes, but she refused to let them fall. "That's not your choice to make."

"I know." His voice gentled, which somehow made it worse. "I know it's not. But I'm asking you to think about what you're really after. Is it justice? Or is it just pain for pain? Because one of those things might give you satisfaction for a moment. But the other one will haunt you forever."

"You don't understand," she said again, but this time her voice was barely a whisper.

"Then help me understand." He reached for her, his hand hovering near her shoulder but not quite touching. "Tell me what you think will happen when Sholto dies. When your mother's murderer dies. Tell me how it ends."

Brynja closed her eyes. She'd imagined it a thousand times—her blade sliding between Sholto's ribs, the shock in his eyes, the way he'd fall. Or the ghost that haunts her every night. She'd imagined standing over his body and feeling... what? Relief? Victory? Justice?

"I don't know," she admitted finally. "I don't know what happens after. I just know that I can't move forward until he's dead. I can't sleep, I can't rest, I can't—" Her voice broke. "I can't be free until he's gone."

"What if you're wrong?" Hagen's hand finally settled on her shoulder, warm and steady. "What if killing him doesn't set you free? What if it just trades one cage for another?"

"Then at least I'll have tried." She opened her eyes, meeting his gaze. "At least I'll know."

He studied her for a long moment, his expression unreadable. Then he sighed, his hand dropping away. "And what about us?"

The question hung between them, heavy with meaning.

"What about us?" she echoed.

"If you go after him, *when* you go after him, I'm going with you. You know that, aye?"

"I can't ask you to do that."

"You're not asking. I'm telling you." His jaw set in that stubborn way she was coming to know.

"If you walk into danger, I walk into it with you. That's what this is. That's what we are."

"Even though you think I'm wrong."

"Even though I think you're wrong." A ghost of a smile touched his lips. "Love doesn't mean agreeing with everything someone does. Sometimes it means standing beside them even when you think they're making a mistake. Because you'd rather be there to catch them than let them fall alone."

Her breath caught. "Love?"

Color crept up his neck. "Aye. Love." He met her eyes squarely. "Did you think it was something else?"

"I..." She didn't know what she'd thought. "We're arguing."

"Aye, we are. And we'll probably argue again. But that doesn't change how I feel." He stepped closer, his hand coming up to cup her cheek. "I love you, Brynja. All of you. Even the parts that are bent on revenge. Even the parts that scare me. I just... I don't want to lose you to it."

Tears finally spilled over, hot against her cold cheeks. "I don't want to lose myself either. But I don't know how to let it go. I don't know how to just... stop wanting what I want."

"I'm not asking you to let it go." His thumb brushed away her tears. "I'm just asking you to think about whether revenge is really what you want. Or if mayhap what you really want is to stop hurting."

The words hit something deep inside her, some truth she'd been avoiding. Because he was right, wasn't he? She didn't want Sholto dead because it would bring her mother back. She wanted him dead because she was in pain, and she didn't know how else to make it stop.

"What if you're wrong?" she asked quietly. "What if you're telling me not to seek revenge while you would do exactly the same thing in my place?"

Hagen was silent for a long moment. Then he said, "You're right. I don't know the answer. Because if someone hurt you, I wouldn't hesitate. I'd hunt them to the ends of the earth, and I wouldn't stop until they were dead. So mayhap I don't have any right to tell you not to do the same."

"Then why are you?"

"Because I can see you more clearly than I can see myself. Because I can see what it's costing you, even if you can't. And because—" He drew in a shaky breath. "Because sometimes love means telling someone the hard truth, even when you know they don't want to hear it."

Brynja pressed her forehead to his chest, her hands fisting in his tunic. "I'm so tired, Hagen. I'm tired of being angry all the time. Tired of watching the horizon. Tired of waiting for him to come. But I don't know how to stop."

His arms came around her, solid and sure. "Mayhap you don't have to stop. Mayhap you just have to decide that revenge isn't all you are. That it's not the only thing that defines you."

"What else is there?" The question came out muffled against his chest.

"Everything." His voice was fierce. "There's you learning to ride. There's you laughing at midnight on the parapets. There's you being fierce and brave and stubborn. There's you standing here letting me see you cry. There's you and me and whatever future we might build together." He pulled back just enough to look at her. "There's so much more than revenge, Brynja. If you'll let yourself see it."

She wanted to believe him. Wanted to believe there could be a life beyond this consuming need for Sholto's death. But the anger was so familiar, so much a part of her now. How did you let go of something that had kept you alive?

"I don't know if I can," she whispered.

"Then don't. Not yet." He pressed a kiss to her forehead. "Just… promise me you'll think about it. Promise me that when the time comes, you'll ask yourself whether revenge is really what you need. Or if mayhap you need something else entirely."

Brynja pulled back to look at him. His eyes were troubled, his expression open and vulnerable in a way that made her chest ache. He loved her. This complicated, stubborn man loved her. And he was asking her to think. Not to give up her quest, not to forgive, not to forget. Just to think.

"I'll think about it," she said finally. "I can't promise more than that."

"It's enough." He pulled her close again, and they stood there in the cold wind, holding each other.

Brynja managed a small smile. "Mayhap we're

both broken in the same ways. And mayhap that's all right."

He whispered, "If we work on it together, we might do it right."

Together.

A word Brynja didn't know much about, but she was willing to learn.

CHAPTER TWENTY-EIGHT

CONNOR

THE GROUP STOOD out near the gates the next day, readying their trip to Tiree.

"Da," Dyna said. "I still think you need more guards to go with you."

"Dyna," said Connor. "I have the best swordsmen we have. Hagen, Broc, and Alaric. I'm leaving Maitland, Jowell, and Paden with you. And all three can switch to bows with Merryn if we need to. Brynja can shoot her daggers or switch to a bow. She's been practicing enough to send arrows out to scare them."

"I should go with you, Da!" she cried, tears running down her face. "I have this feeling, but I can't see clearly."

Sela said, "Exactly why you're staying here. Dyna. I'll not lose my husband and two of my bairns at once. Your father and I agreed to that years ago. No more than two at a time."

Connor strode over to his eldest daughter and kissed her cheek. "You need to stay here with Mama. And your bairns need you. I'll not risk my grandbairns losing their mother. Besides, this is just a patrol. I wish to see how many they have and how skilled they are. We'll be back late on the morrow. I hope to go over later this eve. We'll spend the night at MacQuaries and then return. I promise we will not attack."

Dyna ran into the stables and brought out several apples, moving from one horse to the next. She stopped at Midnight Moon and whispered to her favorite horse, "You are carrying my father. Bring him home to me like Midnight did Grandda."

They left at high sun, the weather gray but agreeable. The trip to MacQuarie land was uneventful with little conversation. Hagen rode with Brynja tucked in front of him, something he liked. "At least I know I'll be warm," she said. "You're like the warmest hearth on the coldest day in winter, Hagen."

Merryn overheard her and laughed. "It must run in the family. Broc is the same."

Alaric led the way. "Connor, if Eli wasn't thick with a bairn inside, she would be here. It's killing her to stay back. But with Brenna and Logan both there, she can't sneak away."

"How was Hildi this morn, lass?" Hagen asked.

"Better. She seemed more alert, but her head still pains her something fierce. I asked Brenna about it, and she said as long as she had that bump, it would still hurt. The bump was definitely smaller. And Hildi was eating porridge when I left. Tora and Sylvi were busy playing healer with her, something Hildi thought was endearing. She loves the bairns like I do."

"Dyna said the bairns are improving too. They had nightmares for a long time after they were stolen away. I hope they don't remember what happened to them. Not like poor Magni. He'll always remember."

They were nearly to MacQuarie land when Alaric slowed his horse. They came over the crest, heading down toward the coast to the front of the castle when a small form stood in the road.

"Nay, nay, nay," Alaric said. "What do we do? Go back?"

Connor asked, "Alaric. What is the problem?"

"She is the problem." He turned back to everyone and pointed ahead of them in the path. "Lia is here. That's bad. You know it's bad."

Broc said, "Nay, Lia. Go away!"

Connor said, "I don't consider it bad. Have we lost anyone when Lia is around?"

"Nay, but you know if she's here, trouble is coming," Broc said. "We've seen it enough times, Uncle Connor. Mayhap we should turn around."

Connor stopped his horse and said, "I will not allow a Comming to scare me away. If anyone wishes to go back, please do. I'll take the lead." He headed straight for the wee lass waiting for them in front of the curtain wall.

"Greetings to you, Granthams. And I see you have many Grants with you. Welcome to all."

Merryn asked, "What is going to happen, Lia?"

Lia said, "I don't know what you mean, Merryn. I'm just visiting MacQuaries. I would like to speak with you all about Yule. Magni is verra troubled still, and I'd like to find a way to convince him to move to Thane's castle. I thought you could help me."

"We'd be happy to," Connor said.

Broc whispered behind him, "Good. It's about Magni, not us."

A voice carried to them from the top of the wall. "Come on in, Grants. We just finished the evening meal and have stew and bread left."

"Enough for Broc? You know how much he eats," Merryn said with a laugh.

"Plenty. Come in through the gates, and I'll meet you at the stable."

Thane and Artan greeted them as promised, near the stables. Lia smiled and greeted everyone. "I'll be pleased to see you all in the great hall. I wish to plan an event for the bairns at Yule."

Connor said, "If you make a trip to Duart Castle, you'll learn of our Yuletide Festival. It's planned for the first two nights of Yule. We hope you and Magni will come. Everyone on Mull is invited." He paused, then added, "And Iona, of course."

"Many thanks to you, Chief Grant. We will do our best to convince Magni to come. I think we will plan one here also. Magni does not wish to leave Iona, but I'm hoping we can get him here. His mother is here healing from a back pain."

Connor stepped away from the group, leaving the young ones to chat with Thane and Artan. "Lia, may I speak with you privately?"

"Of course."

"What can you tell me of the group on Tiree. Are they operating Kelvan's previous atrocity? Are they stealing and shipping bairns?"

Lia said, "That is their plan. It has not happened yet. There have been a couple of groups who have tried to take over Kelvan's work, but they have all failed. One of the groups took Brynja and Hildi. This is a new group, but one or two are the same. You are headed there?"

"Aye, I'm seeking information on the man who claims to be the grandson of Niles Comming. Know you who that is?"

"Nay, I do not. I can seek out that information, but I think you'll find out as quickly as I can. I am the protector of bairns, so I focus on that. And I will tell you there are no bairns on Tiree at present. None being held against their will. They are hoping to start the operation up again."

Connor nodded, crossing his arms. He still had difficulty listening to a lass of six summers as though she were thirty. However, he did note that her gaze was one of an old, wise woman. That much he was certain.

"Will you come with us?" He was fine without her, but he heard the apprehension in both Alaric's and Broc's voices.

"Nay, not this time. There are no bairns who need you, so I must stay here."

"Do you know where the new group is congregating?"

"Hagen and Brynja will show you. They have been there. It's her home. It is on the far side of the island. If you land on this side of Tiree and cross it, you'll pass the same cottage where Broc found the bairns before. It stands empty."

"Would it not behoove us to land on the other side? We'd be closer to them?"

Lia shook her head. "Nay, you will be able to surprise them better from this side. And the sea on the other side is much rougher. You'll need to navigate quickly from there."

Connor frowned at the last comment, wondering exactly what she meant, but Lia ran up the stairs to the keep with a wave. He knew he'd get no more information from her.

He was on his own now.

CHAPTER TWENTY-NINE

HAGEN

———~~~———

HAGEN LED BRYNJA down the path to the boat they were taking to Tiree.

Brynja said, "I've never been on a ship this big."

"Thane said the Norse left it hidden in the bushes. When Artan found it, they discovered the hole in it, patched it up with new wood and it's been beautiful for them. It takes six rowers to make it move."

"And they're underneath?" Brynja asked, peeking into the bottom of the boat.

"Aye. Thane has his men row it. Bearnard loves it, says they love the sea air. Wait until you see how fast it moves," Hagen said, ushering her to one of the seats built along the inside of the boat. The boat rocked gently beneath them as Thane's men settled into position below deck. The salt spray hung in the air, mixing with the scent of fresh-cut wood from the pines they were cutting for winter nearby.

"Where should we land, Brynja?" Artan asked. "I'm going with you."

"Gott Bay," she answered. "It's the closest. Then it's a short distance to our cottages."

Once they headed toward Tiree, Connor pulled the group together, giving instructions. "This will be a quick trip, I hope, because our goal is to learn more about Dugan and his plans. There are six of us. I'd like Broc and Merryn to return to the cottage you found the bairns in before. I'd like to be certain there are none that need saving. If you are outnumbered, just return with the information and we'll retrieve them when we're together again. Alaric, Hagen, and Brynja will go with me. I need your guidance because I have no idea where this hut is." Connor's hand rested on his sword hilt as he spoke, his eyes scanning each face in turn, ensuring they understood. "I would guess they have guards with them at this point. You said there were two huts together?"

"Aye. Two huts and one small outbuilding for cold storage behind them."

"How far from the water? Or a bay to launch a boat from?"

"A short walk. We lived up on a small hill to protect us from the sea. It was just a short jaunt to the beach."

"Is there a way to come up to the cottages without being seen?"

"Aye, there is a crest on one side. The beach has plenty of rock formations, but that would be the other side of the huts from here. We'll be coming down a crest and there is one copse of trees to hide behind."

As they approached, Tiree announced itself

with the thunder of surf against hidden reefs, the
white spray leaping skyward where the sea swells
met submerged rock. Then the island emerged
from the sea mist, so low and flat it seems barely
to rise above the waves, as though one good
storm might wash it away entirely.

But what it lacked in height, Tiree made up
for in light. The shell-sand beaches glowed almost
white, stretching in long, sweeping crescents
around the island's edge.

Connor said, "I'll never cease to be impressed
by the beauty of the isles around Mull."

They landed a short time later, Broc and
Merryn heading in the direction of the cottages
they were familiar with.

His father said, "Be back within the hour. We'll
plan to return by then."

A group of fishermen gathered not far away,
chatting, so his sire approached. "Greetings to
you. Have you noticed a group of new islanders,
the kind you don't like to see on your isle?"

"Who is asking?" one man asked, the creases in
his face evidence of years of fishing expeditions,
the deep crevices unable to hide the sharpness in
his brown eyes.

"Connor Grant, son of Alexander Grant, Clan
Grant of Dulnain Valley of the Highlands."

One man whistled, while a third man said,
"You're a long way from Dulnain Valley, but you're
as big as your reputation says you are, Grant."

"I am visiting family on Mull. I was advised
someone on this isle has planned an attack on my
clan allies at Duart Castle."

At the mention of Duart Castle, one man nodded to another, and they broke out in smiles. "Bastards think they'll steal some of our bairns, but they won't. We've been watching them."

The oldest man, the first one they spoke to, nodded to his father. "You were here before, drove Kelvan off our isle. I remember you."

"I was."

"Welcome back." Connor's shoulders relaxed slightly, though his hand never strayed far from his weapon. The fisherman pointed toward the other side of the isle. "Follow that path. Fools are hiring mercenaries and bringing them here. We don't like it."

Another stepped forward and asked, "Brynja? Is that you?"

She stepped forward, nodding, then ran over to hug one of the men. "Och, lass. We are glad to see you are hale. Where is Hildi?"

"We found our way to Iona. Have lived there. But I wish to get rid of the scum in our old homes."

"Go, lass. They're evil men. We'll follow at a distance, see if you need any help."

Artan said, "We'll stay back, but whistle and we'll come running."

Connor nodded and the four headed across the isle.

Once they were close, Brynja motioned for them to hush, moving them over to a crest as protection.

They hid and listened, pressing themselves low

against the rocky crest. The wind carried voices toward them, harsh laughter and the clatter of weapons being moved. Hagen's heart hammered in his chest as he counted the speakers. He guessed there were four men and held that number of fingers up to his father, who nodded, his jaw tight. Then Hagen caught another voice, deeper, from farther away. He held up five fingers.

A voice carried to them and Brynja said, "That's Dugan."

The voice was closer than the others. "Four score? I think he lied. I think they have only two score. I've asked, and I don't think Granthams are that strong."

"That's what he said. And two score more coming."

"It will be a long time before they can get two score here. You think they have a fleet of Norse boats for the men and their mounts? I say we go now."

"What is your rush? I thought you were going after bairns first?"

"Nay, we don't have anyone to care for them yet."

"We don't need anyone to care for young lasses."

"I'll care for the young lasses."

A slap sounded. Hagen felt his father's body go rigid beside him. The air between them crackled with barely contained rage.

Hagen caught the fury in his father's eyes—a murderous gleam he'd only seen a handful of times in his life. He shook his head at his father, his own hand clamping down on his sire's forearm in warning, because that was his fear.

"Da, control." Hagen's whisper was urgent, desperate. His father's head was full of vengeance for what the man's grandfather did to his mother, the beloved Madeline Grant. Connor's breathing had gone shallow, his muscles coiled like a spring about to snap. "He's not Niles, either. Focus."

True, Hagen recalled his grandfather Alexander enough to know that he would want the man killed without another thought, without hesitation or mercy. This was vengeance, no different than the vengeance Brynja harbored for the men who killed her mother. The realization struck him cold.

Were they the same? Was vengeance ever righteous, or did it always cloud judgment?

Dugan snorted. "You'll care for the young lasses. Like the ones you did on Iona? She got you, you never got her."

A third man said, "You should have seen the two who lived here with their mothers. We almost got a taste of them."

Dugan said, "You cannot ruin the merchandise. And they got away from the two watching the cottage."

"And now we have no one to watch the bairns. You didn't need to kill them, Dugan."

Hagen glanced over at Brynja, whose face had turned red. She'd heard. These were the men who killed her mother and aunt. He squeezed her hand, and his father shook his head at her.

Dugan chuckled, "I can't wait to see Connor

Grant's face when I stick my sword deep in his belly. But first I'll tell him how my grandfather enjoyed ripping into his grandmother."

And then his father did exactly what Hagen didn't want him to do.

And what he'd sworn not to do.

Connor Grant rose from their hiding place, his massive frame unfolding to its full height. The movement was deliberate, controlled—the calm before the storm.

"See if you think you can do it now, Comming."

His father's voice rang across the space between them, cold as winter steel.

And everything happened at once.

Brynja stuck her head up, her movements fluid and practiced. Two daggers flew from her hands in rapid succession, silver flashes in the afternoon light. The first struck the third man in the throat—he made a wet, gurgling sound as he clawed at his neck and dropped. The second blade buried itself in the fourth man's belly. He looked down in disbelief, wrapped both hands around the hilt, and yanked it free. Blood erupted from the wound, spraying across the dirt in a dark arc. He stumbled backward, pressing his hands uselessly against the flow.

And the battle began in earnest.

Dugan charged after Connor like a maddened bull, his sword already drawn and gleaming. Hagen moved instinctively to protect his father, his own blade clearing its scabbard, but his sire bellowed at him with a voice that could shake mountains.

"Do not dare to step in front of me!"

The command froze Hagen mid-stride. His father wanted this fight. Needed it.

Sholto grabbed a fallen sword and ran at Brynja, murder in his eyes. She loosed two arrows in quick succession—the first whipped past his ear, close enough to draw a thin line of blood. The second embedded itself in the wooden doorframe behind him. Sholto skidded to a halt, then wheeled around and dove back into the hut, disappearing into its shadowy interior.

Movement erupted from behind them. Two more men came charging from the trees— mercenaries by the look of them, their weapons already drawn and their faces twisted with battle rage. They were suddenly outnumbered, surrounded.

Alaric moved to intercept one attacker, his sword meeting the man's blade with a shower of sparks. The clang of metal on metal rang out across the hillside. Hagen spun to face the other swordsman, a hulking brute with a scarred face and dead eyes.

Behind him, Dugan went after his father with relentless fury. Connor fought like a man possessed. Nay, like a man who'd been waiting thirty years for this moment. The sound of their swords clashing was deafening, a rhythmic thunder that everyone on the isle could have heard. His father's movements were powerful, brutal, each swing carrying the weight of decades of grief.

Hagen's opponent came at him with an

overhead strike that would have split him from crown to jaw. He threw his blade up, catching the blow, feeling the impact shudder through his arms. The mercenary was strong but reckless. Hagen sidestepped, letting the man's momentum carry him forward, and slashed across his sword arm. The blade bit deep into muscle and the man screamed, his weapon clattering to the stones. He clutched his ruined arm and ran off down the hill, leaving a trail of blood behind him.

But Sholto had reemerged from the hut, and he was still headed for Brynja.

She saw him coming and her hand went to her belt, coming up with another dagger. The blade flew true, sinking into his shoulder. Sholto roared in pain and fury.

"Bitch, I'll kill you!" He kept coming, ripping the dagger free and casting it aside, blood streaming down his arm.

Hagen turned to go after him, his legs already moving, but two more men materialized from around the side of the cottage. He didn't know which bastard to go after first, his mind racing to calculate the threat. Brynja or his father?

Then, suddenly, the air sang with arrows.

Four shafts flew over their heads in perfect formation, finding their marks on the two new attackers. One took an arrow through the eye and dropped like a stone. The other caught two in the chest and staggered backward, mouth open in a silent scream, before collapsing.

Merryn and Broc had arrived, Artan with them, bows still raised and ready.

But then the worst happened, and Hagen's world tilted on its axis.

Another man—one they hadn't seen, hadn't counted—attacked Connor from the side. His father spun, catching the strike on his blade, and shoved the man backward with brutal efficiency. The attacker stumbled and fell.

But that split second of distraction was all Dugan needed.

The evil bastard lunged forward, his sword point finding the gap in Connor's defense. The blade slid beneath his ribs, punching through leather and plaid and flesh. For a heartbeat, everything stopped. Connor's eyes went wide—not with pain, but with the terrible understanding of what had just happened.

Dugan twisted the blade and pulled it free, dark blood coating the steel.

His father crumpled to the ground, both hands gripping the wound in his side, trying to hold his life inside his body.

"Da!" The word tore from Hagen's throat, raw and agonized.

Hagen went after Dugan with murder in his heart, but at that point Alaric had already charged after him while Broc, and Merryn had scared the rest off. The remaining mercenaries took one look at their fallen comrades and the fresh reinforcements and broke. They scattered, running down toward the beach in full retreat.

Dugan ran with them, and his voice carried back up the hill, triumphant and mocking.

"Grandfather, vengeance is ours! I've killed Connor Grant!"

The words echoed across Tiree like a curse.

His father lay on the ground, both hands pressed against his side. Blood seeped between his fingers, too much blood, spreading dark across his plaid.

"Da!" Hagen dropped to his knees beside him, his hands shaking as he ripped a piece of his plaid free. He wadded the fabric and pressed it hard against the wound, but he could feel the warmth soaking through immediately, could feel his father's life bleeding away beneath his palms.

His father's hand shot out and grabbed Hagen's wrist, his grip still strong despite everything.

"Too late." Connor's voice was a rasp, thick with pain. His face had gone gray, his lips taking on a blue tinge. "Tell Mama I'm sorry. And your sisters and brother. I thought I had him. My emotions took over…"

His eyes drifted closed, and Hagen felt panic claw up his throat.

"Da!" He pressed harder, desperate, heedless of the pain it caused.

Then his mind cleared, snapping into the cold clarity of command he'd learned from this very man.

"Broc and Merryn, go for help. Ask the fishermen to find a healer—the best they have. Hurry!" His voice cracked on the last word.

"Alaric, go take the boat back and bring help. We need Brenna, we need—"

"Nay," Alaric interrupted, dropping to his knees on Connor's other side. His face was pale, stricken. "We'll have to get him on the boat first. We can't leave him here."

His father's eyes fluttered open again, focusing on Hagen with effort. He grabbed his son's hand with blood-slicked fingers.

"I'll never make it." The words were barely a whisper, but they hit Hagen like a physical blow.

Broc and Merryn were already running. "We'll find a healer!"

Artan stood, his face grim. "I'll get more men from the boat. It's going to take at least four men to carry him safely. Meet us at the boat, Broc."

Hagen nodded, unable to speak past the lump in his throat. "Go, he doesn't have much time."

He turned to Alaric. "Make sure the ones on the ground are dead. We don't need anyone sneaking up on us while we're vulnerable. Protect our backs."

Alaric hesitated, clearly not wanting to leave Connor's side, but duty won out. He nodded and moved away, checking each fallen man with methodical care.

And then they were alone—Hagen, his dying father, and Brynja.

Hagen looked at Brynja, and she must have seen the devastation in his eyes.

"I don't know what to do." The admission felt like failure, like betrayal.

His father's eyes opened again, and for a moment the old Connor Grant was there—the teacher, the warrior, the man who'd trained Hagen since he could first hold a wooden sword.

"Push hard. Brenna's teachings. Stop the

bleeding." Each word cost him, but his voice was clear.

Hagen set both hands on his father's wound and pushed down with all his strength. In his heart, he knew this wasn't going to work. The wound was too wide, too deep, he could feel the edges of torn flesh beneath the blood-soaked fabric. This was a killing blow, and they both knew it.

His father bellowed in pain when he pressed down, his back arching, his hand clawing at the ground.

"Da, I'm sorry, but you can't die on me. I haven't married yet. I want my bairns to have a grandda like I had, like you were to me. You taught me everything. You can't leave now. You cannot die." The words tumbled out, desperate, pleading.

"I was foolish, Hagen." His father's voice was growing weaker, thready. "I let my emotions control me. I should not have…"

His eyes drifted closed again.

"Da!" Hagen shook him gently, terrified that if he closed his eyes this time, they wouldn't open again.

Brynja knelt beside them, her hands hovering uselessly over Connor's body.

"What can I do to help? There must be something. Tell me what to do."

Her voice was thick with anguish—this man was dying because of her vengeance, her need to return to Tiree.

"Alaric will be back soon," Hagen said, forcing himself to think, to plan, even as his heart was breaking. "And we can get him in the boat.

Mayhap they'll bring the boat around to this bay, and we can put him in it quickly. Get him to Brenna faster."

But even as he said it, he could see the truth. His father's color was not good—ashen gray where it should be ruddy. His breathing had gone shallow and rapid, each breath a labored wheeze. Blood continued to seep between Hagen's fingers despite the pressure, pooling dark beneath his father's body.

Tears ran down Hagen's cheeks, hot and unchecked.

"Nay, Da. You're invincible. No one can hurt you. You're the strongest warrior I've ever known—the strongest warrior who ever lived."

A small voice startled him from behind, but he heard her loud and clear.

"Your father is dying, Hagen."

CHAPTER THIRTY

DYNA

D YNA STROLLED TOWARD the hearth
where the bairns played with their fabric
puppies, her mother nearby. A sharp pain caught
her in the belly, so strong her knees buckled.
Then a headache struck unlike any other. "Da!"
She crumpled to the floor.

Tora began to run in circles. "Gwandda.
Gwandda. I need Gwandda. Where is Gwandda?"
Her mother ran over to Tora and shouted
to Derric above stairs, "Derric, help Dyna.
Something's wrong."

The door burst open and Logan stepped inside.
"What the hell is happening? You should see the
cloud formations outside, something strange." His
gaze swept the hall. "What the hell? This cannot
be good."

Gwyneth, in a chair by the hearth, said,
"Sit down and shut up, Logan. Something *is*
happening, and you don't need to make it worse."

Sylvi sat on the floor and cried, "Grandda. Bad
man stabbed Grandda. Someone save him. Help

Grandda. Help him." She lay back flat and cried and kicked her feet. "Grandda!"

Avelina entered from the kitchens. "Dyna, my head. Drew? Where are you? Find my potion." She collapsed into a chair.

Maitland and Maeve entered with Grant tied to Maitland's chest, now crying and kicking furiously. "Bwia, Wia, Bwia, Wia."

Maeve reached for Grant. "Here, help your mother. I'll take him, Maitland." She held him on her hip so he could look out over the hall, shock covering her face as she stared at the chaos unfolding in front of her. "What is happening?"

"Wia, Wia, Bwia." Wee Grant's hands were both in tight fists. "Wia!"

Derric ran over to Dyna. "Diamond, are you hale? Is this a feeling or real? What is happening? The bairns are screaming for your father. Do you see something?"

Dyna rolled over onto her back, holding her head. "Something is wrong. Da is hurt. I can feel it in my belly. Oh, Da. I hope it's not too bad. I'm sure they'll get him back here as quickly as possible."

Brenna entered, picked up Sylvi who was sobbing on the floor, and moved straight over to Dyna. "What's wrong? It's Connor, isn't it? How bad?"

Sylvi began to sob. "Grandda hurt. Grandda. Lia, help him."

Dyna looked at Sylvi and asked, "Is Lia there, Sylvi? Tora, is Lia with Grandda?"

Tora broke free from her grandmother, who

looked like she was about to pass out, and ran to her mother. She leaned over, cupped her mother's cheeks and said, "Lia and Bwia are there. They twyin to save him."

Her mother paced, a sick look on her face.

Then Tora ran over to her grandmother and said, "Uppy. Gwandda hurt. Lia dare too."

Her mother fell into a chair. "Dyna, is this real? Is your father dying? Oh my Heavens, nay. Please say nay. I can't live without him."

Dyna didn't know what to think. Derric picked her up and sat in a chair by the hearth, cuddling her. "Take your time, Diamond. Do what you must. We've got the bairns."

Sandor began to run in a circle, giggling furiously. "Top it, Unca Shakee. Top it!"

Dyna heard that and had to find out the truth, pushing herself to a standing position, ignoring the pain battering her head. "Jake! Uncle Jake. What is happening to your brother? You cannot take him yet. Do you hear me, Jake?"

Sandor ran over and stopped in front of her. "Unca Shakee say Gwandda hurt."

Dyna twirled in a circle, staring at the rafters. "Stop it right now, Jake, and you listen to me. Are you listening? You. Cannot. Have. My. Father. Not yet! Do you hear me? He's too young! Leave him be. Do something to save him, Jake. Get over there. We don't need you here. You need to help your brother! Aline, Grandda, Grandma, not yet. You can't have him yet!"

Sandor followed his mother and pressed on her leg, "Unca Shakee twyeen." Then he sat down.

He broke into a giggle immediately, then stopped and said, "Awex say he comeen. Awex bwinging Gwandda hewe."

Sylvi stopped crying and said, "Lia is with him now. Do not worry, Mama."

Tora cupped her grandmother's cheeks and said, "Gwandda need Brenna. He comeen home now."

Dyna said, "Start saying your prayers."

CHAPTER THIRTY-ONE

LIA

HAGEN SPUN AROUND as Lia stepped closer. "Do something, Lia. He is dying."

Lia strolled over to stand behind Brynja, who was now kneeling opposite him on the other side of his sire. She set her hand on Brynja's shoulder. "I cannot fix him. I don't have the ability to do that."

That was too much for him. He shouted, "You always fix people. You save them. You tell us where to go. You make sure no one dies. Do something. I cannot lose my father. Help me, Lia."

Hagen stared up at the sky, his hands slippery with his sire's blood. "Help us, please, God. Someone help him. He cannot die here!"

His father had always been one of the clan's leaders, he and Uncle Jamie, the two everyone looked up to. Now it was Alasdair, Alick, and Els leading. He thought of his aunts, Kyla, Maeve, and Elizabeth, who all adored their baby brother.

Hagen swiped angrily at the tears on his cheeks. His father's eyes were closed, his color pale. He looked defeated. Weak. Growing weaker by the moment.

His father loved to lead Clan Grant into battle, riding one of the Midnights, carrying a banner, bellowing the Grant war whoop when they came home after a win.

This was not a win. One of the worst losses ever.

"Lia, help me, please." His voice came out in a whisper.

Lia said, "You can save him, Hagen. You don't need me."

"How? Tell me. I'll move all of this isle if I must, just tell me what to do. I'd do anything for my father. Please."

Lia leaned over and said, "Set both hands on his wound."

"What? I did this before. I tried to stop the bleeding, but it's too large a wound."

"Do it, Hagen," Brynja whispered, locking her gaze on his. "Do what Lia said. Trust her. I do."

He did what she said, trusting the faery lass with all of his being. He didn't know what else to do.

"You must believe in each other for this to work," Lia said, her gaze going from his face to hers.

"What?" Brynja looked over her shoulder at the lass as confused as he was. "I don't understand."

"You two are a special power together. Alone, neither of you can fix him. Together you can." Lia squeezed Brynja's shoulder. "Put your hands on Hagen's and look into his eyes."

She did as Lia said, tears now rolling down her cheeks. "Hagen, I don't understand."

"I don't either, just do what she says, Bry."

Lia continued, "You must be calm and believe in your power together. If you do, your hands together will heal him."

Brynja placed her hands on top of Hagen's and gazed into his eyes.

Something intense happened.

A surge of power moved through her hands into his and into his father's belly, a force so strong that both of their hands shook.

"Keep your hands locked. Don't let go," Lia shouted.

Alaric came up behind them and whispered, "Holy Heavens."

Lia barked, "Do not interrupt them, Alaric."

Still locked on Brynja's gaze, he saw something there he hadn't seen before. A calmness, a confidence he didn't have, but she did. She smiled at him, sending him a more powerful message than words could ever do, and dark clouds filled the sky just before a lightning bolt shot down and struck behind his father, shaking the ground underneath them, thunder rolling all around them.

Lia yelled over the din of the storm, "That is a sign of how powerful your father's spirit is. Keep going. It's working. You're doing it."

Hagen kept his hands on his father, Brynja's hands still locking onto his, praying this would work. His hands tingled and shook, and he let out a large roar from something happening that he didn't understand, but then he looked down at his father, and his eyes were open.

"You can let go now, both of you," Lia said. "Well done." She hugged Brynja from behind. "Remember this, you two together have a power unlike any other. Never forget it."

His father asked, "What the hell did you two do to me? I saw that lightning, and your hands. The roar of thunder. Something coursed through me from your hands, something as potent and intense as that bolt that landed behind me." He looked down at his wound, blood still everywhere, but the skin, while not completely healed, was bound together.

Alaric asked, "What the hell was that? That lightning looked like it hit you. And it came out of nowhere. No rain, no nothing. Just one bolt and the thunder. And you two. What you did. What she said…"

Hagen said, "Hush. We cannot deal with that right now. Forget it until we get my father home. I don't want everyone else to know. Just say Lia helped for now."

Alaric nodded. "Agreed. We get him home. Let's go. The men are all dead except Dugan and that other one."

Brynja cursed. "Sholto. I'll take care of him later."

Lia pointed toward the boat. "You cannot wait. Get Connor home. Chief Grant, your work is not done yet. You have much time left."

Artan approached with two other men. "We can lift him. He's a big man." Then he looked at Connor and said, "What the hell? What happened? That thunder was the largest I've ever heard."

"I don't know what it was, but it healed Da. Lia. It was Lia." Hagen didn't dare mention his hands and Brynja's, that together they'd healed his father. It sounded as daft as anything he had ever heard. He'd talk about it later. Now he wished to get his father the hell out of there. "We need to get him to Brenna. Lia said to hurry."

Merryn and Broc followed. "We'll help carry him."

His father sat up. "No need. I can walk. Slowly, but I can walk if you'll help me up."

Hagen and Alaric got his father to his feet, and his father said, "Do not be upset, Alaric, but I'd like to have Brynja on one side and Hagen on the other."

"Understood, Uncle." Alaric stepped aside and Brynja took his place.

They made their way back to the boat, all quiet.

Hagen looked back over his shoulder. "Where did she go?"

Broc asked, "Who?"

"Lia. She was here with us."

Broc said, "I never saw her."

"She's gone," Brynja whispered. "She went down the beach."

"Da? Do you feel healed on the inside?"

"I do. I feel verra weak, but the pain is nearly gone. I can't manage a horse on my own, but I can ride. I've never seen anything like it."

Artan said, "You bled worse than anyone I've

ever seen. That will weaken anyone. How did you heal so quickly?"

Alaric said, "I can't believe it myself, but I saw it with my own eyes. That surely was a death blow. You should be dead, Uncle Connor."

His father looked at him and said, "It was the lightning. Lia and the lightning."

It was as if his father had overheard all she'd said, but he was telling them to keep it quiet. He nodded at Hagen and squeezed his shoulder.

Hagen was more confused than ever, but he had his beloved father walking next to him. He and Brynja had healed his father, with Lia's help.

But no one would believe them.

And what kind of power did he and Brynja really have? He peeked over at her and winked.

Brynja smiled.

Hagen was in love. There was no doubt in his mind now. They were meant for each other.

CHAPTER THIRTY-TWO

CONNOR

CONNOR HAD RIDDEN in front of Alaric, and he'd held him strong. In fact, he slept part of the way. It was nighttime, not the best time to travel, but they knew the way well enough.

The battle had humbled him. He'd done exactly what his father had warned him against. He had let his emotions overpower him. His father had warned him once that such an error could be deadly.

He'd nearly died.

And how was he to explain exactly what had happened?

He'd had to change his stance because another fool had come at him from the side, then Dugan had grabbed at the opportunity, aiming for his belly. The pain had been the worst he'd ever felt in his entire life, and the blood.

There had been so much blood. He'd felt the warm liquid as it covered his hand, there to try to stop the bleeding, though he'd failed because he had no strength in his hand.

He recalled Hagen's distress, how Brynja had stayed by his side. And then he'd seen Lia.

And two others.

He'd seen his father and mother. He pushed that from his mind until he had someone like Sela or Aunt Brenna to talk with. It had been so real.

But then he'd opened his eyes to see Hagen and Brynja's hands on his belly, Lia behind Brynja talking, and a strange force shot through him at the same time a bolt of lightning came right at him.

He thought he'd been hit, but yet he'd lived.

How? How had he healed so quickly?

There were things on this isle that never made sense, but he was too tired to think on it.

They'd arrived to cheers from the parapets, Dyna squealing, Sela sobbing.

Tora had shouted, "Gwandda comeen. See, Gwanmama."

Even though it was late, the bairns were still awake. They couldn't sleep, something inside them knowing they needed to see their grandfather.

Hagen, his first-born son, whom he was so proud of, shoved everyone aside and shouted, "He needs Aunt Brenna. Alaric will explain. Brynja and I will take him inside."

And the crowd had spread apart, giving them the room they needed. Connor had managed to dismount with only one knee buckling, Hagen catching him easily. The lad was stronger than he would have guessed. But hellfire if the boy wasn't a wee bit taller than he was now.

His father would be proud.

Sela sobbed and leaned over, Hagen allowing his mother to kiss his cheek. Then he said, "Follow us inside, Mama. We cannot stop."

Connor whispered to Hagen as they approached the keep, "I can't make the steps." But his son had scooped him up and carried him up the stairs without even a grunt.

He'd immediately remembered the day he'd had to do the same with his father when he came back from the battle with Buchan. When his mother had fashioned a bed for his father in the stables at Clan Cameron, as if she'd known he'd come home weakened.

"I remember, Da." He could picture his mother and father as if it happened two days ago.

"What?" Hagen asked.

"Naught." Hellfire, he was talking to ghosts now. His mind was playing trickery on him.

Maitland opened the door and walked next to him. "If he's too heavy, Hagen, I can help, and Alaric is right behind you. Don't try to set him down alone. We'll help.

"Welcome home, Grant. Glad to see you here," Logan shouted.

Maitland opened the door to the healing chamber, and Aunt Brenna pointed to the bed. "I've been waiting for you, Connor. I was going to return home, but something told me to stay a wee bit longer. I'm glad I did."

Hagen moved to set his father down on the bed. "Maitland, catch his other side. I can't maneuver him."

"He's too tall, I've got this side," Maitland said, the two men lowering him to the bed.

Maeve squeezed in and kissed his cheek. "I love you, Connor."

Connor grabbed her hand. "Stay, Maeve. I need to speak with you and Sela and Brenna."

Aunt Brenna said, "Not until I hear about the wound. Everyone out except Maeve, Sela, and Hagen. If you were there, Hagen."

"I was."

People shuffled out, but at the last minute, Connor yelled, "Stay, Brynja."

Aunt Brenna arched a brow in question at him, Sela staring at him wide-eyed. He held a hand up to tell them to wait.

Maeve and Sela stood back, Aunt Brenna on a stool next to him, already doing the things he'd seen her and Aunt Jennie do so many times. Looking and touching and feeling and looking again.

When the door closed, he said, "I'll tell you what happened."

Aunt Brenna put her hand to his chest and said, "Nay, you will be silent until I tell you that you can speak. Hagen and Brynja will explain."

The door opened and Logan stuck his head in. "Beware, she can be an ornery witch when she wishes to be."

Aunt Brenna said, "Unless you'd like me to make certain you are on a pallet next to him, you'll close the door, Logan."

The door slammed. Connor caught Aunt Brenna's smirk.

His beloved aunt said to Hagen, "Tell me exactly what happened. Leave nothing out."

Connor said, "I can…"

"Connor, shush. I'll not tell you again," his aunt said.

Sela said, "Connor, do what she says. You're too weak."

So he relented. He settled his eyes on Hagen, who sat on a stool in his line of vision, and listened.

"We were behind a crest, and Da heard Dugan—and aye, Dugan Comming—say he was going to kill him if he ever saw him. I tried to stop Da, but he stepped out and the battle just began. Just like that. His men of ten or so were everywhere. We only had Brynja and me and Alaric. Broc and Merryn had gone to look for bairns. And another came at Da's opposite side. He cut him down, but Dugan got his belly when he cut the other man down. Da crumpled to the ground and there was blood everywhere…"

"Hagen, I see the blood, his, Brynja's, and your tunics and plaids are all saturated, but there's no wound." Aunt Brenna looked at him and said, "Where, Connor? Where were you stabbed?"

Connor used his hand to point to the spot, and he watched his aunt lift his tunic, looking for an open wound, but there was none. "I only see a scar that looks like a lightning bolt." Sela looked over Aunt Brenna's shoulder. Hagen paled and squeezed Brynja's hand.

"Where, Connor? Point to the wound."

He did, and then said, "It healed. Lia was there."

Sela gasped and Maeve flopped onto a stool.

"Lia healed you? But there's so much blood." Aunt Brenna looked at Hagen and Brynja. "Is all that blood on you and Brynja Connor's blood? Neither of you are wounded? Anyone else with a wound? Alaric? Broc?"

"It's all from Da." Hagen nodded, Brynja nodded, and Aunt Brenna looked back at him. "That's impossible."

Connor took Brenna's hand and said, "Listen to me. And you are all sworn to secrecy. Lia told Hagen to set his hands on me, then told Brynja to put her hands on Hagen's. And this heat shot through me just before the lightning bolt hit over my head. The pain disappeared."

The three look stupefied, then he said, "Hagen, you and Brynja may go. Get something to eat."

The two left, holding hands. "I'll be back, Da."

"My thanks to both of you," he said. "And we've only told everyone that Lia healed me. That's it."

Once the two were gone, he looked at Maeve and his wife and said, "I saw Mama and Da."

"What?" Maeve asked, leaning forward.

Aunt Brenna said, "It's not unusual for people who are nearly dead to have seen loved ones. It's common. Probably as a dream."

Connor grabbed Aunt Brenna's hand and said, "Nay, Da said to forget Dugan. That I would not be taken yet, that I was to help gather the group who were to work with Lia."

"Lia? Da knows Lia?" Maeve asked.

"He said Hagen and Brynja are bound together, that they will have special powers, along with

Grant and John. And others too, but I woke up. They were so real. Da yelled at me for allowing my emotions to drive me. He said to forget Dugan. Said there are worse things happening."

Connor's cheeks dampened from the tears that he hadn't known had fallen.

Aunt Brenna patted his hand and said, "Connor, it sounds like you had quite an ordeal, but you are pale and weak, and you need rest. I'm going to treat you as though you had a huge wound that you lost all that blood from. Mayhap Lia put some odd stitches in you. I don't know. You're wounded and you'll do what I tell you. I want you to drink first. Maeve, would you get him some broth, please? Drink the broth, then sleep. Your body, even though there is no more blood, has been through an ordeal. If you wish to heal to do whatever my brother wants you to do, then you must stay here and do what I say."

Connor smiled and whispered, "He said that too. And Mama. Said to listen to Aunt Brenna, so I promise to do whatever you say. I'm going to close my eyes now. When Maeve brings the broth, awaken me. I'll drink it. Please say naught about what I said. I'll tell Kyla and Jamie when I see them."

He closed his eyes and snored lightly before Aunt Brenna could cover him with a plaid. Maeve left for the broth, and Sela looked at her. "I don't know what to believe, but I'm grateful. He and Hagen and Brynja are all covered in blood."

"I'm going to say Lia did it. I don't know about the other, but for now, we've all known Lia has special powers. I'm grateful, as you are, Sela. If not for Lia, he never would have made it back here. He would have died in a boat."

Aunt Brenna got up to fetch water in a basin to wash the blood from her nephew, and Sela just sat on the stool and set her cheek to her husband's chest.

CHAPTER THIRTY-THREE

BRYNJA

B RYNJA SHOT UP in bed, shocked at what she'd just seen.

Duart Castle was under attack. Men were everywhere, and right in front were Sholto and Dugan, the latter yelling for Connor Grant.

She jumped out of bed, wiping the sweat from her brow. Hildi lay in the bed next to her, fast asleep as though nothing had happened. She was nearly back to her old self, something that pleased Brynja verra much.

But nothing had happened. *It was a dream.*

She paced a bit, not wanting to awaken Hildi, but she had to do something. There was no possible way she could lie back in that bed and fall asleep, with such a horrid nightmare fresh in her mind.

Brynja grabbed a blanket, donned her wool hose and opened the door as quietly as she could. How she needed Hagen, but she could not knock on his door and awaken him either, especially with his two cousins in the chamber with him.

She was about to head down the stairs to the

hall when the door at the end of the passageway caught her eye, beckoning her. That's it. She needed to go up.

So up she went to the parapets, hanging on to the door when the wind caught it so it wouldn't bang shut. She closed it quietly and turned, surprised to see Hagen sitting on a stool there.

He broke into a smile and held his arms open for her, and she flew into them, allowing the soft kisses he rained all over her face and neck, tucking her into his heat.

"Lass, why are you here?"

"Nightmares," she said, leaning her head on his shoulder as he settled her on his lap.

"About what?"

"Are you sure you wish to know? Mayhap I ask you what you think of Lia's words before we talk about my nightmare."

"All right. You mean her words that we are a special power together? And alone we're nothing?"

She peeked up at him. "The special power together part. Have you heard of anything like that before?"

"Nay, never. And as you know, I have cousins who are seers and all kinds of odd things. But their powers are all separate. None are tied to anyone else. Do you believe her?"

She sighed. "I believe everything that wee lass tells me. Lia is quite unique. She knows things, predicts things. Disappears and no one knows how she gets across the water sometimes. They say she is a guardian angel, and I believe it."

"Guardian angel and protector of bairns. Those are two amazing titles."

"She's saved many bairns already."

"And my father, with your help."

They said nothing for a while, staring out over the land, the sea, and the clouds. The breeze had finally died down, and the night was quiet, a beautiful crescent moon winking at them.

"The water? What makes that sound?"

"Fish jumping. Sounds like they are having a party." He chuckled, "What think you of us being together forever?"

She lifted her head to look into his eyes, brushing some of his wild hair back. "Your hair is sooo long."

"It is. I rarely touch it, just wash it."

She cupped one cheek and kissed the other, rubbing her lips across the short stubble with a giggle. "I like the idea of us being together forever. You comfort me, yet excite me at the same time. You encourage me, but appreciate me too. Most people only see a foolish lass with odd braids. That's what I love most about you."

He arched a brow at her, a smirk on his face. "What?"

"You see me for who I am, not something I'm not."

"I do love you for who you are, Brynja Nyberg. The Norse half and the Scottish half. Which half said they love me?"

She giggled like a wee lassie. "Both halves love you. We are perfect together, are we not?"

"I think so. And you surely won my father over by using your hands on him."

She gave his arm a playful slap. "Did I need to win him over?"

"Nay, he already liked you. Now, about that nightmare."

"I would dismiss it, but after Lia telling us we are special, it makes me wonder."

"Tell me, then we can decide together. I think that's best."

She took a deep breath and leaned her head back on his shoulder. "I was near a battle, and it was huge, men dying everywhere. And I only recognized a few people."

"Who?"

"Sholto and Dugan. They came for Connor. Your father came out and fought with Dugan again. That's when I started crying, but then Sholto yelled to Dugan. Told him he was going to Iona for the bairns."

Hagen said nothing, closed his eyes, kissed her slowly, his lips warming hers, sucking on her bottom lip before stopping. "I was afraid that was what you were going to say."

"How would you know that?"

"I had the same nightmare."

CHAPTER THIRTY-FOUR

SHOLTO

THE TWO MEN sat in the cottage the next morning, both holding their heads from all the ale they drank.

Sholto said, "He's not dead, I'm telling you. Just because you stabbed his belly doesn't mean he's dead. His body wasn't there when we returned."

"He's dead, fool. That was a killing blow." Dugan got up and punched the wall with his fist, cursing afterwards. "They carried him off to bury him on their land."

"Then why did I see him walking when I returned?"

"What?" Dugan came over and grabbed him by the shoulder, whipping him around. "He walked away?"

"Aye. They were halfway across to Gott Bay. There were two with him, and that one wee annoying lass was there too. But she went down the beach. Why does a lass so young walk around alone?"

"Forget her. Who helped him?"

"The man with the long hair and that other

bitch. The one on Iona who hit me with the dagger. Why was she with them? That's what I want to know, though it explains why I haven't seen the bitch on Iona lately. I'm going to kill that bitch. If I'd had any more men, I would have gone after her."

Dugan kicked his stool over, then righted it to sit down and hold his head. "I cannot go on this day, but we have to go to the Granthams. I have to kill him. He must be weakened at least."

"He was. He didn't walk unaided. But you know there's a problem."

"I do. Multiple problems. We don't have enough men. They killed or scared most of our men away. And the next group won't arrive for two days. And someone found my stash."

"What stash?"

"The one I found buried in the back. I've been using that to hire the mercenaries. Did you take it?" He slapped Sholto hard.

"Nay. If I did, I'd be the hell away from you. What is wrong with you?" He rubbed his cheek and moved away from Dugan.

"We'll have to wait. Fortunately, I kept enough of that coin with me. But we're going to Duart Castle in two days. I'm calling him out to the gates to fight me. One on one."

"Good, because I'll not help you. I'm going for the bitch and then I'm going for the bairns."

"The bairns can wait until later."

"Nay, the first ship arrives in three days. I'm going for them, but not until I kill that bitch first. Then I'm heading to Iona. You take care of your foolish vengeance for your grandfather. I care naught about that."

"Well, I do. And we're going. And you're going with me. Understood?"

"Understood."

Sholto would go to Duart Castle, but he was after the lass. The hell with the Grants.

CHAPTER THIRTY-FIVE

BRYNJA

THE FOLLOWING DAY, Brynja found Hildi in the great hall, sitting by the hearth with a piece of embroidery in her lap. Her cousin looked stronger now than she had in days—the gray pallor gone from her skin, the awful stillness replaced by quiet vitality. She was healing. Slowly, but healing.

"May I join you?" Brynja asked.

Hildi looked up, her expression softening. "Please. I've been hoping you'd come. We've hardly had the chance to talk, since I've slept so much. But I'm finally feeling like my old self."

"I'm so happy, Hildi. I've missed you so."

Brynja settled into the chair beside her, noting the way her hands worked with the needle on a pair of leggings, confident and sure. Her old friend was back.

"How are you feeling?" Brynja asked, though she could see the answer in Hildi's face.

"Better. Stronger." Hildi set her needlework aside. "The headaches have mostly stopped. I can walk without getting dizzy. Lia says I'm healing well."

"I'm glad." And Brynja was—the guilt of Hildi's injury still sat heavy in her chest. If Brynja hadn't wounded Sholto, if they hadn't traveled to Ulva, if she could have fired her dagger to stop him, Sholto would never have thrown Hildi against that tree.

"Stop that," Hildi said gently.

"Stop what?"

"Blaming yourself. I can see it in your eyes." Hildi reached over and took Brynja's hand. "What happened to me wasn't your fault. It was Sholto's. Just like what happened to your mother wasn't your fault. It was Dugan's. Aye? You think it was him?"

Brynja's throat tightened. "Aye. Dugan killed our mothers, and that is one thing. But if I hadn't struck Sholto that night, this may never have happened to you."

"If you hadn't what? Defended yourself? Refused to be a victim? If those two men had found Sheona, they would have looked for another lass too. I'm certain they would have grabbed all three of us from our bed chamber." Hildi's grip was firm. "Brynja, you can't spend your life taking responsibility for the evil other people choose to do. That's not guilt. That's giving them power over you even when they're not there."

The words hit something deep. Brynja had never thought of it that way—that her guilt was another form of Sholto's control.

"I've been watching you," Hildi continued, her voice soft but steady. "These past few days at Duart. I've seen you learning to ride. Training with everyone in archery and horseback riding. Laughing with Hagen Grant."

Heat crept up Brynja's neck. "It's not what you think. I'm not in any kind of relationship with Hagen."

"You are." Hildi's smile was knowing. "And I'm glad. You deserve happiness, Brynja. You deserve to heal."

"I don't know if I can." The admission came out barely above a whisper. "Heal, I mean. I don't know if I know how."

"Neither did I." Hildi turned to look out the window, her expression distant. "When I woke up after Ulva, I couldn't remember what had happened at first. Then it all came back to me. I remembered Sholto's hands on me, his dagger pricking my neck, flying through the air, the tree, the pain. And I was so angry, Brynja. So angry at him for hurting me. At you for bringing him into our lives. At God for letting it happen."

Brynja's chest ached. "Hildi, I'm so sorry—"

"Let me finish." Hildi's voice was gentle but firm. "I was angry. And that anger kept me alive at first. It gave me something to hold onto when the pain was unbearable. But then… then I started to heal. And I had to decide what to do with all that rage."

She turned back to Brynja. "I could have let it consume me. Could have spent every waking moment thinking about Sholto, hating him, planning revenge. But lying in that bed, barely able to move, all I could think about was that I almost died. And if I had died, what would my life have been? Just fear and anger and pain?"

Tears pricked Brynja's eyes. "What did you do?"

"I chose to let it go." Hildi's voice was steady. "Not forgiveness. I'll never forgive him for what he did. But I chose not to let him steal any more of my life than he already has. I chose to focus on healing. On the people who loved me. On building something new instead of just dwelling on what was broken."

"I want Sholto dead," Brynja said flatly. "I want to watch the light leave his eyes. I want him to know it was me who killed him."

"All right. And after?" Hildi's gaze was steady. "After he's dead and your revenge is complete, what then? What does your life look like?"

Brynja opened her mouth, then closed it. She'd spent weeks imagining Sholto's death. But she'd never imagined what came after. It was as if her life stopped at the moment of his dying, as if there was nothing beyond that single point of vengeance.

"I don't know," she admitted.

"Then mayhap that's what you need to figure out." Hildi's voice was soft. "Because revenge might satisfy you for a moment. But moments end, Brynja. And then you're left with the rest of your life. The question is, who do you want to be in that life?"

Brynja pulled her hand away, moving over to the door to peer at the weather. Outside, the sky was darkening, storm clouds gathering. "I don't know how to be anyone other than the woman who wants the men who killed our mothers dead. That's who I've been for over three moons. That's what's kept me alive."

"I know." Hildi rose more slowly, wincing slightly as her body protested. "But you're more than that, Brynja. I've seen it these past weeks. You're the woman who learned to ride a horse even though you were terrified. You're the woman who makes Hagen Grant smile. You're the woman who brought me broth when I was recovering and sat with me when I couldn't sleep."

Brynja joined her friend at the hearth, so glad to see her standing up strong.

"Cousin, you're not just vengeance. You're also courage and kindness and strength. You're also capable of love, even though you're afraid of it."

"I'm not afraid of love, Hildi."

"You are." Hildi's tone was gentle but unyielding. "You're terrified. Because love means vulnerability. It means letting someone close enough to hurt you. And you've been hurt so much already."

Tears spilled over, hot against Brynja's cold cheeks. "I can't. I can't let him in. What if something happens? What if I lose him too?"

"You might." Hildi's honesty was brutal but necessary. "Life doesn't come with guarantees. I could have another accident on the morrow. You could lose Hagen. We could all die in our sleep. That's the cost of being alive. We all die eventually."

She turned to face Brynja fully. "But the question isn't whether we'll lose the people we love. The question is whether we're brave enough to love them anyway. Whether the joy of having them is worth the pain of potentially losing them."

"I don't know if I'm that brave," Brynja whispered.

"You are." Hildi wiped Brynja's tears with her thumb. "You're the bravest person I know. You survived things that would have broken me. You kept going when anyone else would have given up. If you can do that, you can do this."

"But what if revenge is all I have left? What if I kill Sholto and there's nothing inside me afterward? What if I'm just... empty?"

"Then you fill yourself back up." Hildi's voice was fierce. "With love and laughter and ordinary moments. With morning rides and honey baked apples and arguments about nothing. With Hagen's smile and Jowell's gruffness and Grant's giggles. You fill yourself with life, Brynja. Because you're alive. And that's what living people do."

Brynja pressed her forehead to Hildi's shoulder, her cousin's arms coming around her. "I'm so tired of being angry all the time."

"I know. I know you are." Hildi held her close. "But anger doesn't have to be all you are. It can be part of you, but not the whole story."

They stood there as the storm began outside,

rain pattering against the stone in the courtyard. Finally, Brynja pulled back, wiping her face.

"What if he comes for me?" she asked. "Sholto. What if he finds me here?"

"Then you'll face him." Hildi's expression was steady. "But you won't face him alone. You'll have Hagen. Jowell. Paden. Maitland and all his warriors. You'll have an army at your back instead of just your rage."

She took Brynja's face in both hands. "But promise me something. Promise me that when the time comes, you won't throw away your chance at happiness just to satisfy your need for revenge. Promise me you'll think about what comes after. About who you want to be."

"I…" Brynja struggled with the words. "I can't promise I won't go after him if I get the chance."

"I'm not asking you to promise that. I'm asking you to promise you'll think about what you're choosing. That you'll ask yourself if revenge is really what you need, or if what you actually need is to be free of him. To stop letting him control your life."

Brynja met her cousin's eyes—so much like her mother's, so full of love and concern. "I promise I'll think about it."

"That's all I ask." Hildi pulled her into another embrace. "Because I love you, Brynja. And I want you to have the chance I almost didn't get—the chance to choose life. To choose joy. To choose love, even when it's terrifying."

"I love you too," Brynja whispered. "And I'm so glad you're healing."

"Me too." Hildi pulled back, smiling through her own tears. "Though I'll admit, watching you train with daggers and bows makes my head hurt. You're terrifyingly good at violence."

Despite everything, Brynja laughed. "Years of pent-up rage have to go somewhere."

"Well, mayhap you could channel some of that energy into being happy instead." Hildi's expression turned mischievous. "Hagen Grant is verra handsome. And the way he looks at you makes me giggle."

"Hildi!"

"What? I'm injured, not blind." She grinned. "Besides, someone needs to point out the obvious since you're so determined to ignore it."

"I'm not ignoring Hagen." Brynja started to say something else, then stopped. Because she was ignoring it. Ignoring the way her heart raced when Hagen smiled. Ignoring how safe she felt when he was near. Ignoring the fact that for the first time in months, she could imagine a future that wasn't just about revenge.

"See?" Hildi's smile was knowing. "You're thinking about it now. Good. Keep thinking about it. And when you're ready—when you're brave enough—let yourself have it."

"What if I'm never ready? What if I'm never brave enough?"

"Then pretend." Hildi's expression was fierce. "Pretend to be brave until the pretending becomes real. That's what I did. Every day I woke up and chose to get out of bed even when my head was splitting. Chose to walk even when I was dizzy. Chose to live even when dying felt easier. And eventually, the choosing became easier. The pretending became truth."

She squeezed Brynja's hands one more time. "You're stronger than you think. Braver than you know. And you deserve happiness, even if you don't believe it yet."

"Thank you," Brynja said softly. "For this. For understanding."

"Always." Hildi smiled. "That's what family does." She glanced around at the few people chatting in the hall. "This is a large one, but a clan who loves hard and is loyal to their core. We've found a good place, Brynja."

"This place is special, for certes."

"And now I have a question for you."

"Anything."

Hildi dropped her voice to a whisper. "Does Jowell have a girlfriend?"

Brynja nearly squealed with glee, but managed to hold it in, her hand over her mouth. "Nay, but I adore him. You would be perfect together. He's the serious one and perfect for you, Hildi. Paden is too silly. I love him too, but he has a different personality. Jowell is a rock."

"I'm not ready yet. I'm still healing. But mayhap someday."

They returned to their chairs by the hearth, listening to the storm rage outside. But inside the hall, there was warmth. There was hope. And for the first time in a long while, Brynja allowed herself to imagine what might come after revenge.

A life. Not just survival, but an actual life. With

Hagen and laughter and ordinary moments. With morning rides and quiet conversations and the gradual healing of old wounds.

It was terrifying. But perhaps it was worth being terrified for.

Outside, the storm continued. And somewhere across those dark waters, Sholto was still alive, still planning, still waiting.

But for now, in this moment, Brynja chose to focus on the warmth and the hope. On Hildi's recovery and Hagen's smile and the possibility of something more.

The storm would come soon enough. But she didn't have to face it alone.

CHAPTER THIRTY-SIX

BRYNJA

———— ✦ ————

BRYNJA WOKE IN darkness, her heart hammering, the scream trapped behind her teeth.

Not again.

She lay rigid in the unfamiliar bed, counting her breaths the way Sister Ada had taught her. In for four. Hold for four. Out for four. The dream clung to her—blood on stone, her mother's hand going cold in hers, rough voices speaking of golden braids and the coin they'd fetch.

Moonlight filtered through the fur covering the window of her chamber at Duart Castle. She'd been here over a sennight now, and still she couldn't quite believe the luxury of her own room, her own bed, walls of stone that kept the world at bay.

Except walls couldn't keep out memories.

She pushed back the covers and reached for her boots. Sleep wouldn't return now—it never did after the dreams. Better to walk, to move, to remind her body that she was here, alive, safe.

Safe. What a strange word. She'd thought she was safe at the nunnery too, until men came in the night for Sheona.

And a boat with two men patrolled the isle constantly, looking for something.

Or someone.

Brynja pulled on her mantle and belted her dagger at her waist. The weight of it was familiar, comforting. She eased her door open, grateful when the hinges didn't creak, and slipped into the corridor. She wanted to make sure she didn't awaken Hildi, now that she was finally sleeping in a true bed chamber again.

The castle was quiet at this hour, most residents long asleep. She made her way down the stairs, past the great hall with its banked fire, and out the door to the courtyard. Fresh air might help clear her head.

She was halfway across the courtyard when she saw him.

Hagen sat on a bench near the stable, Freya's reins in his hand. The mare stood beside him, already saddled, her coat gleaming silver in the moonlight.

Brynja stopped. He hadn't seen her yet, his attention on the horse, murmuring something too soft for her to hear. What was he doing out here at this hour?

Then he looked up, as if sensing her presence. No surprise crossed his face. Instead, he simply said, "Couldn't sleep either?"

"Nay." She moved closer, confused. "Why is Freya saddled?"

"Thought you might need her." He stood, holding out the reins. "You've been restless these past few nights. I hear you walking the corridors."

Heat crept up her neck. "I tried to be quiet. I didn't mean to wake you."

"You didn't wake me. Besides, it's not your steps that I hear. It's something deep inside me that I sense. I can tell when you're troubled. I don't sleep well either." His smile was crooked, self-deprecating. "I think Lia is correct. We have some kind of connection."

She took the reins, still bewildered. "But why Freya?"

"Because walls can feel like cages sometimes," he said quietly. "And I thought you might want to run."

Something in her chest cracked open. He understood.

He understood.

"I saddled Midnight Star too," Hagen continued, gesturing to where his own mount waited in the shadows. "Da said to take him for a ride. That is, if you want company. Or I can stay here, if you'd rather go alone."

The offer hung between them. No pressure. No expectation. Just... understanding.

"Come with me," Brynja heard herself say.

His smile was worth the vulnerability of the admission.

They mounted and rode out through the castle gates, the guards waving them through without question. Hagen must have warned them, Brynja realized. He'd planned this. Not just tonight, but other nights too, keeping her horse ready in case she needed an escape.

The path he chose led away from the village, toward the cliffs overlooking the sea. The moon painted everything in shades of silver. The view was glorious: the rolling hills, the dark ribbon of water, the distant outline of other islands.

They rode in silence, but it wasn't uncomfortable. The rhythm of hoofbeats, the cool night air, the vast open sky above, all of it slowly unknotted the tightness in Brynja's chest.

When they reached the cliff edge, Hagen dismounted and walked to the very edge, looking out over the water. Brynja joined him, leaving Freya to crop the grass nearby.

"Better?" he asked.

"Aye." She drew in a deep breath of salt air. "How did you know?"

"About needing to run?" He was quiet for a moment. "My cousin Derric, Dyna's husband. He came back from war different. He fought with King Robert for a few years. Couldn't stand to be indoors for long after that. Used to ride out at night, just to feel like he could breathe. Took him a long time to find peace again."

"Did he? Find peace?"

"Aye. But not by forgetting what happened, or by having someone tell him to just let it go. He found it with Dyna's help, and having three bairns keeps his mind busy, he says."

Brynja's throat tightened. "The sisters used to tell me I needed to forgive. To find peace through prayer and absolution."

"And did that help?"

"Nay." The admission felt like sacrilege, but also like relief. "It just made me feel like I was failing at healing. Like there was something wrong with me because I couldn't just… move past it."

Hagen turned to face her fully. "There's nothing wrong with you, Brynja. What happened to you was evil. Your mother was murdered in front of you. You were dragged away, nearly sold. That's not something you just move past. It's something you carry."

"But for how long?" The question burst out before she could stop it. "How long do I have to keep carrying it? When do I get to just… be free?"

"I don't know." His honesty was startling. Most people would have offered platitudes, false comfort. "Mayhap never completely. Mayhap that's not how it works. But I think…" He stepped closer. "I think freedom isn't about forgetting or forgiving or any of that. It's about choosing what you do with what you carry."

"Like riding out in the middle of the night when the walls get too close?"

"Aye. Like that." His smile was gentle. "Or like learning to trust someone new, even when it's terrifying. Like staying at Duart Castle even though you could run back to Iona. Like letting yourself imagine a future that's different from your past."

Wind swept up from the water, tangling in Brynja's braids. "Is that what you think I'm doing? Imagining a different future?"

"I hope so." His voice dropped lower. "Because I find myself imagining one too. One where you're in it."

Her heart stumbled. "Hagen—"

"I'm not asking you to be anything you're not," he said quickly. "I'm not asking you to be healed or whole or any of those things people say. I'm just asking… if mayhap you could see yourself staying. Here. With me. As you are."

As you are. Not as some idealized version of herself. Not once she'd overcome her trauma or avenged her mother or learned to sleep through the night. But as she was, nightmares and rage and all.

"You keep Freya saddled for me," she said, the words thick in her throat. "Every night?"

"Every night since you named her. After the first time I heard you pacing, I asked the stable master to keep her ready. Just in case you needed her." He looked almost embarrassed. "I know what it's like to feel trapped. I thought… I thought having a way out might help you feel less caged. Even if you never use it."

"But you come with me."

"Only if you want me to." His expression was open, honest. "If you'd rather ride alone, I'll stay behind, though I'll admit I'd probably send guards behind you for safety reasons. This isn't about me, Brynja. It's about you having what you need."

Something inside her shifted, like a locked door finally opening. All her life, people had wanted something from her—the men who'd killed her mother had wanted her body to sell, the sisters had wanted her to be pious and forgiving, even Hildi sometimes wanted her to be the strong cousin who always knew what to do.

But Hagen just wanted her to be herself. Broken pieces and sharp edges included.

"I want you with me," she said. "Tonight. And on the morrow night, if the dreams come again. And the night after that."

"Then I'll be there." Simple. Certain.

Brynja stepped closer, close enough to see the way moonlight caught in his eyes, turning them silver. "You don't try to fix me."

"You're not broken."

"Aye, I am. A little bit." She reached up, her fingers brushing his jaw. "But you don't mind."

"I don't mind." His hand covered hers, warm and solid. "We're all broken somewhere, Brynja. Every person who's lived through anything hard. The question isn't whether you're broken. It's whether you're brave enough to keep living anyway."

"And you think I am?"

"I know you are." He turned his head, pressing a kiss to her palm. "You got on a boat after seeing your friend attacked and left for dead. You came to a strange keep full of warriors. You learned to ride a warhorse. You wake up every morning and choose to keep going even when the nightmares make you want to hide. That's not broken, Brynja. That's the bravest thing I've ever seen."

Tears pricked her eyes. She blinked them back fiercely, but one escaped, tracking down her cheek.

Hagen caught it with his thumb, gentle. "And if you need to ride out at midnight every night for the rest of your life, I'll saddle your horse. If you need to keep a dagger under your pillow, I'll sharpen it for you. If you need to curse men in Norse and imagine terrible fates for them, I'll learn the words to help you do it."

A laugh burst from her throat, watery but real. "You'd do that?"

"Aye." His smile was crooked. "I might not be verra good at the pronunciation, but I'd try."

She kissed him then, rising on her toes, her hands fisting in his tunic. He made a surprised sound against her mouth, then his arms came around her, pulling her close.

The kiss was salt and wind and promise. It was acceptance and understanding and something that felt dangerously like hope.

When they finally broke apart, both breathing hard, Hagen rested his forehead against hers.

"Stay," he whispered. "Not because you're healed or because you've dealt with your past or any of that. Stay because you want to. Because mayhap we could be broken together and still build something good."

Brynja closed her eyes, breathing him in, leather and horse and something uniquely Hagen. Behind them, the sea crashed against the rocks, eternal and unchanging. Above them, stars lit up the winter sky.

She'd thought safety meant walls and weapons and keeping everyone at arm's length. But mayhap it meant this too, someone who saw your scars and didn't look away. Someone who kept your horse saddled in case you needed to run, and who ran with you when you asked.

"Aye," she said, opening her eyes to meet his. "I'll stay."

His smile was like sunrise, slow and transforming. "I hoped you'd say that."

They stood there for a long moment, wrapped in each other, the wind whipping around them. Then Hagen pressed a kiss to her temple and stepped back.

"Want to ride back? Or stay here a while longer?"

Brynja considered. The nightmare's grip had loosened, replaced by this strange, fragile warmth in her chest. But the night was beautiful, and she wasn't ready to return to stone walls just yet.

"Stay," she decided. "Just a little longer."

So they sat on the cliff edge, shoulders touching, watching the moon's path across the water. Freya and Midnight Star grazed nearby, peaceful and patient.

"Tell me something," Brynja said after a while. "Something true."

Hagen was quiet for a moment. "I was afraid to talk to you at first. When you came to Duart. You looked so fierce, so… untouchable. I thought you'd see right through me. See that I'm just a third generation warrior trying to live up to a grandfather's legend, with a sister who's already chieftain of a clan."

"You're more than that," Brynja said firmly.

"Am I?" He smiled ruefully. "Sometimes I

don't know. Everyone sees Alexander Grant when they look at me. Everyone expects me to be as powerful with a weapon as my father and grandfather..." He broke off, shaking his head. "Sorry. You didn't ask for this."

"I did." She bumped his shoulder with hers. "Something true, I said."

"All right then." He took a breath. "I'm terrified I'll never be as good as my father. Or Grandda. That I'll fail somehow, and everyone will realize I'm not the warrior they thought I was."

Brynja turned to face him fully. "Hagen Grant. You saddle a horse every night for a woman with nightmares. You teach her to ride without making her feel weak. You don't try to fix her or change her or make her into something she's not. You just... see her. And accept her." She reached for his hand, lacing their fingers together. "That's what makes a good man. Not how well you swing a sword."

His grip tightened on hers. "You see me too."

"Aye. I do. Even though you've been overbearing before. And you growl at me sometimes."

They both chuckled, and he rolled his eyes. "Take every growl as a compliment, lass. It's meant to be."

They sat in comfortable silence as the moon tracked its path across the dark sky. Eventually, the cold started to seep through their cloaks, and they rose reluctantly, mounting their horses for the ride back to Duart.

As they approached the castle gates, Brynja felt something she hadn't experienced in four months, a sense of homecoming. Not because of the stone walls or the warm bed waiting for her, but because of the man riding beside her. The man who understood that safety wasn't about fixing what was broken but about accepting it and moving forward anyway.

On the morrow, she knew, Dugan might show up outside their gates. She'd felt it in her dreams, seen glimpses of him riding hard across the winter landscape. Whatever news he brought would change things. Would set events in motion that couldn't be stopped.

But tonight, she had this. This moment of peace, hard-won and precious. This man who kept her horse saddled and didn't try to heal her, who simply loved her as she was.

It would have to be enough. Because on the morrow, everything could change.

On the morrow, there could be an attack.

CHAPTER THIRTY-SEVEN

BRYNJA

$$\text{---}\infty\text{---}$$

TWO DAYS LATER, Brynja knocked softly on the chamber door, a bowl of venison stew balanced in one hand. Sela had asked her to bring it because Connor was finally eating again, and he needed to keep his strength up.

"Come," Connor's voice called, stronger than she'd expected.

She pushed the door open. Connor sat propped against pillows, still pale but no longer bearing that gray, death-touched look from a few days ago. The wound on his side had healed, thanks to Lia, as the tale was told. She still had a difficult time believing that it had been her hands intertwined with Hagen's that had healed that horrible wound.

"Sela said you need to eat," Brynja said, crossing to set the bowl on the table beside his bed. The old warrior's coloring was the opposite of Hagen's, dark hair peppered with gray strands, but the blue cycs were the same, calculating and always alert. His hair fell to his shoulders, like most men in the clan instead of like Hagen's hair that fell well past his shoulders.

It fit Hagen. She thought of Hagen's father as an old warrior, but he appeared only a bit older than her mother had been. Old was not a word she'd ever use to describe Sela.

"My wife is a tyrant." But Connor's smile was fond. "My thanks to you, lass. Will you sit with me for a moment? Or do you have somewhere else to be?"

Brynja hesitated. She'd expected to leave the bowl and go. She wasn't comfortable with the easy intimacy of the Grant family, wasn't sure where she fit among them. But Connor's eyes were kind, and there was something in his expression that made refusing seem rude.

"I can stay," she said, settling into the chair by his bedside.

Connor reached for the stew, his movements careful. "You were there, on Tiree. When I was wounded."

"Aye." She watched him taste the stew. "You fought well."

"I got stabbed. That's not fighting well." His mouth quirked. "But I'm alive, so I suppose it could have been worse."

"Much worse," Brynja said quietly. She'd seen the wound, seen how close he'd come to dying, felt his blood on her hands. Another finger to the left and the blade would have found something vital.

Connor studied her over the rim of his bowl. "Sholto got away. How does it feel?"

"I don't know," she admitted. "Different than I expected. I'm angry, but there were too many for us. I don't think I could have done any better, so I'm upset, but I have faith I'll get the chance again. I will still stick my blade in his neck someday."

Connor nodded slowly, unsurprised. "I would wager you will. Vengeance has a way of sticking with you."

"You sound like you speak from experience."

"I do." He set the bowl aside, his expression turning distant. "I've killed men for vengeance, lass. More than I care to count. Some deserved it. Some... well. Battle makes monsters of us all, if we let it."

Brynja leaned forward. "Did it help? Killing them?"

"Sometimes. For a moment." He met her eyes. "And then the moment passed, and I was still left with whatever I'd lost. Still left with the hole in my chest where someone used to be."

"But you kept doing it. Kept fighting."

"Aye. Because sometimes vengeance isn't about filling holes. It's about making sure the bastards who hurt you can't hurt anyone else. It's about drawing a line and saying this far and no farther." He shifted against his pillows, wincing slightly. "But there's a difference between necessary vengeance and poison."

"What's the difference?"

"One you can walk away from when it's done. The other consumes you until there's nothing left." He paused. "Which one is Sholto for you?"

Brynja opened her mouth to answer, then

closed it. She'd thought she knew. She'd spent days convinced that killing Sholto was necessary, that it was justice, that it would set her free. And now she knew that Dugan was the man who had killed her mother. That fact would forever haunt her if he continued on his villainous ways.

"I don't know," she said finally. "I guess I won't know until I see the light leave his eyes. Hagen thinks revenge is always wrong."

Connor snorted. "My son is young and idealistic. He'll learn."

"Learn what?"

"That the world isn't black and white. That sometimes you have to do dark things to protect the people you love. That vengeance isn't always wrong, it's just complicated." He looked at her steadily. "You have the right to kill Dugan, lass. He murdered your mother. He would have sold you and your cousin. Justice won't come from any magistrate or lord, so you became justice yourself. There's no shame in that, and there's no one in the land who would say you were wrong."

Something in Brynja's chest loosened. She hadn't realized how much she'd needed to hear that from someone she trusted, that her choice was understandable, even justified. Not wrong. Not shameful. Just… complicated.

"But?" she prompted, because she could hear the unspoken word in his tone.

"But then you'll have to decide who you are after vengeance." Connor's expression was serious. "You've spent four moons being the girl who would kill Dugan. Then you met Sholto and have had to deal with his cruelty. When the two are finally dead, what will you do with your life?"

The question hit harder than it should have. Because she didn't know. Her entire identity since that day on Tiree had been wrapped up in her need for revenge. It had shaped every decision, every thought, every nightmare. Without that consuming purpose, who was she?

"I'm not sure yet," she whispered, thinking of how she'd answered Hildi and Hagen.

"Then that's what you need to determine." He reached out, his hand covering hers. His grip was weak but warm. "You're not just vengeance, Brynja. You're also the woman who learned to ride a warhorse. Who can use a spear and a dagger and is now learning archery. Who makes my son smile in ways I haven't seen in years. Who brought me stew when she could be anywhere else. That's who you are too."

Tears stung her eyes. "What if that's not enough?"

"It's more than enough." His voice was firm. "But you have to believe it. You have to choose to be more than what was done to you."

"I don't know how." Her voice came out in such a whisper, she wondered if he heard her.

"One day at a time. One choice at a time." He squeezed her hand. "You wake up in the morning, and you choose not to let the past define your present. You choose to build something instead of just tearing down. You choose love over hate, even when hate feels easier."

"Is that what you did?"

"Eventually. After a long, dark time of not doing it." His smile was sad. "I've made a lot of mistakes, lass. Hurt people I loved because I was too consumed by my own pain to see theirs. It took me longer than it should have to learn that vengeance isn't the same as healing. That you can get your revenge and still be broken."

"But you're not broken now."

"Nay. Because I chose to build a life instead of just destroying my enemies. I chose Sela. I chose my children and grandchildren. I chose to be more than my rage." He met her eyes. "And that's what I'm telling you to do. Not to forget what happened. Not to forgive Sholto or Dugan, they won't live much longer anyway. But to choose what comes next. To choose the life you want instead of just reacting to the life you were given."

Brynja sat with that for a long moment. Outside the window, she could hear the sounds of the castle, voices calling, horses whinnying, the clang of metal on metal from the lists. Life continuing, heedless of her internal struggle.

"Hagen wants me to stay," she said quietly. "Here. With him. Build a life together."

"And what do you want?"

"I want…" She paused, searching for the truth. "I want to stop being afraid. I want to sleep through the night without nightmares. I want to wake up and not immediately reach for a weapon. I want to feel safe. And I wish to be happy again."

"And do you think staying with Hagen will give you that?"

"Mayhap. I don't know." She looked down at

their joined hands. "He keeps my horse saddled at night. In case I need to run. He doesn't try to fix me or make me be something I'm not. He just… accepts me."

Connor's expression softened. "That's love, lass. Real love. Not the kind the bards sing about, but the kind that shows up every day and does the work. The kind that saddles horses and holds you when you wake up screaming and doesn't ask you to be anything other than what you are."

"I don't know if I can be what he needs."

"What does he need?"

"Someone whole. Someone who isn't broken by her past."

"Brynja." Connor's voice turned stern. "Listen to me. We're all broken. Every single one of us. I'm broken by the wars I've fought and the people I've lost. Sela's broken by what was done to her before we met. My wife still has occasional nightmares. Hagen's broken by the weight of expectations he can never quite meet. Being broken isn't the problem. The problem is thinking you have to be perfect to deserve love."

"But—"

"No buts. If Hagen wanted someone perfect, he'd have chosen someone else. He chose you. Nightmares and all. Rage and all. Past and all." He squeezed her hand again. "Don't insult him by deciding for him what he can handle."

A watery laugh escaped her. "You're quite blunt."

"I'm older and I nearly died. I don't have time for pretty words." But his smile was kind. "Besides, you need someone to be blunt with you. You've been living with pain for too long, making up stories about what you deserve and what you don't. Time to stop thinking and start living."

"Just like that?"

"Just like that. One choice at a time. Today, you choose to stay instead of run. On the morrow, you choose to let yourself be happy even though it feels dangerous. The day after that, you choose to trust that Hagen means what he says when he tells you he loves you." Connor's expression grew serious. "And eventually, if you keep choosing, you'll look back and realize you've built a life. Not the life you thought you'd have. Not the life without pain. But a life worth living anyway."

Brynja sat with his words, feeling the truth of them settle into her bones. Sholto would be dead. Her mother's murderer would be dead too. She would see to it. The revenge she'd spent months pursuing would be done. She'd made that vow to herself and would see it through.

But what then?

Not the girl who watched her mother die.

Not the woman consumed by vengeance.

But perhaps the woman who learned to ride and laugh and love despite everything. The woman who kept a dagger under her pillow but didn't let that be all she was. The woman who had been broken and chose to build something new from the pieces.

"My thanks to you, my lord," she said softly.

"For what? Lecturing you after you brought me stew?" Connor's eyes twinkled. "You're welcome.

Come back on the morrow with more food and I'll lecture you again."

Despite everything, Brynja smiled. "I'll consider it."

"Good." He released her hand and reached for his stew again. "Now go find my son and tell him you're staying. Put the poor lad out of his misery. He's been moping around like a kicked puppy for days."

"He has?"

"He has. Trust me, I know what Grant men look like when they're in love and terrified." Connor's expression turned knowing. "I looked the same way when I met Sela. Like I'd been hit in the head with a mallet and couldn't quite remember my own name."

Brynja stood, smoothing her tunic. "I'll think about it."

"Don't think too long. Life's short. I just learned that lesson again, rather painfully." He gestured to his wounded side. "Don't wait for a sword to the gut to figure out what matters."

"Wise words from a man who nearly died."

"The best wisdom usually comes after near-death experiences. Makes you focus on what's important." He settled back against his pillows. "Now go. Let an old man rest."

Brynja moved to the door, then paused. "Connor?"

"Aye?"

"Do you ever regret it? The vengeance you took? The men you killed?"

He was quiet for a long moment. "Some of

them, aye. The ones who didn't need killing. The ones I killed out of rage instead of necessity." He met her eyes. "But the ones who hurt people I loved? The ones who would have kept hurting if I'd let them? Those I don't regret. I'd kill them again if I had to."

"So vengeance isn't always wrong."

"Nay. It's just not always right either. It's like anything else in life, complicated. Messy. Sometimes necessary. Sometimes poison. The trick is knowing which one you're dealing with." He smiled faintly. "And you, lass? You are dealing with the necessary kind. So stop second-guessing yourself and start living."

Brynja nodded, something settling in her chest. Not peace, exactly. But perhaps the beginning of it.

"I'll see you on the morrow," she said.

"With more stew?"

"Or porridge," she agreed.

She slipped out into the hall, closing the door softly behind her. The castle hummed with afternoon life around her, and for the first time since Tiree, she felt like she might actually be part of it. Not just a guest. Not just a visitor waiting to leave.

But someone who belonged at Duart Castle.

She went to find Hagen.

CHAPTER THIRTY-EIGHT

HAGEN

IT HAD BEEN three days since they returned from Tiree. Hagen had awakened in the middle of the night again, bathed in sweat, the nightmare the same as the two previous nights.

There was an attack on Duart Castle and his father went down, but this time, he never got up.

Hagen came in from the lists, half the day gone already, a brutal practice session with Alaric and Broc, wondering what to do about his persistent dream. The same kind Brynja was experiencing, though hers was much more vivid when it came to the bairns on Iona. His focused on his sire.

Alaric came up behind him and said, "You're killing yourself. Don't worry. I have an odd feeling there will be more Grants here soon. Maitland sent word to Jamie and Kyla that Connor had been injured. I bet they'll be here soon. Alasdair too is my guess."

"Nay, Kyla mayhap."

"He used the word Comming." Alaric arched his brow, a growing smirk spreading across his face.

"Oh, shite. That changes everything. They'll all be here. Aunt Kyla, Uncle Jamie, Alasdair. Only Alick and Els will stay back."

He paused when they passed the archery target inside the gates. Brynja, Eli, and Merryn were there with Dyna practicing. Hell, but he was growing more and more fond of the lass, if that were possible.

"You going to marry her?" Alaric asked.

"Aye. Once this all settles down. But she's having the same nightmares as I am. That worries me more."

Alaric paused for a moment, watching the lasses shoot. "I'll never get over that day, seeing you and Brynja with Lia telling you what to do. Telling you about this special power the two of you hold but only if you're together. And the lightning. Hell, if I were you, I would have married her as soon as you got back. You can't argue with the Heavens."

"You haven't told anyone what you saw, have you?"

"Nay. If I said anything, they'd think me daft. I just say it was Lia. It's up to you to mention the other. How's your sire this morn?"

"He's out with Midnight Star, brushing him down. Aunt Brenna won't allow him in the lists yet, but he has to keep busy. He likes the peacefulness of the stables."

Alaric looked toward the gates. "Did they take some horses out for a run?"

"Nay, there were two patrols that went out, but that was a while ago. Why?"

"Listen. I hear horses and they're getting closer."
Alaric tipped his head, both men now listening.

"Who's on the gate?"

"Jowell and Paden."

The horses stopped and Hagen heard the voice.
"I'm here for Connor Grant."

Alaric looked at him. "That can't be Dugan,
can it?"

Hagen said, "It sounds like him. He wouldn't
be that daft to come here, would he?"

"They won't let him in."

Hagen took off on a run toward the gates,
glancing over his shoulder. "Jowell and Paden
never saw Dugan on Tiree. They might let him
in."

His father heard Dugan. He could tell because
the old warrior was saddling his horse.

Hagen's blood ran cold. He had to stop this
before it escalated. He mounted his horse and
yelled at the stable lads. "Get more saddled and
ready to go."

Before he could ride out, he yelled back to
Alaric, "Get everyone out of the hall and make
sure the bairns are inside."

Alaric ran at the keep shouting for assistance,
Eli joining him. Logan, Maitland, Drew, and the
rest of their guards were already mounting up.

Dyna raced up the stairs to the curtain wall,
full quiver in hand and bow over her shoulder,
Merryn and Brynja following. His sister would
be a definite help on the wall.

Hagen rode through the gate first, heading

down the path to meet the fool. "I'm here, Comming. You want a Grant? Face me."

Dugan's eyes lit with malicious glee. "The whelp thinks he's a warrior now? I'll carve you up just like I did your father."

"My father lives, so think again about that power behind your blade. You'll find I'm not so easy to cut down."

Dugan raised his sword and came at him.

The battle was on.

Hagen met Dugan's first strike, the clash of steel ringing across the hillside. The man was strong, but Hagen had trained with the best—his father, his uncles, men who'd fought in countless battles. He parried and deflected, his movements fluid and sure.

Behind him, he heard the thunder of hooves as the Grantham guards poured through the gate. The group fought in a spot down the path a bit, and the Granthams had about thirty men at the ready while Dugan had around a score joining him up the path. Maitland had sent a score on patrol, and they had left for different areas. How had they missed them?

Hagen pressed his advantage against Dugan, driving him back. For a moment, he thought he might end this quickly—until three of Dugan's men broke away from the main fight and charged toward him.

An arrow whistled past Hagen's ear and struck the lead attacker in the shoulder, spinning him sideways in his saddle. A second arrow found its mark in another man's thigh. It had to be Brynja.

Her aim was as deadly as ever. The third man hesitated, glancing up at the curtain wall where more arrows were already nocked, and that moment's distraction was all Hagen needed.

He wheeled his horse, engaging the nearest attacker. His sword work was clean, efficient. One man fell. Then another. But the third—the one with Brynja's arrow in his thigh—rallied and got past his guard, blade aimed at Hagen's exposed side.

A black destrier crashed into the fray.

"Get away from my son!" Connor's voice rang out, his sword deflecting the blow meant for Hagen.

"Da! What are you doing? You shouldn't be here!"

His father said nothing, positioning Midnight Star between Hagen and the immediate threat. But Hagen could see it immediately, the way his father favored his one side, the slight hitch in his movements, the set of his jaw that meant he was fighting through pain.

Dugan turned his attention to Connor with savage delight. "I knew you couldn't stay away, Grant. Come to let me finish what I started?"

Connor's response was steady, though Hagen noticed how his father's grip on his sword was tighter than usual, compensating. "Leave him be, Comming. Your quarrel is with me."

"Nay, Da!" Hagen tried to intervene, but two more of Dugan's men engaged him, forcing him to defend himself.

Through the chaos of combat, Hagen kept his

father in his peripheral vision. Connor's parries were strong, his technique as sound as ever, but his stamina was flagging. Each strike came a fraction slower than it should. His breathing was labored, evidence that he wasn't healed completely.

Hagen dispatched one attacker, then the other, and fought his way closer to his father. "Leave him be, Comming. I'm his son, you bastard. See if you can take my sword down."

Dugan swung toward Hagen, engaging him for several rapid exchanges, then the weakling did a cheap move and pivoted suddenly, trying to cut Connor down while his guard was down.

His father retaliated with a false move, pretending to be hurt worse than he was and almost falling off his horse, drawing Dugan in.

At least, Hagen prayed he was pretending. "Dugan, I'm coming for you."

But Dugan went for Connor, his full attention on finishing the older warrior, giving Hagen the perfect opening. He struck Dugan in his flank, a death blow for sure. The man turned to glare at Hagen, shock on his face, and Hagen's father gave him a shove with the flat of his sword, knocking him off his horse.

Connor swayed in his saddle, his face pale beneath the grime and sweat.

"Da, get back inside. I'll handle this." More men came at Hagen just as ten Grantham horses joined from inside the gates. One of their patrols of five men was coming from the left, blocking Dugan's men in.

The battle was not over yet, but his sire moved

his horse back, one hand pressed briefly to his wounded side.

Connor Grant had regained his honor, not by seeking glory, but by protecting his son.

And Hagen Grant had earned his reputation by fighting alongside his father as an equal.

CHAPTER THIRTY-NINE

BRYNJA

———～～———

BRYNJA HEARD THE commotion and stopped Merryn and Dyna. "Something is happening."

The trio ended their practice to listen.

Brynja had a sick feeling deep in her belly. It was happening again, but this time it was just like her nightmare. The Grants and Granthams were under attack.

Dyna screamed, "Grab as many arrows as you can."

She did the same and raced up the staircase behind her, nocking her arrow and firing into the group once she made it to the top and set her position.

Merryn was right behind her with Eli. Poor Eli, big belly obvious, sent so many arrows that Brynja was stunned. Dyna and Eli's accuracy was something to see. She knew exactly who she needed to watch to improve her skills, but this wasn't the time. She fired too, catching an occasional leg or shoulder, but shaking the confidence of their attackers.

Her belly flopped when she saw Hagen jump into the fray doing his best to protect his father. At one point, two men came at Hagen so she fired at them, hoping to catch one of them. And when his father played a move that surprised them all, Hagen taking Dugan down with a death blow and his father knocking him to the ground, a cheer went up from the group, Logan Ramsay shouting, "You can't beat the Grants' swords, men. Run while you still have both arms."

And many did run off after Dugan went down.

Including Sholto. He left and headed in the opposite direction than she expected. They came from MacVey direction, but he headed toward MacLane Castle. And in that instant, Brynja knew what she had to do because the nightmare was happening just as she'd seen.

Sholto was headed to Iona and the bairns.

"Dyna, tell Hagen I had to go after Sholto. He's going for the bairns and Iona. I'm going to Tristan's. I have to go after him."

Dyna said, "Go. We'll follow."

Brynja found Freya already saddled and waiting, glad that she'd spent some of the last few days practicing her horse skills with Hagen. She'd ridden enough now to have the confidence to ride alone.

She made her way around the remaining men still fighting and headed toward MacLean land. Hagen shouted after her, "Go! I'll be behind you."

How she prayed he would. Darkness was falling fast, and she didn't wish to be alone against four fools. She would need help to take the bastard down. She noticed three of his men followed him, so there were at least four she'd have to deal with. She could not, would not, allow that bastard to steal any of those innocent bairns away.

She prayed Artan and Simone were on Iona to help her.

It took forever to travel the path down to Tristan MacClane's place, and when she got there, she noticed a ship already heading toward Iona, with six men, if she was correct. There was another one that just pushed off down the coast a bit. Did Sholto have two boats of men? How she prayed he didn't, but they headed straight toward Sholto's boat.

Tristan stood on the coast watching the two boats, then whirled around when he heard her approach. He came toward her. "Are there more coming? I'll go with you because someone has to stop those fools. I came out when I heard them talking about the bairns, but they headed out so fast, I couldn't do anything. I don't know them, do you?"

"I know one," she said, gasping to catch her breath. "Sholto, the one who I hit with my dagger when he tried to go after Sheona. He's a slimy bastard. He's after the bairns on Iona. Have you a boat I can take? Any men who can go with me? I can't row myself."

"We'll take this one," he said, pointing to a boat. "Let's ready it. I can grab two more men to go with us."

"No need!" A shout came from the top of the crest.

Brynja spun around, her heart leaping with joy when she saw Hagen come over the ridge and down toward shore, Logan, Maitland, Dyna, and Alaric behind him. How she adored this man and how blessed she was to have found him.

She squealed and clapped, but then she helped Tristan move the boat, loading her quiver into the vessel while Tristan gave orders to his men to care for the horses.

Hagen kissed her quickly, then handed his horse over.

Tristan said, "Menzie, I wasn't expecting to see you, but glad of it."

Maitland gave a loud growl. "I don't like weak men who pick on innocent bairns. Move this boat. Heartless bastards."

The six climbed in with Tristan and headed toward Iona.

Hagen pointed a good distance ahead of them. "Is that Sholto's boat?"

Brynja nodded and pointed to the second boat. "Aye, I think he has five or possibly six with him. And there's another boat coming along. They have to be his men too."

Tristan said, "I noticed the ship down the shore earlier. There were two men fishing so I didn't think anything of it. That was the boat that followed him."

Brynja asked, "Where the hell is he going?"

Looking back over his shoulder since he was rowing, Hagen said, "They're landing somewhere else. Why?"

Logan said, "Because the spineless trolls are afraid of Simone and Artan. I think that's them standing near the shore, is it not? I see someone but can't make out who it is. It's getting dark."

Alaric peeked over his shoulder and said, "That's Simone. And Artan isn't far from her. They see the boats coming and are protecting the bairns, like they should. How many bairns are living there now, Brynja?"

"Nine with Tenney and Magni."

Logan said, "I let her know there was a new group causing trouble, so she's been on alert. They're going to approach from the beach shore on the point, thinking to sneak up on them, because Simone's reputation with her bow precedes her. She's firing arrows as we speak. I think I hear that sweet sound over the water. I hope Magni is sleeping."

"But where are they going to land? There's no good place that far down. It's too rocky." Tristan glanced back while he was rowing. "I don't like this."

"I know where they're headed," Brynja said. "There's a spot on the opposite side where the beach is flat and not many rocks. There's a direct path straight to the cottages. Geva's husband fishes off that shore often."

"Don't slow down," Logan said. "We might be able to beat them there if they're coming from the other side. The boat just disappeared around the point."

Maitland glanced over his shoulder. "And the other group of hedge-born toads are waiting to see what we do. I'd wager they'll land down shore."

Brynja nearly cried, praying Magni wasn't awake.

Hagen glanced at her and winked. "We'll get them. You can count on it, Bry."

They neared the shore when the one thing Brynja dreaded came to fruition.

Magni screamed so loud it echoed across the water, sending shivers down her back.

CHAPTER FORTY

MAGNI

⟞⟀⟝

"BUT WHY ARE you here now, Simone? It's dark out. Usually you go home before dark." He stared up at his favorite lass. Well, besides Brynja and Hildi. And Sylvi. And Tora too. And their mother. And…

"We're just enjoying the night. The water is calm and there's no breeze. It's lovely, Magni. Go play with your brother."

"He went to bed. Do you think my mama will come back soon?"

"I'm not sure," Artan said. "Her back is much better sleeping on that bed than sleeping on the floor here. Next summer we'll build her a better bed, but it's hard to do now."

Simone gave her husband an odd nod, tipping her head toward the sea, then Artan said, "Magni, I left my favorite fishing pole behind Beatris's cottage. Would you get it for me, please?"

"Sure. I know which one it is." And he took off to fetch Artan's pole.

Magni hoped his grandsire would come back for another visit on the morrow. He felt bad for turning him down the other day. He'd come to invite him to Yuletide at Duart Castle, but Magni had refused.

Grandsire nearly got angry with him. Magni could see it in his eyes. He never raised his voice, but his grandsire had a way about him that sometimes made him want to run and hide. "Dammit, Magni!" But then he'd calmed down and asked him quietly, "Why not? Did you know that the Grants give a gift to each bairn at their Yuletide festival? It was Maddie Grant's way."

"A gift? Just for me?" He pictured a big boat he could play with on the shore. Or a bigger sword than the one he had, one that was sharper than his wooden one. Or mayhap he'd get a wooden horse or two to play with. Or a new fabric horse to take to bed. He'd nearly worn out the one he had that his mama made for him a long time ago. It took a lot to get himself to fall asleep some nights.

"Magni, what do you think? I'll come and get you for Yule?"

Leave Iona? Absolutely not. "Nay, I'll stay here for Yule."

Then he'd seen Grandda's fists clench, but he whispered, "Why not, lad? I promise to keep you safe."

He had to think hard. Then he came up with it. "Because Lia is not here. She's helping someone else so I cannot leave. She wouldn't know where I was. I can't leave my sister alone for Yule."

"But how would she be alone if she's not here?" his clever grandfather had asked.

He'd scowled about that one, turning away, surprised to see his father standing behind him. "Son, I wish to go to Duart Castle with your mother. We both want you to visit us there."

And then Thane had invited him to Yule.

And Connor Grant.

And Simone.

He stopped behind the cottage to stare up at the stars. Someone else had asked him too. Who was it?

Lennox! Chieftain MacVey had invited him too.

And Chief Rankin said they were going.

And then Dyna came and invited him too. She brought Sylvi with him, and she had begged him to come. He remembered how she had taken his hand and said, "Please, Magni. We miss you. Sandor and Tora miss you. And Rowan will be there. And Alana and Shealee too."

He couldn't help but smile about that. He did have many friends.

But he couldn't leave. God would only protect him if he was close to the abbey. Someone had told him that once. That the monks would protect him forever.

"I have to stay near the monks, Grandda."

And his grandsire had asked, "When was the last time you saw a monk here protecting you?"

His grandsire was a wise man.

But he'd answered everyone the same way. He wasn't leaving Iona.

Ever.

He'd been alone and afraid before and didn't wish to have it come back ever again. He'd never forget when he'd been stolen away by those evil men who lied and told him they killed his parents and set off in a boat and left him on Ulva. He'd escaped and made it to Mull, but there he was, alone, on the isle of Mull until he'd found his dear sister Lia hiding under the fronds. She was truly the faery of the woods, the faery of the green meadow, but she promised to protect him and stay with him forever.

He picked up Artan's fishing pole, then turned because he heard something. There was a boat behind him at the spot where Henry always went fishing. Not where Simone and Artan were.

There were never any boats back there.

He crept down the path to see if he was wrong, creeping closer, closer, until he saw the boat. Who was it? He took a few more steps forward, noticing the boat was full of men, and listened.

"Grab as many bairns as you can."

His eyes widened.

He dropped the fishing pole.

He let out a scream that could be heard all over the isle.

"Lia! Help me!" And he ran back toward the cottage and out toward Artan and Simone.

Still screaming.

Sobbing.

Begging for his dear sister to help him.

"I'm coming with you, Thane! Or Grandda!"

He wished he could run faster.

"Someone help me, please."

He tore around the cottage still screaming. Expecting to see bad men everywhere.

Instead, he saw more boats. One small boat, and three large ones.

Were there bad men everywhere? He had to find Simone.

But then he saw them—his grandfather and Brynja ran straight toward him.

"Grandda! Brynja! Save me!" He couldn't stop the scream that exploded from his body, the sobs right behind it.

Brynja grabbed him by the shoulders and said, "We're here, Magni. Where are they? Tell us."

He pointed behind him, mumbling, "Henry's fishing spot." She took off faster than he'd ever seen her run.

His grandfather shook him and said, "Lord above, stop screaming, Magni. We're here. We'll protect you. Now who and where? How many did you see?"

He closed his mouth, gasping for breath. "On the coast behind us. Straight down the path. Six or eight of them. I couldn't count them. I was bouncing too much." Then he threw his arms around his grandda.

Logan barked some orders to everyone coming off the boats and then pulled him off to the side, tugging him close. "I told you we'd protect you."

And they did.

He stood on the side while he held his grandfather's hand and cried like a wee bairn as he watched them pass him by, some waving, some going right on past him.

Some said, "We'll protect you, Magni!"

He just couldn't stop the tears.

Artan, Simone, Dyna, Hagen, Tristan, Alaric, Eli, Jowell, Paden, Maitland, Broc, Merryn, and some he didn't know.

They came and came and came.

All for him.

Last was Thane who came straight to him.

Magni looked up at him and asked, "Can I still move in with you, Thane?"

"Aye, lad. You're always welcome. You can come home with me in a little bit, if you like."

He wrapped his arms around Thane's waist and said, "I'm coming with you."

Logan said, "And you're coming to our Yule Festival. No arguments."

And he looked up at this man he adored and said, "All right."

And it didn't matter if they gave him a gift or not. He needed to be inside a big castle.

Safe.

Someday, he'd be a big Ramsay warrior too.

CHAPTER FORTY-ONE

BRYNJA

———❦———

BRYNJA RAN PAST the houses but then took a detour, moving over to one of her hiding places. She glanced over her shoulder, Sholto and his men still a distance away and moving slowly. There it was. Her mother's armor. She'd hidden it here in case she ever needed it. She donned the heavy armor, tying the strings behind her back to hold it in place. Then she picked up her weapons.

One spear and three daggers.

She made her way to Sholto and stood in front of him, a distance away, making sure he could see her. She called out, "Remember me?"

Sholto's eyes widened. "I'm going to kill you, bitch." He motioned to the other men. "Get the bairns and I'll meet you back here."

Brynja took off on a run. She headed toward the heavily forested area, one she knew well, but he didn't, especially in the dark. She went a ways in, then hid in some bushes, listening to the man call out his empty threats. "I'm going to stab you right between the legs too. And then I'll cut your breasts off. See how that feels."

He approached the area heavy with brush and slowed his walk. "Come on out. We can talk about this." She heard him draw his weapon, his arm pushing the branches aside as he crept through the trees.

How she wished to run out and chase him, but she'd learned from Hagen. Patience. Her hand flexed on her weapon as she took a deep breath to help herself focus.

She waited until the right moment, stepped out, and said, "Here I am." Then she lifted her spear with every bit of strength she had, driving it into the area just below his ribs. And the weapon sunk in deep.

Reflexively, he jerked his sword and tried to stab her in the chest, but he hit metal.

Her mother's armor protected her.

The man's eyes closed as he slumped to the ground, taking his last breath, never to hurt another bairn again.

She whispered in her mother's tongue, "May all the devils that could fill your boat rise up from hell to drag you down, you evil piece of scum."

And she let the tears flow but then told herself she had to go help Magni and the bairns. Walking out of the forest, she saw Hagen running toward her. "Are you hale?"

"Aye, see for yourself." She pointed to Sholto's dead body a distance behind her.

He looked at the body and said, "Brynja, well done. The spear. What a deadly weapon. How did…" He stopped and saw her tears and instead, returned to her, wrapping his arms around her. "You're a hell of a warrior, and I'd be honored to have you by my side in any battle."

"We make a fantastic team, Hagen. You killed the man who killed my mother and my aunt. I didn't want to say anything when your sire was so sick, but when I saw Dugan on Tiree, I recognized him. He's the one. A killer and a molester. Many, many thanks to you and your sire."

He leaned into her, kissed her tears, and whispered, "We can finally both let go of our vengeance."

"Aye." She let the tears fall and asked, "Magni?"

"Magni is blubbering in Thane's arms, asking if he can still live with him. He's fine." He struggled against her and drawled, "I have to admit, hugging you without the armor is much more enjoyable."

She broke into giggles, and he took her by the hand as two more huge ships arrived at shore near them.

"Who is that?" she asked. "Those ships are huge."

"My uncle's idea when he heard my sire was injured. Hired the biggest galley ship he could find, especially because he heard it was a Comming. They're ready for a huge battle. One of his ships landed on the other side and helped take care of the other six men who were there. Another of Dugan's ships landed, and they were taken care of quickly. Come, meet my uncle."

He took her hand, and they raced over to

the ship. "Uncle Jamie. Welcome! I think we've managed for now, but we can check."

"Hellfire, I was ready for battle. My brother, Hagen? How is he? As soon as we were close to Craignure, Drew was there waiting, sent us over here to save some bairns. He climbed into Alasdair's ship to show the way. You have too many islands."

"Da's fine, though weakened. He ran into Dugan Commings and put an end to his threat earlier this eve. You just missed the battle."

Another ten men came behind him, and Uncle Jamie waved them on. "Go check to see if they need any assistance on the other side of the cottages."

"Uncle Jamie, this is my betrothed, Brynja Nyberg."

Jamie made a small bow and said, "The pleasure is mine, my lady. There's naught we love more than a strong Norse warrior. I'd love to take a look at your armor later, if you don't mind. I see it protected you well already."

Brynja looked down at the dent in her armor. Hagen bent down to stare at it, his eyes widening. "What the hell happened?"

She shrugged her shoulders. "Sholto. He tried and failed."

CHAPTER FORTY-TWO

CONNOR

———✺———

WITH ALL THE family that had arrived, and Yule only a few days away, they'd decided to start the Yuletide festival with the wedding of Hagen and Brynja. From there, they were headed into a huge three-day celebration.

Jamie, Gracie, and Kyla had arrived with various other Grants, all worried about Connor. Two ships of guards had gone home, with one ship left for the family members.

Gracie swore she was waiting until Eli had her baby.

Connor enjoyed spending time with his brother and sister. They'd sat up on the parapets last eve, and he'd shared with them his near-death experience of seeing their parents. Kyla had sobbed through the entire story.

He'd kept the secret about Hagen and Brynja's true gift, afraid no one would believe them. In true Hagen nature, he'd refused to wait to marry Brynja, so they'd arranged the wedding, Kyla and Sela enjoying every last bit of making all the

arrangements. They'd had a great, successful hunt
with Sloan, Thane, and Lennox along with them,
Merryn catching her first pheasant while Dyna
grabbed two and Eli one. There would be lamb
and venison meat pies aplenty, even a slab of boar
meat brought over by Jamie, and the MacVey and
Rankin cooks had helped out with extra bread.

It would be a wonderful celebration.

The wedding had begun in the packed great
hall, so many bodies there that some had to stand.
Connor sat off to the side of the couple as the
priest rambled on. Hagen and Brynja, their hands
intertwined, stood together, ready to say their
vows for their marriage.

His gaze traveled fondly back to his son,
besotted and smitten, but also proudly wearing
his father's sword. Connor had given it to him
earlier in front of his siblings, surprised not by his
own tears, but those of Sela's and Hagen's. Kyla
and Maeve had cried buckets, but that much he
had expected.

Oh, Connor would still fight, but he didn't
need the most powerful sword. The best weapon
belonged with the strongest swordsman, and
Hagen had proven his worth. All of Hagen's
cousins had noticed as soon as they'd joined
them, pats on his back and taunts aplenty.

Sela sat next to him, as beautiful as the day he'd
met her in Inverness, a bit teary-eyed, but smiling.
Kyla sat on the other side of him, Jamie on the
other side of Sela, and Aunt Brenna sat in front of
them, insisting that it might all be too much for
Connor. She refused to leave his side, along with

a few chastisements for fighting before she told him he could.

The priest's voice carried across the hall while a group of musicians played their strings, but Connor had his eye on one spot.

There was an odd light in the healer's chamber. The chamber was empty and the door sat open, Aunt Brenna sitting not far from the door of her chamber.

Connor couldn't take his eyes from the small light inside, and it finally drew him in. No one else appeared to notice it but him, mayhap Sela and Kyla could if they turned, but neither one could take their eyes off the couple.

He squeezed Sela's hand, leaned over and said, "I need something to drink to settle myself. I'll be right back." He hoped it would suffice. He'd told her that the battle had weakened him again, and it surely had, but Comming was done. He moved into the healing chamber, pulling Aunt Brenna with him, hoping that it would cover his absence if anyone else noticed. Kyla followed, whispering to her brother, "What's wrong?"

But he also wanted his siblings to see what beckoned to him along with Aunt Brenna. If he was correct, it would mean as much to Kyla and Jamie to see them as it would be to Aunt Brenna to see her brother again.

It was dark, no light inside except for the one in the middle. Connor motioned to Jamie to follow him. He held the door until Jamie and Maeve came in behind him. "What's wrong?" Jamie asked.

"Naught, just a feeling. Come in closer. I wish for you to see something."

Once Connor closed the door, they appeared in front of them, their parents, shimmering with a glory unimaginable.

Alexander and Madeline Grant.

Kyla whispered, "Mama? Da?"

Maeve gasped, tears flooding her cheeks.

Aunt Brenna said, "Oh, Alex. I miss you so." Then she looked to Maddie and said, "And you, my dear sister." They weren't true sisters, but Aunt Brenna had always said Maddie was as close to a sister as one could get.

Connor grabbed a chair, sat down, and nodded to both. "My thanks for visiting again one more time. I knew it was you when I saw the light, Da. And I wished to bring Jamie, Maeve, and Kyla with me."

"Connor," his mother said. "We're here to see Hagen get married and you're missing it."

"It was the musical part, Mama. No worries. And I promise to be there for their vows. My thanks for saving me on Tiree."

His father stepped closer, so close he could nearly touch him, but he had such a transparency to him that he knew better than to reach out to him. His sire's hair was as dark as night, the aging, gray-haired Alex Grant gone, replaced by the fierce Highlander chieftain they all remembered so well. "Hagen and Brynja saved you the first time, Connor. You were lucky. You and Hagen did a great job the second time using your wits instead of your emotions. Well done. You took care of Dugan, Connor. Fear not. You will heal," his father said. "It's not your time yet, you have much more to do. Lia will tell you later."

That comment surprised Connor. "You are familiar with Lia?"

His mother gave him that smile as if she were watching him stuff his mouth with her holiday sweet breads. "Of course, we know Lia. You'll see."

His father said, "Don't let the lass fool you. She's a wise old soul inside that faery."

Their mother clasped her hands in front of her chest. "We're so proud of you all for the way you've raised your bairns. And Brenna, our thanks for always taking such good care of our clan."

Their father added, "And my thanks for bringing the clan to the power you have. And most importantly to me, a clan with the honor all Scots would be proud of. I have one more question, Connor. Have you accepted the truth about your son yet?"

Connor grinned, tears filling his vision. He knew what his sire asked, referring to his special skills, but he also knew his sire well enough to know that skill needed to be kept a secret. So he answered in the way that would entertain his siblings. "Aye, Hagen bested me, Da. He now has the stronger sword."

His father erupted in a hearty laugh, the sweet sound bringing so many memories to all of them that Kyla let out a low squeal.

A head popped up behind Alex and Maddie.

Jake smiled. "He is better than you, Connor.

Just as Alasdair beat me long ago. Greetings to you all. Happy Yule, especially to my twin."

Jamie said, "You're missed more than you know, Jake. Hellfire…so much." It wasn't often Connor saw Jamie cry, but he shed a few tears with him.

Maddie Grant lifted her hand in a wave. "We're leaving. Our time is always short. Go back out there with everyone. We love you. Godspeed, all."

Their light faded and Aunt Brenna leaned over and hugged him, none of them saying a word before returning to the ceremony. Kyla wiped her tears away and leaned over to kiss both brothers' cheeks, then hugged Aunt Brenna. Maeve sopped up her tears that appeared to be never-ending, the others hugging her.

They didn't need any words, their hearts were full.

CHAPTER FORTY-THREE

LOGAN

~~~

THE FESTIVAL STARTED right after the wedding with tables and tables of food. Pheasant, boar, and lamb meat pies, venison stew, fruit tarts, bread, and baked apples filled the tables. The hall was decorated with greenery, pinecones, and ribbons, and everyone from Mull was there.

Logan sat near the hearth, Gwyneth next to him. "Do you feel bad we're not at Clan Ramsay, Gwynie?"

"Nay, we have enough friends here. But aye, I do miss our bairns and our clan. We see Simone often enough, and Eli is here, plus your special guest whom I adore is outside. It's always good to see him again. This was a special year. Look at all the weddings."

"Too many to count," he said.

"I'm not sure who I think is the happiest. Who do you think is?"

Logan snorted. "Lennox and Meg because he's always staring at her arse, Gwynie. Have you noticed? And Sloan couldn't be happier to be married and to have his sister married and his father."

"Rut and Dermot look verra happy. I hear Lennox and Taskill were overjoyed when Rut moved out to live with Dermot."

Logan laughed. "But then Rut went home. Every time they argue she goes home, so Lennox says."

Gwynie said, "I know who I think is the happiest—Thane and Tamsin. Their story is the best of all. He's so happy with her, and he found his parents again. Plus, they caught those cruel bastards who abandoned those children on the shore. What a terrible story that was."

"Merryn's story is something too. Broc adores her." Logan took his wife's hand and kissed her fingers. "I just thank the Lord above that Connor made it through."

The door opened and someone motioned to Logan.

"I'm up, Gwynie. I shall return."

"Go ahead, you big softie."

Logan nodded to Dyna who had Maitland whistle to quiet everyone. Dyna and Maitland stood in front of the crowd and called all the bairns up front, seating them before everyone. The crowd moved back to make room. Up came Alana with Magni, Shealee with Sylvi, Tora, and Sandor, Rowan with Tenney, and Maeve holding Grant.

Logan said, "After all you bairns have been through this year, you deserve some special gifts for Yule. Dyna, Sela, and Gwynie have worked hard to create new fabric animals for you. Dyna? Go ahead and hand these out."

Dyna, Eli, and Sela handed out the various handmade bunnies, squirrels, and puppies, letting each child select their favorite. The wee ones giggled and hugged their gifts, faces glowing.

Then Logan said, "But this year, you all get a second gift and it's a special one. I had my special friend bring your gifts across the water." He turned around and opened the door, two tall men entering, one clearly older than the other, carrying a big crate between them.

"This is my nephew and Chieftain Torrian Ramsay for those of you who don't know him. He's here with his son Lucas, the new chieftain, and they brought you special gifts."

Torrian took the top off the big crate, one too tall for the bairns to peek inside. "I know what it's like to have a difficult time, and I hear you bairns suffered too much this year. So, I offer you something that helped me forget about the bad parts of the world. Mine was named Growley, and not only did he help me grow, he also protected me many times when I was young."

Magni asked, "What could protect you that is small and sits in a box?"

"You'll see, lad. Be patient."

The lads and lassies waited, odd squeaks coming from the crate. Torrian played with whatever was inside, then said, "Magni, Lia tells me you need something warm and large. It's not large yet, but it will grow. Magni, would you like to come up and be first?"

Magni crept up to Torrian and said, "Aye, my lord, if you please."

Torrian pulled out a basket with a gray puppy and handed it to Magni.

Logan said, "His name is Liam, Magni. So when Lia has to leave for a while, you have another protector, Liam."

"My verra own?" he cried, looking from Torrian to Logan. "I can keep him?" Both men nodded as Lucas lifted the puppy out of the basket and handed it to him, the furry beast promptly licking his cheek. Magni giggled and spun around to Thane and asked, "Can we keep him?"

"Aye, because Alana is getting one too." Thane squeezed Tamsin's hand while she patted her growing belly.

Torrian said, "Every home needs two dogs. They like to sleep together."

Torrian and Lucas handed out the puppies, the bairns all ecstatic with their gifts. Once they finished and joined the group, Logan said, "Wait. One more surprise. And this one is for Gwynie."

Someone knocked on the door and Logan opened it. In came two of their bairns, Sorcha with her husband Cailean, and Gavin with Merewen. Some of their grandbairns followed with squeals of excitement, and they all surrounded Gwyneth: Ysenda and Lewis, Ceit and Brin Cameron, Cadyn and Tryana.

Just when they thought everyone was here, the door opened and a tall, fair-haired lad came in, slamming the door behind him—Errol, Gavin and Merewen's youngest son. Eli hurried over to give her youngest brother a hug.

Connor stared at the lad. "He's the exact image of you, Logan."

Logan nodded and beamed. "Aye, he is."

"Happy Yule to all," Logan said.

Hagen and Brynja watched from the back while the bairns received their gifts. "Can you believe we're married, lass?"

"Nay, but I'm happy. So happy. I understand what you and your sire were trying to tell me."

"About?"

"Vengeance. I'm still sad and angry about losing my mother and my aunt, and I'll never forget Sholto or Dugan, but I won't let them take over my mind. They really did do exactly that."

"What?"

"Vengeance consumed me. But that hate, that anger, is replaced with something else."

He tipped his head at her, then nuzzled her neck.

"Love. For you, Hildi, your clan, the people of Mull, even the nuns. They were only trying to help us."

"I love you too."

She scowled, her gaze scanning the hall. "Speaking of Hildi, where is she? Have you seen her since the ceremony?"

He shook his head, frowning with her. "Now that you mention it, have you seen Jowell? Paden is over there flirting with Mora, but I haven't seen him."

Brynja broke into a grin and took his hand. "Hush, I think I know where they are."

"They? You mean together?"

She nodded and held her finger to her lips to shush him, then led him over to the healer's chamber. A small candle flickered inside, but not enough to light up the entire space. She cracked the door open and heard a gasp.

"Hildi?"

Hagen peered over her shoulder. "Jowell, you scoundrel. What are you two doing in here?"

The two were kissing and jumped apart, both a bit short of breath.

"Naught," Jowell said. "Hildi was feeling lightheaded, so I brought her in here."

"Of course," Hagen drawled. "I'm sure holding her that tightly kept her from dropping. Try seating her next time, Jowell."

His cousin shrugged, grinned, then sat down and hauled Hildi onto his lap. "I was just convincing Hildi to stay at Clan Grantham now that you're married."

"And?" Brynja's whisper ended in a light squeal.

"And I agreed." Hildi's face glowed.

"Hildi, I'm so happy. We belong together."

"I know. I'll never leave you, Brynja."

Hagen tugged his wife over, took a seat across from Jowell, and settled Brynja on his lap. "The priest is here for the night." He tipped his head at his cousin.

Jowell shook his head and said, "Nay, we've discussed it. We're not ready yet. We wish to wait a while. Mayhap next Yule."

"That sounds perfect," Brynja said. "And I promise to show you where I hid the treasure left by our mothers so we can both enjoy it."

EPILOGUE

LIA

THE DAY AFTER the festivities were over, Lia had called a specific group into the solar. "I needed to have a meeting with you all. I have some important words for you."

She looked out at the group in front of her: Connor, Sela, Hagen, Brynja, Maitland, Maeve, Grant, Alasdair, John, and Dyna.

Connor said, "Lia, I need to understand something. And since it's just this small group, I would like an explanation of what happened when I was injured on Tiree. How was I healed so quickly? I thought I was dying."

"You were verra close. It allowed me the chance to explain to Hagen and Brynja what powers they hold. As you can guess, they are a powerful couple. Everyone can see it, but I needed them to know that I will ask them to help me in the future. It's my job to protect the bairns, but I cannot do it alone. I need helpers in the universe. And they, along with others in your clan, have been chosen.

"As time goes on, we'll have more bairns to

protect, but I will need you two together. Hagen and Brynja," she turned to them, "I am binding the two of you until the end of time. Together, you will travel and help me fight the evil of the world."

Hagen whispered, "Why us?"

"It's not just you, but I'm starting with you. To be the most powerful, you will have to stay together as a couple. Are you willing to commit to each other? I'm pleased you are married, but you must commit to support each other when you are needed."

The two looked at each other and both nodded. "Of course," Brynja said, Hagen nodding next to her and kissing her cheek.

"As for the rest of you, this is why you are all here. It's not just Hagen and Brynja. The group will consist of John, Grant, Tora, Sylvi, Sandor, and Magni. Dyna, you and Alasdair are the only other adults who will play a large part. You are among the chosen ones whose job will be to help me battle evil. Connor, I may call on your assistance too."

Maitland set a kiss on his beloved son's head. "Grant is a wee bit young, Lia."

"Maitland and Maeve, I needed to ask you here because Grant will be needed at a younger age than the others, so you will be involved. He and John have a special power with the sapphire sword. They will both have the power to use it, but not until John is an adult."

"Why tell us now if this won't happen for several years?" Alasdair asked.

"Because enough strange things happened here in the last year, Alasdair. There were many questions about Tora's and Sylvi's abilities, Sandor's ability to speak with Uncle Jake, John's sapphire sword, Grant's attraction to me…"

"And his ability to touch a sharp sword and not bleed?" Maeve asked.

"Grant has many skills to build yet. He is indeed one of the special chosen ones, he and John will be called upon often. It's hard to say exactly how this will play out, but your bairns will all build their skills, and I felt it important to let you know that you shouldn't discourage the oddities you will see but instead encourage them. Encourage Tora's and Sylvi's ability to see, and John's skills with his sword."

"All right," Maitland scratched his head, staring at the wee lad in Maeve's arms. "That all makes sense to me, and Maeve and I will do whatever we can do to help our son meet his greatest potential."

"That's the reason I didn't have the other bairns here. I'll ask you not to talk about this outside of this group. And this isn't going to happen for about ten years. But sometime in the future I will call all of you together. I can't give you an exact time, but your time is coming. I ask that you all stay close and in the same clan."

Dyna said, "Finally, I understand why our bairns are special. Many thanks to you, Lia."

"You may tell Derric, Dyna."

The group took a moment to look around at

each other, taking in the information that was just given.

Then Lia said, "As I said, all will be quiet for a while. If you ever need me, I'll be here. Magni will surely let me know. And please don't tell Magni. He won't be able to understand it yet. But expect quiet times for about ten years. Then I shall return."

Alasdair asked, "Will you appear the same to us, Lia? Or will you come looking different?"

"Great question, Alasdair. I can't answer that, but I can promise you that when you need to know it's me, you will. Until then, many happy times to you all."

Lia disappeared.

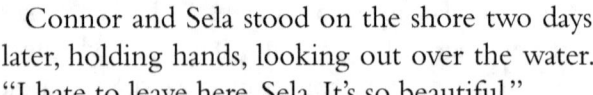

Connor and Sela stood on the shore two days later, holding hands, looking out over the water. "I hate to leave here, Sela. It's so beautiful."

"We'll be back. I know you can't leave forever. Besides, we're just going for a visit. And we'll bring Astra and Morgan back with us. Astra is ready, and Morgan has been begging to come. It's time."

Lia appeared next to them. "Greetings, Grants."

Connor said, "Greetings, Lia. Didn't you just leave us?"

"I did. But I wished to see you two alone."

Sela looked up at her husband, curious, then back at the faery. "Is something wrong?"

"Nay, I just wondered if either of you recognized me."

Connor and Sela looked at each other, Connor shrugging.

Sela said, "We always recognize you, Lia. You're always dressed in that lovely green gown. The faery gown of the meadow. It suits you perfectly."

Lia stepped closer. "And what if I wore something different?"

Connor said, "I will always recognize you, Lia. You saved my life. I'll never forget you. I promise."

"Are you sure about that?" She had that look on her face that told them something odd was about to happen.

Then she held her arms up and her image changed, her dress fading in color, going from forest green to a white gown, a billowing white skirt flowing to the ground with a blue band at her waist.

They both stared at her puzzled. Sela said, "You still look like Lia."

Then she raised her arms and she grew in front of them, from a wee lass of six to a woman of about twenty summers. "Now do you recognize me?" Her hair turned from gold to an odd shade of red.

Sela gasped, falling back against Connor, her finger pointing. "Oh my Lord in heaven, Connor. The abbey. Lochluin Abbey the night before I left."

Lia held her hand up. "Wait! I'm missing something." Then she swept her hand across her neck, and a string of pearls appeared. She repeated the movement, and the pearls changed to a chain with a red heart at the end. "Does this help?"

Sela whispered, "The protector of the innocent lasses."

Connor could barely speak. He knew her. He'd seen her several times before. Once or twice with Roddy, telling them they had to help Rose. And then when Sela finally came to him. And once with Daniel when she sent them to help Constance.

"Oh, my gosh! Sona Abbey. And then on Grant land. And the time you floated outside our window with Roddy in the middle of that wild storm."

Lia smiled and said, "Finally, you remember. And Sela, great memory. I was the protector of the innocent lasses. Now I've been moved to the protector of bairns." Then she laughed and waved. "I've been assigned to the Grants for a long time. You can tell Maitland and Maeve that I was named Callie once. Don't worry. I'll be back again, but not for a while."

Then she waved and disappeared.

The End

DEAR READER,
Did you guess it? I can't wait to hear how many of you tied the two Lias together!

This is the last book in the series.

So let's take a look at 2026. I have a couple of surprises for the first half of the year. Then I'm hoping to release the first book in the 4th generation of Grants and Ramsays over the summer. As you can see, the book (series possibly) will focus on John, Grant, Hagen, Brynja, Tora, Sylvi, Sandor, Magni, Dyna, and Connor. Lia will be there, of course! I don't know exactly how I'm going to spin this yet, but I've got time to make it great!

The happiest of holidays to all my lovely readers. I can't wait to share what's up next with all of you! I think you'll love it.

Keira Montclair

www.keiramontclair.com

NOVELS BY
KEIRA MONTCLAIR

CLANS OF MULL
THE PLIGHT OF A SCOTTISH LASS
THE BURDEN OF A SCOTTISH
CHIEFTAIN
THE ANGUISH OF THE SCOTTISH
LAIRDS
THE TORMENT OF A SCOTTISH
WARRIOR
THE DEFIANCE OF A SCOTTISH HEART
THE WRATH OF A SCOTTISH BLADE

HIGHLAND HUNTERS
THE SCOT'S CONFLICT
THE SCOT'S TRAITOR
THE SCOT'S PROTECTOR
THE SCOT'S VOW
THE SCOT'S DESTINY
THE SCOT'S WARNING
THE SCOT'S RECKONING
THE SCOT'S LEGACY

HIGHLAND SWORDS
THE SCOT'S BETRAYAL
THE SCOT'S SPY
THE SCOT'S PURSUIT
THE SCOT'S QUEST

THE SCOT'S DECEPTION
THE SCOT'S ANGEL

HIGHLAND HEALERS
THE CURSE OF BLACK ISLE
THE WITCH OF BLACK ISLE
THE SCOURGE OF BLACK ISLE
THE GHOSTS OF BLACK ISLE
THE GIFT OF BLACK ISLE

THE BAND OF COUSINS
HIGHLAND VENGEANCE
HIGHLAND ABDUCTION
HIGHLAND RETRIBUTION
HIGHLAND LIES
HIGHLAND FORTITUDE
HIGHLAND RESILIENCE
HIGHLAND DEVOTION
HIGHLAND BRAWN
HIGHLAND YULETIDE MAGIC

THE HIGHLAND CLAN
LOKI-Book One
TORRIAN-Book Two
LILY-Book Three
JAKE-Book Four
ASHLYN-Book Five
MOLLY-Book Six
JAMIE AND GRACIE-Book Seven
SORCHA-Book Eight
KYLA-Book Nine
BETHIA-Book Ten

LOKI'S CHRISTMAS STORY–Book Eleven
ELIZABETH–Book Twelve

THE CLAN GRANT SERIES
#1– RESCUED BY A HIGHLANDER–
Alex and Maddie
#2– HEALING A HIGHLANDER'S HEART–
Brenna and Quade
#3– LOVE LETTERS FROM LARGS–
Brodie and Celestina
#4–JOURNEY TO THE HIGHLANDS–
Robbie and Caralyn
#5–HIGHLAND SPARKS–
Logan and Gwyneth
#6–MY DESPERATE HIGHLANDER–
Micheil and Diana
#7–THE BRIGHTEST STAR IN THE
HIGHLANDS–
Jennie and Aedan
#8– HIGHLAND HARMONY–
Avelina and Drew
#9–YULETIDE ANGELS

THE SOULMATE CHRONICLES TRILOGY
#1 TRUSTING A HIGHLANDER
#2 TRUSTING A SCOT
#3 TRUSTING A CHIEFTAIN

STAND-ALONE BOOKS
ESCAPE TO THE HIGHLANDS
THE BANISHED HIGHLANDER

REFORMING THE DUKE-REGENCY
FALLING FOR THE CHIEFTAIN-3RD in a
collaborative trilogy
HIGHLAND SECRETS –3rd in a collaborative
trilogy

THE SUMMERHILL SERIES-CONTEMPORARY ROMANCE
#1-ONE SUMMERHILL DAY
#2-A FRESH START FOR TWO
#3-THREE REASONS TO LOVE

ABOUT THE AUTHOR

KEIRA MONTCLAIR IS the pen name of an author who lives in South Carolina with her husband. She loves to write fast-paced, emotional romance, especially with children as secondary characters.

When she's not writing, she loves to spend time with her grandchildren. She's worked as a high school math teacher, a registered nurse, and an office manager. She loves ballet, mathematics, puzzles, learning anything new, and creating new characters for her readers to fall in love with.

She writes historical romantic suspense. Her best-selling series is a family saga that follows two medieval Scottish clans through four generations and now numbers over thirty books.

Contact her through her website:
www.keiramontclair.com